MY GIRLS:

AN ENTREPRENEURSHIP STORY

INTENTIONALLY BLANK

FABRICIO TAKAYASSU

MY GIRLS:
AN ENTREPRENEURSHIP STORY

The S.H.E. Edition

1.0.6

2021

Author e publisher
Fabricio Takayassu
@F42013 (Twitter)

Editorial Support
Fernando F. de Sousa Lima
@fernando.desousalima (Instagram)

Cover design and art
Fabricio Takayassu

International Standard Book Number (ISBN)
978-85-920492-1-8

Dear reader,

you didn't ask for this, but
I took the liberty to sign the
book. I'll be brief.

You probably don't know
who I am, but you can learn
more about me.

How? Just read the book - it's
part of my life.

Send me a message after your
journey.

Your new friend,

INTENTIONALLY BLANK

CONTENTS

DISCLAIMER

This is a work of fiction, really. All characters, names, events, facts, places, and incidents – I mean everything – in this story are fictional. Any similarity with actual persons, living or dead, or actual facts and events is only coincidental and unintended.

However, it is quite possible you can recognize persons, names, facts or events in this work. As I said few lines above, this story is fictional. I have created characters who have eyes, mouths and hairstyles like those you may have met or seen in your life. That does not mean my characters are the real persons you have met or seen in your life.

Although I have tried to create a fictional new world in this story, it is quite possible you can recognize (or imagine) names, places, events or facts. If you do, remember this story is fictional (as I said before, twice).

In addition, you may think you are some character in this fictional work. If that happens, do not think that. If you insist in thinking you are in my story, I would like to tell you this secret: I do not write about my enemies, not even about people I do not like so much. Most of times, I create stories about people I LOVE. Because my enemies – if I have – do not deserve anything from me – not even contempt or hatred. I write stories about persons I admire, love and respect.

If you want to insist in thinking you are any character of my story, see that as a tribute, please. Probably I have met you in my life, and/or I am your (huge) fan. As I said, I write stories only about people I love. If you think you are in this story, it is because I admire you and/or your work. However, I have to say for the fourth time, this story is fictional, then probably you are not exactly described – WHETHER it is you. Maybe only the same eyes color or some attribute as tall or hair color. All the rest, probably and possibly, is fictional. Talk to me before suing me, please. Thank you.

Something also relevant is: although the author (me) and the publisher (me too) have made all effort to ensure all information, as concepts and thoughts about all subjects, in this book was correct, the author and the publisher do not assume any liability for any loss or damage caused by errors or omissions, result from accident, misuse, or any other cause. The short version is: use the concepts in this book at your own risk.

And last but not least, I cite real products and companies in this work. All these products, trademarks and companies names are property of their respective holders, of course.

No people, animals or vegetation were harmed in the production of this story. However, I had many nights without sleeping – because sometimes you NEED to write. Writers will understand this very well.

To my father and my mother, the superheroes,
and to my sisters and my brother, for being my family for so long (it
is a hard job).

And to all women and girls
who have to prove something,
to someone,
every single day.

INTENTIONALLY BLANK

ABOUT THIS EDITION

This "S.H.E." Edition means "Sweet Happy Ending" Edition, and I think I do not have to explain anything else.

When I finished the first edition, available on Wattpad.com, I was not happy about it. If you have read this story on internet, you probably know what I am talking about. I just did not like the result. Because, as you may know, we do not have a happy ending in the internet version of this story.

Then came this idea: a "happy ending" edition. If you have already read this book on internet, please, go to the chapter thirteen or fourteen. After reading the preface, introduction and specially the prologue, of course. And last but not least, do not forget to check the post-credits scene.

INTENTIONALLY BLANK

PREFACE

This story is about incompetence. I have tried over and over to make some business, but in vain. I have tried to start a company, a start-up company. I also have tried to start some projects – and one of them I got it, but I did not end it. I have tried to call people to work with me, as partners, but they gave up. I do not know if it is me, or them. However, this is not important anymore.

The point is: who am I? Am I an entrepreneurship? Am I a manager? Am I a designer? Am I a marketing specialist? Am I the ideas man in a project? Maybe the coder? Or the finance guy?

I would like to be all of them. Actually, I am a little bit, because you can read about all these subjects in this story – and, of course, I have studied all these themes. If you want a start, try Ries, Trout, Drucker, Kotler, Duailibi and Simonsen.

However, at the same time, I could say I am not any of these professionals above. None of them.

I am a storyteller. That is what I do. That is my best part – what is yours? It is what I have chosen to make in my life: telling stories, creating worlds, manipulating the reality as I want – playing God.

And maybe that is why I could not build any company, game or business project (until now). I still have some time on this planet, by the way, and I do not know about tomorrow (not everything).

However, I do not write stories – I LIVE them. I laugh, I cry, I suffer with my characters. They are my sons and my daughters. And we do not want to see our kids in troubles, do we? No, we do not. Because I do not have children in real life. If I would, I certainly would know that having kids is very different than creating characters. But I do not have, and I keep laughing and crying with my children – telling and living their adventures.

As I said, this story is about incompetence. I did not have ability in making business. I just could not. Then, I started to write about what I could not make. It is not a simple story. It is a story about my life, but in a kindly way of telling a story. There are people talking to people, almost like an informal mentoring or coaching (search for these terms on internet, please). There are people helping people. There are parents teaching kids. The characters in this book meet great persons in their lives – as I did. And these characters make friends in their path. True ones, not those kinds of "friends" you need to handle nowadays. I mean, friends forever.

Finally, there are friends helping friends in this book. Because, as I said, it is a story about my life. You can say "Okay, not bad. But I do not want to read about your troubles." But I highly recommend you that you LIVE the story. This is the best way to read any book. Because if do not laugh or cry when you read one, you do not enjoy the journey. That can mean you did not learn anything, you did not enjoy it, you did not live. And life, my dear reader, is our greatest value. Do not waste your time if you will not live the story.

Now, I would like to introduce my kids to you, and invite you to live this journey with us.

Shall we?

INTRODUCTION

Elle is like you and me. She has a best friend. She is studying. Fine, maybe you have finished your studies already. But you know what studying is, right?

Elle has a father. Her father is... well, you must read the story. I think that is why you are here. Let's jump ahead this part.

Elle has problems, like you and me. She has wishes too. And, look at this: she has feelings. Elle also has ideas, good ones, sometimes. And guess what? Just like you and me.

In a beautiful day, Elle has a great idea. That is when her new story starts. And that is where I need to stop telling you and let you read.

But the introduction has not ended yet. You do not know Elle, I mean, in person. But I am sure you know someone like her. Or maybe you ARE like her. Or maybe you ARE her – who knows? Send me a message, please.

As I said, Elle is like you and me. She has troubles, wishes, ideas. Elle has good and bad moments. She also has friends. She has a life, as you and I have.

You can meet this life – hers, mine or yours – right now.

You just have to live.

INTENTIONALLY BLANK

PROLOGUE

In some place in United States, someone is called to the front of the class. The person, timidly, stands up and walks to the front. The classroom with white floor looks like a wild place; the people look like... huh... this is not important. It is a nice afternoon, anyway.

The professor asks to the new student to tell something about the last holidays – if it was good or bad, and what this new person expects from the new colleagues. Then, the freshman starts to tell a story to the new classmates. This person has moved to that place and now is facing new challenges in life – as anyone who relocates. This is the first day at the new college. This is the story she has told.

INTENTIONALLY BLANK

CHAPTER ONE – VERSION 1.0 – WHO I AM AND HOW I GOT THAT.

Meeting Elle and Hailee

Texting:

"Where are you?"

"Guess where I am."

"Jesus, Elle, what happened?"

"My dad… again…"

"Oh, no… is he okay?"

"Yes, but he's at a hospital, Hailee… You know…"

"Oh, Elle, I'm so sorry…"

"It's okay…"

"Are you coming?"

"I don't think so…"

"I'll try to talk to Mr. Johnson!"

"Thanks, Hailee… You're my best friend."

While Elle was texting in the cell phone, she realized Hailee was her best friend. Elle always has seen Hailee as a friend. But in the last days (or months), she started to see the brunette long hair girl as more than that.

When Elle's father goes to hospital, Hailee is always the first person to text or call her. And the blonde girl could see that she had a best friend. Elle has a few friends at college, but Hailee has become close in the last times. Suddenly, between her thoughts, a nurse calls a known surname.

"It's me."

"Good afternoon, Ms…"

"Elle. Just Elle."

"Follow me, please."

"How is he?"

"He's fine. You can talk to the doctor, Elle."

"Thank you."

"Father's companion at a hospital," she thought. "It isn't so bad… It could be worse. I could be my father's companion at a funeral…"

And she was at one. Four years ago, when the blonde girl was eighteen, her mother died. Now it is just her and Charlie. That made them closer, but not always happy. Elle's father had some heart complications after he retired football – a quarterback known as "The Fox".

"Hi, Dad." she is not so happy.

"Hi, Ms. Blonde!"

"How you doing, Dad?"

"Not so bad, not so good, honey."

"Why do you try to play if you can't, Dad?"

"Yeah, that was a mistake…"

"Again?"

"I'm sorry, Elle."

"You know I should be at a class now, huh?"

"Yes… I'm sorry…"

"Doc knows when you can go home?"

"Maybe on Saturday, I don't know."

"Fine. So, I'll come back tomorrow, okay?"

Doctor Alice comes.

"Good afternoon, everyone!"

"Hi! Doctor Alice, right?"

"Yes, nice to meet you! You must be Elle."

"Yes."

"Well, your father has a history of heart attack or heart disease, Elle."

"Yes, Doctor Alice. Is he gonna be fine?"

"Hmm… I'm not so sure… You should take care, Mr. Panning. You are not a superhero, you know?"

"Oh…" Charlie sighs.

"You are not… hmm…" the doctor says.

"Superman!" says Elle.

"Yes! You're not Superman, Mr. Panning!" the doctor completes.

"It's my favorite…" the blonde girl continues.

"Oh, really? And there is that… with a red suit… Hmm… his name starts with a 'D'…" Doctor Alice thinks.

"Deadpool." Elle says.

"Yes! Deadpool! You're not Deadpool, Mr. Panning! Please, take care of yourself!"

"Okay, doc, I will." Elle's father agrees.

"So, I think you can go home on Friday or Saturday."

"That's fine, doc! And thank you." Charlie says.

"Can I talk to you, Elle?" Doctor Alice asks.

"Yes, sure."

They leave the room.

"Your father has a complicate disease, Elle. He has a weak heart and he must watch that."

"Yes, I know, Doctor Alice. But… he… he's a man… you know…
They hate to feel useless."

"Okay, but, anyway, you should talk to him seriously. Because he
can't do what he is doing. I mean, if he pushes too hard, you know,
huh? He can…"

"Die?"

"Yes. And that will be abrupt. No time to help or anything."

"I'll talk to him, Doctor Alice. Thank you!"

"You're welcome! If you need anything, please talk to me, Elle.
I'm one of the directors here, and I'm monitoring your father's case.
It's a very complex case."

"Thank you again, doctor!"

"Hmm… Shouldn't you be at a class now?"

"Yes… that's the problem number two…Actually, I was waiting
to talk to you, Doctor Alice…"

"Oh, I have a hard schedule sometimes, Elle, I'm sorry!"

She goes to the room one more time to see her father and then
she leaves. The clock is ticking, but maybe she has some time to go
to the class – and make an exam.

Chapter One – Version 1.1

At college.

"Excuse me, Mr. Johnson, may I come in?"

"You're late, Ms. Panning…"

"Yes, Mr. Johnson, I'm so sorry…"

"Fortunately, Ms. Steamfield has told me about your father. Come
in, please. We are just starting the test. Not all the teachers are evil,
Ms. Panning."

"Thank you very much, sir!" she smiles.

She sits down near from Hailee.

"Oh, God, Elle! It's so good to see you! How is your father?"

"He's fine, I think… I've talked to the doctor, she said…"

"Silence, please. Let's start!"

"We'll talk later, Hailee. Thanks for notifying Mr. Johnson about me!"

"Friends are friends, Elle!"

Backing home, the blonde and the brunette start to talk about
the test.

"God, I think I got a 'C'…"

"Really? Lucky you, Hailee! I got a 'D' or worse…"

"Didn't you study?"

"How? I mean, when? My father is always in trouble! Oh…"

"You should take care, Elle! We're in the last year at college! And we promised to complete it together, remember?"

"And there is that…"

"Hey! It's not a bad thing!"

"I mean, it's a commitment, Hailee…"

"Oh, you say that as if it was the worst thing we have together! Ouch, Elle!"

"No, I didn't say that! I'm stressed! So much to think and study and worry about! I'm still a teenager!"

"Actually, we are 22, Elle, sorry… ha ha ha!"

"And there is that too…"

"Isn't it exciting? We'll be in the adult life soon!"

"You mean jobs, taxes and children?"

"Ha ha ha! It's not that bad, Elle! Come on!"

"I think I'm in the adult life already, Hailee."

"Why? Because you have to take care of your father?"

"Yes…"

"We're always taking care of someone, Elle, always. Luckily, you have a father to take care of."

"I'm sorry, Hailee… I always remember you when I'm complaining of my father."

"It's okay, Elle… Just remember there are worse things than that. He could be dead like mine."

Hailee's father died when she was very young, four years old. She did not know him so much. And when Elle used to complain about her own father, the brunette girl always reminded the best friend.

"Yes, it could be worse…" she thought.

However, neither of them is complaining. They are having different lives: one of them has only the father, the other one lives only with mother and an older sister. They were not complaining about that, because, they knew, it could be worse.

The girls go home soon. Tomorrow would be another day – a better one, they would expect, and they still had homework and many things to do at night – that means, huh… talking.

Chapter One – Version 1.2

At night. Texting (as always).

"Hi!"

"Hi, what's up?"

"I had a nice dinner with my mom and my sister. You?"

"I had a nice dinner: pizza."

"LOL!"

"Are you in the bed already?"

"Yes. You?"

"I still need to take a shower."

"Hey, about your father, Elle. He's gonna be okay, don't worry. He'll be home soon."

"I'm not worried about that, Hailee. It's about what comes next. He knows he can't do any effort, but he keeps pushing harder and harder. I'm worried because he can die. And... I'll be by myself! I don't want to live with my uncles. Some of them are boring!"

"Easy, Elle! You won't live with any uncle!"

"Too many questions for a teenager, Hailee! Ha ha ha!"

"We are not teens anymore!"

"Oh, I forgot, we are 'young adults'..."

"Yes!"

"It's almost the same thing; that's stupid! What is the difference between 19 years old and 21? Next to nothing! Ha ha ha!"

"Well, when you're 21, you can watch some hardcore porn movies. LOL!"

"Oh, I forgot that... so useful..."

"You should date someone, Elle!"

"For what? I don't even have time to study, Hailee!"

"You should meet Tyler!"

"Long hair? Earrings? Sandals? No, thanks, Hailee! I'll pass!"

"But he's tall! And he plays in basketball team!"

"And he is a dumb! He got an 'F' in the last exam, remember?"

"Oh, you can teach him... that's your cue!"

"I have more pressing things to worry about, Hailee!"

"Oh, come on..."

"I'm not you, Hailee, with all your boyfriends! Ha ha ha!"

"Ouch! I didn't change my boyfriend THIS MONTH!"

"Oh, that's an 'improvement', Hailee! Congrats!"

"I'm just testing them! To meet someone who is worthy!"

"You're testing ALL of them! LOL!"

"Not everyone... yet! LOL!"

"Oh, better I go, Hailee...I still need to take a shower!"

"OK, and I'm gonna sleep!"

"And I think we have a problem, Hailee."

"What?"

"My father goes to hospital many times, you know. And every time he does, I have to count on you for something…"

"That's not a problem! I'm your friend, Elle!"

"No, I'm sure we have a problem, Hailee. What if something happens to you? What if I can't count on you? What if my father dies? What if I have to live with my uncles? Any of them?"

"Too many 'what if' in one phrase, Elle! What you wanna do?"

"I don't know. I'm thinking about."

"Okay, same time tomorrow?"

"Sure. After school, I need to go to the hospital again."

"Okay, I can go with you if you want."

"Thanks! If I had some way to talk to Doctor Alice, Hailee… It would be great."

"Oh, there is something called 'telephone', you should get know…"

"Very funny, Hailee, I'm laughing loudly here…"

"You can ask her to send you a message."

"Yes… but I still need to see my father. It must be more than a message, Hailee."

"A picture, maybe?"

"Yes, a message and a picture, or a short video. That's a good beginning."

"What are you thinking, Elle?"

"I still don't know, Hailee. But I'll tell you when I get that."

"OK. Same time tomorrow?"

"Yes, same time."

"Good night, Elle."

"Good night, Hailee."

Chapter One – Version 1.3

Every morning, Elle wakes up very soon. She likes to be very alert before going to college. And the blonde girl hates to get out of the bed in the last minute. She is a right girl. That morning, however, Elle stayed a little more in the bed. She was thinking about last day, when she talked to Hailee about a problem. Elle remembered every word they said and she was ready to do something about. No way to keep going in that life. Her father at a hospital, trespassing his health limits and she was almost losing her last year at college. "I need to do something," the girl said to herself. "Mom could be here to help me," she continued.

The daylight comes into the bedroom and she realizes it is time to go. Sometimes, Elle started to think a lot about life and the relationship she had with her mother. Deborah Annie Panning was a so nice mother: tall, blonde like Elle, same small mouth with bright red lips, same blue eyes, same smooth and almost pale skin, and same way to try harder again and again when life was not so good to them.

The girl – or the young adult – gets out of the bed and goes to the bathroom. The clear walls try to talk to her without any answer. She is busy with some thoughts: thinking about father, mother, family, friends, college, and life. It is hard to a twenty-two years old girl (or young adult, as the best friend said before). She brushes her teeth after washing the face. We can say she is a beautiful person. Not so much as she wanted to be, but she is. The long legs, a "registered trademark," and the blonde hair could confirm that.

Elle eats anything at the breakfast – there are no parents to advise her about healthy eating, and the girl is not completely sad about that. Actually, most of times, she used to eat properly to keep everything in the right measurements – except for the cookies (do not tell that to anyone), one of her favorite food. She is really a right girl.

At the same time, Hailee comes.

"Hi!"

"Hi! Did you do homework, the writing?"

"Yes! What about you?"

"Me too! Can I see yours? I think mine is average... and I need a 'B'."

"Oh, a 'C' is fine to me, Elle."

While the girls are going to college, they are thinking about the last conversation. Hailee is 1.73 meters tall, only one centimeter taller than Elle. Her hair is dark brown – she is a brunette, as I said, with hazel eyes. Sometimes, Elle used to kid the best friend: Hailee has "smokey" and "dense" eyes – thanks to long and dark eyelashes (with a makeup help). Hailee looks like she is never with her eyes fully opened – and that is funny, at least to Elle. Her long hair is beautiful. Both the long hair are beautiful, I mean, thanks to hours at hair salon – they do not complain.

Hailee has a lovely smile – that is the first thing people notice. She looks younger than she is, but not so much. She is Elle's best friend and she knows that. The brunette girl tries to help her friend as much as she can, just because she is a good person. Hailee does not expect for help or gratitude – she is just trying to be a better person to her friend. We have good people in this story.

Hailee has a sister, two years older, Emma, and they live with their mother. Hailee's father died when she was four years old (I said that before), in a car accident (I did not say that). Then, the three girls live as close as they can – that is the first rule at Hailee's home.

They finally get to college, just in time. Today's class is not so interesting, but they are sure (or not so sure) that class will be important in the future, as many others – that is what teachers used to say. Anyway, they pay attention to learn a few interesting things.

Elle's mind is in somewhere else – she is thinking about her problem. Life can be short to some people, and the blonde girl does not want to wait for some better. She really needs to do anything. Her father Charlie could die anytime. And then, what? At present, the girl and her father have an insurance, some kind of indemnity from the football team that Charlie used to play for. It is not a bunch of money – not really –, but the family can live in a satisfactory way. Not with expensive travels or buying cars every month, but they have a decent life. Charlie, smart and forewarned man and father, asked for a life insurance to the employee. "Just in case," he said. The football team agreed and helped him. Only with that insurance policy, he could feel safe and peaceful.

"Ms. Panning, would you like to read your writing to the class?"

"Oh, God," she thinks, "why me?" she says to herself. "Yes, Mr. Johnson."

The blonde girl gets up with a forced smile to Hailee and goes to the front of the classroom. She does not want to read any writing. Elle is concerned about her life, not about writing or class or anything else. But she reads:

"Power and sharing," she announces the title.

The teacher shows some impressed face and Elle goes on.

"Last weekend, I watched a movie in which a woman was shooting people. She was kicking some asses too," she starts. "Oh… sorry for this dirty word, Mr. Johnson…"

The teacher smiles, not so happy, but he allows that; the long blonde hair girl continues.

"I do not think that was a strong woman. I do not want to take the worst facet from the men, I mean the physical violence. We are more than that. We can make more than shooting people or hitting them, because we are women. And women can do much better. However, this is not a competition. It is not women against men. It is not who is the fastest or the strongest. In addition, it is not about intelligence. We are building a place to live. Men and women can do their own role in the society, like a great community, like partners in a huge corporation called Earth. In real life, I do not see girls shooting boys or beating them, except when my friend Hailee hit her last boyfriend – but he was such an idiot." She stops and smiles a little, but not showing the bright teeth. "I was about to take off this piece, Mr. Johnson..." she shows a forced smile to the professor.

"Sorry for that, Hailee." she turns to the class.

The brunette girl lowers her head with a laugh and the blonde one keeps reading.

"But I am not here to read a feminist discourse. I am not here to fight or ask for anything. I am not here to beg for my rights because you know them – or maybe you just forgot. I am here to show how people can be unwise when they think men and women, women and men, are rivals. We are not. It is not about giving all the power to us, the women; it is about sharing. We live together here, and we can share the power as we are sharing the world already. Women deserve more. And if we are not doing this for us, let's do this for our children. We can make a better world; we can live in a better place. We can build (or rebuild) our planet if we have respect, tolerance and goodness. We can do this. Together." she finishes.

Professor Johnson starts to applause the young girl saying words like a woman – any woman. She is right, totally right, but who cares? She is living in a "men world," so what can she do?

Elle thanks timidly to the class and then she goes back to her desk. Hailee smiles and blinks an eye with a mouth snap at the desk beside. The girls are happy.

After the class, Elle goes to the hospital.

"Nice writing, Elle! I'm impressed! You should be a politician!"

"Oh, I can't! I think I'm too much honest! Ha ha ha!"

"Ha ha ha! And now, what?"

"Now, I'm going to the hospital to see my father. Are you coming?"

"Yes, sure!"

"Fine!"

"Hmm... About what you've written, Elle... do you think we can change the world? I mean, by ourselves?"

"I think we can start something, Hailee. We can't change the entire world, but we can start small, here, with simple things. We can start with you and me, and then go bigger."

"What do you mean?"

"I can't change people if I can't change myself, right?"

"Completely right!"

"So, if we want to change anything, we must to start changing ourselves."

"What do you want to change in me?"

"Oh, it's just a way of speaking, Hailee. Everything I say, I put you right into it. It's always me and you, remember?"

"Yeah!"

"But, now you're saying that…"

"Oh, I knew it! What is it? Is it about my boyfriends?"

"Oh, so you do care about so many boyfriends! I'm just kidding! I got you! Ha ha ha!"

"Ha ha ha!"

"But I think we can start some change here, Hailee."

"What are you thinking about?"

"Well, we have a problem. We've talked about that last night."

"Yes, but what we're gonna do?"

They get to the hospital.

"Hi, I'd like to see my father, Charlie Panning."

"Room number eight, second floor. You'll see stairs at the end of the row."

"Thank you."

They go to the second floor. Hailee does not like hospitals – I think no one does –, and everything looks unusual, smells included, but she is doing a favor to her friend. Elle, in the other hand, already sees the place like a familiar one. She has come to a hospital almost every month in the last year. She does not care, because it is for her father.

"Hi, Dad!"

"Hey, Ms. Blonde, how are you?"

"I'm fine, Dad! What about you?"

"I'm going home tomorrow."

"Oh, that's great, Dad!"

"Hi, Mr. Panning!"

"Hey, Hailee, how are you doing?"

"I'm fine, Mr. Panning! Thank you!"

"Well, if my father can come back home tomorrow, I think we can celebrate!"

"Hmm… not with beers, I think, Elle…"

"No, of course not, Hailee!"

"Elle has made a great speech today, Mr. Panning. You should have seen her."

"Really, Ms. Blonde? Tell me about it!"

"Oh, it was not a big deal, Dad…"

"It was, Mr. Panning! Mr. Johnson had applauded her!"

"Hey, do we have a speaker in the family? What was that about?"

"It was a writing, Dad. About power and sharing and things people forget every day. It was about girl power."

"That is just you, Ms. Blonde… Exactly like your mother taught you."

"People like, smile, applaud, but they go home and they forget. I don't think that's right, Dad."

"And what are you gonna do about, Ms. Blonde?"

"I don't know…"

"Think about what your mother would do."

"I'm not mom, Dad…"

"Of course you're not! You're my Ms. Blonde! Just remember her. And make better."

The blonde girl with long hair lowers her head and starts to think. She goes deep in her memories and tries to remember something, anything. The girl takes a breath and waits, she almost closes her eyes. And then come the memories of her mother, like a voice inside her mind. It is like thoughts, but they come too fast (too fast for a thought). That makes Elle doubts whether she is really thinking all that or something else is trying to talk to her, to send her a message. Her fingertips start to sweat. Was that power of intuition? She does not know and that is not bothering her.

Elle wants to do something to help herself and her father. And if she can help people in that process, it will be great. But, first, she is thinking of herself. It is not selfishness, it is just self-protection.

She raises the head and sees her best friend. The blonde girl smiles, the brunette, always the best partner, smiles back. Elle looks at the man on the bed and she says:

"I know what to do, Dad."

CHAPTER TWO – VERSION 2.0 – WHAT DO I NEED?

Hailee, we have a problem – having an idea

"What do you mean?"

"Exactly what you've heard, Hailee."

"Is that a good idea?"

"What's the problem? Everybody does that!"

"We're not, huh… 'Everybody', Elle…"

"Why not?"

"I don't think we can do that."

"So tell me why, Hailee."

"Well, first, I don't think I can do that, and I'm talking about the technical issues."

"Can't you learn or search?"

"It can take a while…"

"How long?"

"Just… long! Very long!"

"So, we'll look for somebody to help us. What about that?"

"Yes, that can be reasonable."

"We have the idea already, Hailee!"

"Yes, but an idea can be duplicated, you know…"

"Oh, and there is that…"

"But… maybe we can present the idea to a professor. How about Mr. Johnson? He likes you, I think."

"Yeah, great!"

"We can talk to him next week."

"Yes! For now, we can… huh… plan, I think. I mean we can design and plan."

"Sure, and I can look for someone to help me. Because that will be a huge job."

"But that will be cool, Hailee! And fun!"

"Fun? That will be a lot of work, Elle!"

"Job and work can be fun, you'll see!"

"Okay, if you're saying that…"

"Oh, come on, Hailee! We're in the last year, what can go wrong?"

"Well, there is a bunch of things… First, we can spend our time and get nothing; second, we can lose this last period at college; third, we can look for people and nobody join us. Or somebody can steal your idea. And I didn't say anything about production yet."

"Just think about: I solve my problem and other people's problem too! We do that, we sell it and we'll be rich! We help people and we get rich, what do you think?"

"Okay, Elle! I don't think I can make you go back, I know you! I just know you! I know that face!"

"We're doing something here, Hailee! Something important to me and to other people! Just imagine how many people live with that in the world! We can help them! We must do that!"

"Fine, I got it! But I'm just warning you, that will be a very hard job. It's not only design and then everything is ready. We must plan a lot. It's not homework, Elle!"

"Let's see like a big homework then! I already have everything in my mind, Hailee!"

"Yes, I know! But when you sit down in front of your computer... that's when things get complicated!"

"We are planning, Hailee! We always plan in design, you know!"

"It's not only the design this time, Elle!"

"Do you want to give up?"

"No, I don't! We don't give up! Never!"

"Tell me about what you are thinking. Tell me the pros and cons, tell me your plan."

"Well, we'll need somebody to help me. That's the first of all. Second, we need... huh... I don't know! We need to talk to Mr. Johnson to know more about that."

"We need to show him something like a planning or some sketch. Maybe a previous design. What do you think?"

"Hmm... yes and no. The design can change because we don't know all the features yet."

"So it's better we present only the idea and a sketch. I mean a very first sketch."

"Yes, a low-resolution one. I mean, still on a paper."

"Yes!"

"And then we can start when Mr. Johnson heads us."

"Fine! So... we're starting to make our app now, Hailee!"

Chapter Two – Version 2.1

At night, they are having a dinner together. Charlie, Elle's father, was still hospitalized at, huh... the hospital. So, the dynamic duo was enjoying the night without adults. This time, however, with hard work, of course. But they do not bother (this time).

"So what now?" says Hailee.

"Hmm… we need a plan. I mean, we need to list all the features in the app."

"What about the design?"

"That comes later. And we need a list of new features, to implement later."

"Isn't it too early to think in new features?"

"Hmm… yes, you're right. But we can put that in another list."

"Okay, so I'll start to write the features. What do we need? What are you thinking in this first moment, Elle?"

"Well, we need a blank field to write the message, right? Or… we need options, so the doctors can choose and send the message. That will be easier to them."

"Options like what? I'm writing."

"I don't know, maybe 'the patient is: good, stable or dead.' "

"Dead?" Hailee frowns.

"Just kidding! Ha ha ha!"

"Ha ha ha! Okay, so what's next?"

"Next is about the remedies the patient must take. And now we need a blank field. I don't want so many blanks here, Hailee. Everything must be easy. We must avoid blanks and typing, what do you think?"

"Yes, I agree, Elle! This must be the easiest way to send a message. Because if you have to type, you can use other options like messengers or something."

"So we leave this blank field for now. The second question is about… visits?"

"Yeah, that would be good. You mean 'Visits: yes or no?' "

"Yeah!"

"And we need something to say when the patient is leaving the hospital, an expectation of discharge."

"Yes!"

"How many questions?"

"I don't know, actually, Hailee. Enough questions."

"And that means…"

"Hmm… five."

"Good. What next?"

"Hmm… I think I'm stuck here… What exactly are we doing?"

"Huh, I think we're doing an app, right?"

"Yes, but what for? Do we need to write that?"

"I don't know! I've never made an app before!"

"Should we search about this?"

"I don't know. I don't think so."

"Okay, let's move! Let's make it and we'll see what happens."

"Yes, I've read in somewhere that you can't plan too much. Sometimes it's better to make things fast. I mean, you make the minimal and just sell it."

"I've heard that too… Okay. Where were we?" the blond girl forgot.

"Hmm… the questions. We have two questions already. And we need five, at least. No, wait… we have three."

"Is this the best way to make an app? I mean, don't we need any process or software? Maybe some software to put the questions into it and everything will be done easily."

"I don't think so. We can create our own way. But I think it starts in the paper, like a… hmm… sketch. We don't need software or app yet."

"Oh, yes! Like Mr. Johnson said! We always start on the paper, like design, right?"

"Yeah! We go to the PC when we are ready, when we know everything. The computer is for making; paper is for planning."

"Okay, so we're doing right! Sometimes I forget these simple things, ha ha ha!"

"Ha ha ha! We can't forget the basics, Elle! We're in the last year!"

"Oh, sometimes I feel so old… Like a thirty years old woman…"

"Thirty is not old, Elle! Jesus! Ha ha ha!"

"Ha ha ha!"

"Okay, so we have three questions. Anything else?"

"Hmm… Do we really need five questions?"

"I don't know, you just said that."

"The patient is good, we can visit him, and he is coming home tomorrow. What more?"

"The remedies. And now there will be a blank field. And the virtual keyboard will appear when you touch the screen, like always."

"Can't we make different?"

"I don't know… better we don't change these usual things. People are lazy and stupid, you know."

"Okay. So now we have four questions, right?"

"Yes."

"So we need one more."

"Why?"

"I've heard that, in Japan, four means death. Because it's the same sound." the blonde girl shows some knowledge.

"But we're not selling this in Japan, Elle."

"We don't know, Hailee! We can sell this everywhere! Just see the apps around the world. We must be prepared."

"And what about that conversation about start small and then go bigger?"

"But we are starting small. And this is just a detail about numbers."

"Fine, so we need one more question. How about we ask for something the patient needs? Or a message that he or she is sending? Like, huh… 'I'm fine' or 'Hey, I'll be home soon' "?

"Hey, this is a great idea! And the app won't be so 'serious'! I mean, off course it's serious because we are talking about someone at a hospital. But we can put some 'not so serious' thing. I think that's good."

"So what do we write?"

"How about 'The patient says: I'm fine, I miss you or nothing,' when the patient can't talk."

"Yeah! Good! It's like a personal message, not only the doctor speaking." the brunette likes.

"And then we are done, right?"

"Yes, now we need to put all these in a pretty design. Oh, wait, we need to make a sketch first, remember? And… I think we need to talk to Mr. Johnson for the next steps."

"So let's do that!"

Chapter Two – Version 2.2

Few days later, the girls go to meet Mr. Johnson. They have many questions to ask and the professor is a special one: sympathetic and attentive to the girls, he always likes to answer any doubt from them. And Mr. Johnson is a great teacher. He is a very experienced designer, especially graphic, web and interface design (this means a lot). In addition, he knows about business – what the girls are looking for – because he used to provide consultancy before teaching. After the class, Elle and Hailee come to talk to him.

"Hi, Mr. Johnson. May we talk to you?"

"Yes, sure, Ms. Panning. Ms. Steamfield. How can I help you?"

"Hmm… we are making an app. Huh… for cell phones. And… we'd like to ask you some questions."

"Okay, what is it?" he stops looking his papers and turns to the girls.

"We just understand about design and so we don't know where to go now. We have already written a few questions to put in it."

"Well, first, what is this app for? You need a purpose."

"It's for communication."

"What kind of communication? Because we have many types of it."

"Hmm… it's for communication between a doctor and patient's relatives."

"Good. And what's the problem with a phone call?"

The brunette girl laughs a little bit.

"Yes… Hailee said that…But this app will work like a report to the patient's relatives. Because, you know, Mr. Johnson, my father is always at a hospital…"

"Oh, now I can see! You mean, you get a report about your father, in your case, and you don't have to interrupt your jobs. Your classes, in your case."

"Yes, Mr. Johnson! Yes!"

"That's a good idea, Ms. Panning! Did you say you have already what to put in this app? A few questions?"

"Yes, we've written five of them already."

"Good. And I presume Ms. Steamfield is helping you."

"Yes! We've worked on this last week – Hailee says."

"And what about profit? Are you considering selling this app?"

"Yes, sure!"

"This is a good reason to create an app, ladies. Because I see many useless apps in the marketplace. This one seems helpful. Well, you'll have a lot of work."

Hailee looks at Elle and laughs a bit again because she said that too.

"We are ready for that, sir!" says the blonde.

"Are we?" the other girl says and smiles.

"You have a purpose and some content. Now you need a sketch."

"We have it, Mr. Johnson!"

Hailee takes the sheet of paper and presents to the professor.

"Huh… that's just a sketch, Mr. Johnson."

"Yes, I can see it. Begin with a blank paper is totally correct. As you know, when you are sitting in front of a computer, there are many, hmm… 'distractions.' You try colors and shapes and effects, and the job never gets done. And I didn't say anything about messengers and others amusements."

The senior designer sees the paper and says:

"You have a good start here, ladies. You know already what to ask. And this separation between the first question and the others is very smart."

"Thank you, Mr. Johnson."

"Is it only five questions?"

"Yes, we don't want to put many of them. Because if we do so, it's not a report, it looks like a book about the patient. It's just some things like an overview. Just to know and not to worry about who is at the hospital."

"Fine, it looks good for now."

"And what do we need from now on, Mr. Johnson?"

And then she gets into a completely new world. One thing is access any app store, do the download of an app, and use it. Other thing, very different, is making an app. And when I say "make" is exactly that: building it from zero or from a sketch on a paper. Elle now can see the complexity in making the app. Her graduation course is in Graphic Design and that is just a small, but important, part of the app or software. But she does not feel afraid. She has a best friend and a mentor to help her. And the most important: she has the will, the impetus, and the determination. The blonde girl also has a good reason to work: help herself and her father (and other people too, but she is not thinking so hard about that for now).

"Well, first you need to plan the app. That means all the features, all the purposes, and then how you will build it – I'm talking about coding now. Second, you need to find out who will buy your app, and that means your target audience. Do you know marketing, Ms. Panning?"

"Huh... no, Mr. Johnson..."

"But we know someone who knows, Mr. Johnson!" Hailee says.

"Do we?"

"Yes! My sister!"

"Oh, I got it! Ms. Marketing..."

"Yeah!" Hailee smiles.

"Do you call your sister 'Ms. Marketing'?"

"It's a long story, Mr. Johnson... When she has finished her graduation, she didn't stop to talk about marketing. Everything she was seeing, she could say something about marketing inside of it. Everything, even nonsense or not so important stuff. She always had a theory or a new approach about marketing. And then, we, huh... started to call her Ms. Marketing."

"I see… And I'm sure she doesn't know about that nickname, right?"

"Huh… yes… Oh, no, maybe! I think that's another good story, Mr. Johnson…" Hailee shows a forced laugh.

"Fine. So you have a plan, and it's better you make a schedule. Write everything, this is very important. When you write something on a paper, you see as a commitment. If you just think or schedule in your mind is different. So, don't just think, write everything and, of course, follow the planning as much as you can. Because, in this case, a plan can change, and it will, maybe many times. You will have to adjust it all the time. For instance, let's suppose a new law comes into force and this law has influence on your planning. You will have to change it. So, a plan must be flexible and always opened. It must be manageable."

Now it is a whole new world, a new point of view to Elle. She likes to take action more than planning or scheduling. But, in the last months, she could see that was not the best way to live. She thinks of her father and realizes she must change. Fortunately, in most of times, Hailee used to act as a conscience, someone to stop the blonde girl's rush. Sometimes you need the rush, sometimes you need the rhythm. I think that is why they are so good friends – they need each other and they know that.

The girls say 'thank you' to Mr. Johnson and they leave. Now, there is a new homework: planning. And that is very important, maybe more than usual homework or even studying. And then, suddenly and with no warnings, they start to face all that as a plan to their lives – and that is good. Girls grow up.

Chapter Two – Version 2.3

At night, Elle and Hailee are working at Elle's home.

"So we are planning now?" says Elle.

"Yep."

"And how do we start?"

"Huh… good question! Well, Mr. Johnson said we need to write everything."

"Write where? Was he talking about a paper? Do people still use this? We can use software or some online app. What do you think?"

"Yes, sure. When this grows up, I think we'll need more than a paper."

"I'll use my online agenda. It must have some place to write."

"We can work on an off-line word processor. Let's not worry about the right tool for now." advises Hailee.

"Okay. I'm opening this one in my computer."

"Hey, I've just remembered something!"

"What?"

"What is the name? The app's name?"

"I don't know. Oh, I don't know! I should know that because I had the idea!"

"You don't have to know everything about the app, Elle!" smiles the brunette girl. "Sooner or later we'll need more people here! My sister, for example, is one of these people."

"Oh, it's so many details to think about, Hailee!"

"Oh, really? What did I tell you before we started?" smiles Hailee.

"Okay... you're right..."

"We keep going, lady, we won't give up so soon!"

"So, we start the planning with the app's name. Then we need the questions, and we've already done that. We need a previous design or a sketch; it's done too. And the worst: we need to program the app, I mean coding. And we need a good marketing to sell this, and this is up to your sister. Did I forget something?"

"Hmm... dates?"

"Oh, there is that too! Why don't we just do all the things at our own pace?"

"Because if we do so, this can take a lifetime, Elle. Believe me, it can."

"Fine, so we have already the questions and the sketch. We need a name and we need to talk to your sister about all this. We can do this in one week, what do you think?"

"Good. There are no exams this week."

"And then what?" the blonde girls says.

"And then we go bigger. We need to sell this; my sister must know how to do. I mean who we need to look for. So, we have to talk to Emma. And we need someone to help me to code this. I think this will be the most difficult to find."

"Why?"

"There are not so many coding girls. I mean, there are, but nobody knows where they are."

"Really? Can't we call a boy?"

"Huh... I prefer to work only with girls... if you don't mind..."

"Why?"

"I don't know! We are building this by ourselves. You had the idea, I'm helping you. I don't think we need a boy here. And last but not least, people will think this boy did all the hard work... you know, because we are girls, and people think we can't make a simple app for cell phones..."

"Agreed! I was going to tell you the same. I think we can do this, Hailee. I can see this is gonna be a hard work, but we can do it."

"No boys here. Deal?"

"Deal!"

They shake hands like, huh... boys, and now they have a deal. I do not think they are feminists – or feminazi – or something else, but they did a good deal. The girls live in a "men world" and they always have to prove something to someone. Those girls should be tired to do that all the time. Elle and Hailee are going into a deep and dark new world where people used to think only men can survive, and where a few brave girls have explored: the coding world. However, the blonde and the brunette have friends.

Chapter Two – Version 2.4

On Saturday, Elle is talking to her father. He is home already.

"Hey, Ms. Blonde, are you busy?"

"Yes, a little, Dad. Why?"

"I'm going to bakery. Do you want anything?"

"Oh, I'd like to have a cake! Huh... there is no fresh salmon cake, right? Ha ha ha!"

"No, Ms. Blonde, I think there is no such cake... I know you love that, but I don't think they make this kind of cake... but I'll ask!"

"Okay, could you bring me a chocolate cake?

"Yes, sure! What kind of chocolate? Black, milk?"

"Milk is fine, Dad, thank you!" she smiles with your red lips and bright teeth.

"You're welcome, honey! I'll be back soon. Will you be at home?"

"Yes, Dad, I'm planning something."

"Planning? This is a whole new to you!"

"Oh, yeah... this is new to me, Dad..."

"What happened? Plans for the future, maybe?"

"I was going to tell you, Dad. Me and Hailee, we are going to make an app. For cell phones. What do you think?"

"You mean a game or something?"

"No, it's a kind of messenger."

"Can you be more specific? What a kind of messenger is that?"

"Huh... First, don't be angry, okay?"

"Okay, promised."

"Well, I was thinking that I could be in my classes if I could talk to Doctor Alice. I mean... without visiting you." the daughter is afraid to say.

Charlie lowers his head and thinks. Yes, the blonde girl is right, totally right. He is an inconvenience in his daughter's life. She is studying, striving for a better life to both of them, and he is just an obstacle in Elle's life. But he said and promised he would not be angry.

"I'm so sorry, Mary Elle. I know I've been a jerk on the last days... or... months. I know you could be better at college. I know, I just know. I'll try harder, you'll see. Well, maybe I can help you! Just tell me what you need!"

"Sure, Dad! Hmm... this app will be like a report. Hailee and I have made some questions and a sketch. And we have talked to Mr. Johnson too. Do you remember Mr. Johnson?"

"The designer? Yes, I do. He looks a nice man."

"Well, Mr. Johnson said we need to plan. So, me and Hailee started to do that. And that's what I'm doing right now."

"But you don't like planning, right?"

"Yeah, Dad... I don't..."

"Well, first thing I'd like to say: do things you like, Ms. Blonde. Sometimes you can't, I know. Sometimes you just do what you need. But, it's very good if you have someone to do what you don't like. How about Hailee? Does she like planning? Why don't you ask her that?"

"Actually I don't want to give all the crap work to her, Dad. I don't think that's correct."

"Did you ask her if she likes that?"

"Nope."

"What if she likes? So you are doing this boring work while Hailee could be happy working on that."

"But I want to make all the things, Dad! I want to build this, and I think it's very important to me if I can do the major part."

"Because you had the very first idea?"

"Yes."

"Well, let me tell you something about football and the coach, honey. Everyone in the team has his own task. The coach? He's fine, he's doing his job, just like everyone else. He's looking at all the players; he's taking care of everyone. The coach doesn't have to do all the jobs like running, throwing or push-ups, because we, the players, know how to do those things. He just says what we have to do, and we do. Because the coach's job, and this is his best part, is commanding, not running or anything else. So, even if you have the idea, even if you are the creator of all this, you have to delegate it to a person who does that better than you do. That's how a team shows its best."

"I see, Dad…"

"And there is more. In the beginning, you'll have to do even those things you don't like; that's usual when you start a company. But when the business gets bigger, you have to delegate. That's usual too. You can't take care of everything, even if you are the chairman or the CEO. Just think about any huge company. Do you think its CEO is looking if someone is playing games inside working hours? No, of course not, because the CEO is busy with more important things. So, at this moment, do what you have to do. But in the future, just learn to delegate."

"I like to see everything, Dad. And if I'm building this, I want to do it all!"

"This will work for now, Elle, but it won't work forever. For now, you have to do a lot of things because it's only you and Hailee, right? So, just do it. Take care of everything, see how those things start, how they work, this is important. But, as I said, in the future, and I can't tell you precisely how much time this is, you'll have to ask people to do those things. That is inevitable. And when I talk about people, there is another thing I have to say: choose good people. I'm not talking about beauty or altruism. Choose people who work hard with no complaints; people who you get along with. Of course, must be qualified people. And call someone to complement what you do in the company. And, if you can, call better people, I mean better than you, more competent. You won't want to do that, but do it."

"Why should I call somebody better than me, Dad? What if he or she takes my place?"

"Because when you have to face people more competent than you, you try harder and you improve. In the other hand, when you work with people worse than you, it's easy, it's a comfort zone. And if you want to be an entrepreneur, forget this comfort zone. I mean… forever."

Entrepreneurship, that's the word, the all new word to the blonde girl. Now she realizes what she is doing. And it looks so important now his father is saying it. But, with no comfort zone? Forever? Elle has the answer:

"Okay, Dad. I got that."

"And when things go bad, don't give up. Never. Just try harder and harder, like your mother did. History gifts those who persevere."

"I will, Dad. I promise."

"And I think you have a plan to sell this, right?"

"Oh, this is for Hailee's sister. We are calling her to join the club."

"Have you thought about why you are doing this, Ms. Blonde? I mean, I know it's because I'm always at a hospital and blah blah blah. But, why are you doing this? Why do you need to do this?"

The long blonde hair girl lowers her head for a moment with no answers. "Why?" she thinks. "Is this for me? For my father? Fortune and glory?" she says to herself.

"I just want to do something good, Dad. Something I've never thought before: helping people. Is this too much to ask? Is this, huh... cheesy or too much sentimental? People will think I'm just a foolish girl trying to be someone..."

"Don't you ever think like that, Mary Elle! You can do anything you want! People will always say what you must do. But only you can choose what you will. It's up to you and only you."

Elle smiles and agrees, and she feels so happy now. Her father is a great man. Charlie could be angry because of that app. Or because of his daughter is thinking like an adult (most of parents think their daughters will be children forever). Charlie is not angry; he just understood. That is the least he could do without his wife: understanding his own daughter – is it so hard to do? I do not see any injuries on Charlie on doing this, by the way.

"Okay, Dad, anything else? Maybe the last but not least advice?" she smiles.

"Yes, of course I have, I'm your father!" he smiles too. "Be a good girl. No matter what life brings to you, be a good person, always."

Those words and his voice would remain inside her head for a long time.

Chapter Two – Version 2.5

At night, still on Saturday, Hailee comes to Elle's house. Charlie went out with some friends.

"Hi, Elle! How is the plan?"

"Oh, it's boring, but it's improving, Hailee!"

"Good!"

"Hey, you said you were going to meet your boyfriend, Hailee. What happened?"

"I already met him. And he's not my boyfriend anymore."

"What? I can't believe that! Jesus, Hailee, you're so... so... Oh, I don't even have a word to say!"

"Oh, come on, Elle! He wasn't so interesting, by the way. And he's not a good kisser, by the way..."

"Oh, don't tell me details, please..."

"Ha ha ha! You should date someone, Elle, it's funny! I mean most of times it is."

"Ok, noted." she smiles.

"But, well, now I don't have any more distractions like a boyfriend, how can I help you?

"We have much work here, Hailee."

"What's first?"

"Hmm... I've talked to my father; he said many important things about delegating jobs. He also said it's important to make a good team. Work with people is complicated, you know."

"Yeah, that's why we always work together in all the scholar projects."

"Yes! And we are going to call your sister to join us, right?"

"Yeah. Why? Do you think my sister isn't easy to work together?"

"I was going to ask you, Hailee!"

"Well, she's my older sister! She doesn't bother me so much... We have a nice relationship... I think she's fine to work with."

"Okay, she's in."

"Oh, is this the interview? Only one question? Are you refusing people already?"

"No! I'm just doing what my dad told me. We're not in that position yet, you know, refusing people. I think we must accept all the help for now."

"You must know you'll make a lot of mistakes, Elle. I mean, we will."

"We can't avoid that, Hailee. We are teenagers! Ha ha ha!"

"Ouch... this talk again... I'm just saying we can avoid some mistakes if we plan. But we can't avoid all of them. Sooner or later we'll miss something."

"Well, we'll avoid all mistakes we can."

"Yes, but don't use this 'we are teenagers' stuff as an excuse, okay? Please." the brunette asks with a gesture.

"Deal." the blonde smiles.

"Well, and what about the good news?"

"Hmm… we need a name, remember?"

"Oh, I almost forgot that! Do you have any idea?"

"Nope, zero ideas now."

"Zero? But you are the ideas girl!"

"Am I? Who said that?"

"Huh… I'm saying like, huh… now!"

"Okay, I didn't know you were delegating already, Hailee! Ha ha ha!"

"Ha ha ha! I'm just learning with you, Elle!"

"How can we start this?"

"Let's make a brain storm!"

"You mean, as that teacher I forgot the name told us?"

"Yes! We start to say everything, we write everything, and then we pick one. Or we can combine the options."

"Okay, Hailee, you can start."

"Why me?"

" 'Why me app' noted."

"It wasn't a name yet, Elle!"

"It doesn't matter, Hailee; everything is correct and useful for now. I say… WhatsApp!"

"Great! We'll start the business being sued… how about MSN? And we can name the company as Nineties Microsoft!"

"Awesome, Hailee! We'll be in jail before we start this company!"

"So I say… 'Good report'."

"Hmm… that's a good one! No puns here."

"It must be something short; so people will remember easily, right?"

"Yeah, that's the problem number two."

"What's the number one?"

"It's finding out an innovative name. Like, huh… Google."

"I would prefer a word that is in dictionary, actually."

" 'Google' is already in dictionary, Hailee!"

"Yes, but it took a little time to be in it. I mean, I prefer well-known, familiar words. Because we're starting something new and if we have to explain the name… that's more trouble."

"Okay, but we'll have to explain the name anyway, Hailee. Whatever we choose, we will." advises the blonde girl.

"That's so hard to make! How do the companies do that?"

"I don't know. I think they have a department to do that. There are some companies that create names too."

" 'Department One'."

"Really?" the blonde doubts.

"Yeah… there is no 'wrong' here."

"Okay, so I say… 'Right and Wrong'."

" 'Batman and Robin'."

" 'Avengers versus Thanos'."

" 'Thanos versus Darkseid'."

" 'Superman and Kryptonite'." the blonde girl mentions her favorite.

" 'Thanos versus Avengers'."

"I said that already!" the blonde girl laughs.

"This is the version 2.0, 'The Return'."

"Ha ha ha!"

"Ha ha ha!"

"Okay, 'Avengers versus Justice League – the clash of universes'."

" 'X-Men versus Avengers'."

" 'X-Men versus New Titans'."

"How about 'X-Men and Avengers versus Justice League and New Titans – The most epic battle ever'?"

" 'Marvel versus DC'."

" 'Marvel versus DC versus the world'."

" 'Avengers and Thanos versus Justice League and Darkseid'."

"How about 'Inhumans, Avengers, X-Men and Fantastic Four versus DC Universe'?"

" 'Funny and useless'."

"Ha ha ha!"

"Ha ha ha!"

"Oh, this is so hard!" says the brunette girl.

" 'Nice and easy'."

" 'Hard work'."

" 'I'm tired'."

"Hey, using phrases is nice!"

"Was that a name?"

"Nope!"

"Nope and nothing!"

"Oh, God!"

"That's a nice one!" someone says ironically.

"Is this working?" says Hailee.

"Yes, it's totally working! I don't know, actually! We'll know when we finish this!" says Elle.

"I think we should direct this. Like, huh… to a target."

"Like what? Maybe to 'messenger something'."

"Not exactly a messenger, maybe a report. I see it like a report."

" 'Medical Report'."

"Too normal, average. How about 'Medkit'?"

"Like that zombie game?" remembers the blonde.

"Yeah! That cooperative zombie game we still play!"

"What do you think about 'Reporting Things'?"

"Hmm… good! And how about 'The patient is fine'?"

"Hey, that's good too! Maybe we should try 'patient and something'."

" 'Healthy Care'?"

"Or 'Healing people'."

"But we are not healing people."

"Well, it's just a name. What is an iPhone?"

"It means internet, individual, instruct, inform and inspire."

"But nobody knows that! We don't need a name everybody knows the meaning at the first sight." says Elle.

"As I said, I prefer well-known names." remembers Hailee.

"Okay, we'll try harder."

" 'Keep silence'."

"Like a hospital warning?"

"Yep!"

"This line of thought is good, Hailee. I like it. How about 'Reporting Things'?"

"Again?"

"Did I say that already?"

"Yes, maybe seventeen or eighteen lines ago."

"Are you counting?" Elle surprises.

"Yes, I'm writing all the ideas!" Hailee informs.

"Okay… 'Be patient'."

"Or… 'Heal the patient'."

"Or 'Be fine'."

"Maybe 'Messaging Health'."

"Or 'A Health Message'."

" 'Health Report'."

"Wow, we're improving this!"

"Hmm… It must be something that explains what we do. And at the same time it must show we care about our relatives at the hospital. I mean it must be a cute name, maybe."

"Cute name?"

"Yeah, why not? We're still girls and that could be like a brand, a trademark."

"I like that! Huh… 'Cute Report'?"

"Huh… not so cute or so explicit. Ha ha ha!"

"I'm just trying, Hailee! There is no 'wrong', right?" smiles Elle.

"God! This is so hard! Remember me not to work at those companies that create names, please!"

"Okay, noted. Maybe we need something to drink. I'll bring some juice, do you want it?"

"Yes, please!"

Elle goes to the kitchen and opens the white fridge with some stuck papers on its door. She takes the orange juice package and puts in two glasses which have small drawings. Soon she comes back to the headquarters, I mean the bedroom.

"What if we try something like 'Orange Report'?" says Elle.

"Not orange, please! It's a kind of military weapon!"

"Oh, I didn't know that! We need to be careful about those things! Can you imagine if we use an offensive or illegal name?"

"Yes, we must be very careful! Do you know what 'Siri' means in Japanese?"

"Nope."

"Japanese people pronounce 'sheeree' and that means 'butt'."

"Ouch! Japanese people talk to the butt? Epic fail!"

"Yes, but it's Apple, they can do that. We don't have this chance."

"So… where are we?"

"Well, the best name until now is… 'Messaging health with a cute orange report and be fine, or call The Avengers and Justice League to save the world'."

"Oh, that's awful…" but the blonde girl smiles.

"Now we need to select from the names." says Hailee.

"What if no one is good enough?"

"We start again."

"Oh, can I handle this again?

"You can, you're the founder of this company!"

"Hey, now I'm the founder?"

"Yep! You've started this. And I…"

"I know! You said this would be a hard job! I know that!"

"Ha ha ha!" they laugh.

There are many laughs before they start again. It is not a simple question – nothing is when you are building a company. Finding a name is a huge and hard work, and sometimes it is the most important element before start producing, selling, managing and monitoring. They are having fun, at least. It is an all new world to both of them, and they are loving it. Sooner or later, the most probably is the present year, they will leave the college. And those new words like entrepreneurship, companies, and names sound like the adult world. The girls are really growing up.

Suddenly, a noise comes from the front door. It is late already, and the time has passed too fast to the blonde and the brunette at that night. Some footsteps come closer, but the girls do not listen anything. They are still thinking and studying, and they are focused (and a little tired). Someone comes to the bedroom's door, knocks nicely, and says:

"Dad's home!"

Immediately the blonde girl raises her head and smiles – and her fingertips start to sweat. Hailee sees that smile, moves an eyebrow and thinks something like "Are you sure?" She smiles too. Elle starts to laugh and her blue eyes are shinning. The best friend smiles again and makes some movement with her arms and shoulders. She says "Okay, then!" and she agrees with Elle.

The app name is chosen.

CHAPTER THREE – VERSION 3.0 – WHO ARE MY FRIENDS? WHERE ARE THEY?

Emma and Lily

"Am I the last one to know about this nickname?"

"Huh… yes, maybe, huh… no… I don't know!"

When Hailee told Emma about the nickname, the Ms. Marketing, I mean, the older sister did not like it, of course. How many years Hailee was using that nickname to speak about her older sister? As Emma has gotten the graduation two years ago, I could say that was how long Hailee has been kidding. Not so long, indeed. I know jokes and cheats between brothers and sisters that take much more time.

"Oh, sisters…" Emma says shaking her head in disapproval, but with a smile.

"I'm sorry! But you were out of control! And… huh…sometimes annoying! Oops! My bad!" Hailee says and grins.

"Okay, so tell me about this app."

"This is the deal, Emma."

Hailee tells her about everything: Elle's father at the hospital, the idea, the app, the sketches, the talk to Mr. Johnson, the brain storm and, of course, Avengers versus Justice League.

"Dad's home? Really? What a kind of name is this?"

"Oh, don't ask me. Elle just picked it. But there is a story, Emma. Elle told me later."

"What is this?"

"Well, there are these Mr. Panning health facts. He's always at the hospital because of some heart complications I can't explain to you exactly. And it's so good when Elle thinks he is coming home… It's only her and her father, as you know. So, it's not about the name or how it sounds, or even whether it's idiot. It's about the feeling, the emotion. It's about how the patient's relatives feel when a patient comes home. Maybe it's not the best idea, if we think from the marketing point of view, but there is more than that: there is a great story to tell. It's about a father coming back home to his daughter."

"I got it. You convinced me. And we can use this in marketing, a touching story."

"And, by the way, we were working hard for hours to find a name! And when Elle's father knocked at the door, Elle just smiled."

"Eureka!"

"Yeah! Just like that!"

"And what is next?"

"Hmm... we need to learn how to sell this. That's why we are calling you. And before that we need a logo and we need to finish the sketch and... Oh, my God! I forgot the code! We need to find someone to help me coding this!"

"Can't you do it by yourself, Hailee?"

"No, of course not! I can do only the front-end! I'm still learning back-end development!"

"Huh... English, please.

"The front-end is how the user will see everything. It's more design and user experience. The back-end is the rest, I mean how the data will, huh... 'talk' to this front-end. And how everything will be managed in the server. To be short, that's how it works."

"And what is a server?" Emma asks while frowns an eyebrow.

"Don't you know what a server is? It's like a... huh... like a big closet, full of clothes and jewelry and... perfume bottles. You are the front-end when you dress up and people see you in a good design, nice and beautiful, and the most important: working."

"I know what a server is, Hailee, but thanks for the comparison." smiles Emma.

"Oh, you're always testing me..."

"Don't bother, it's good to you!"

"Yes, and annoying!"

"Oh, come on, little sister! Ha ha ha!"

They have a good relationship as sisters. Emma is two years older and she can teach and instruct Hailee and Elle. She is working at an enterprise already, and that is very valuable because she has some experiences the other girls do not. Unfortunately, to Emma at least, the younger sister is eight centimeters taller than the older one. It means Emma is 1.65 meters tall. And that difference, my dear reader, means a lot to them when they start to debate (or fight).

The older sister has some freckles on her face. No, I am being nice. There are a million of them on Emma's face (now it is an overstatement), and they are all joined under her eyes. Big eyes, by the way, big dark brown eyes with light brown hair. Someone told me she was blonde, but I did not check that. Emma has a body in shape (maybe some grams to over), even though she enjoys eating thousands of chocolate bars almost every day – her favorite sweet. About the freckles, whatever: a vanity case is always a good friend to her (and to other girls). However, most of times, she does not make up; she likes natural look and this natural look is very attractive already. She has a mysterious thing in her eyes – a charming thing – that could bewitch people. Maybe she had been a sorceress or a little witch elsewhere or in other times, maybe it is just a perfect combination between eyes color and well drawn eyebrows – I do not know!

"You should talk to Elle, Emma. She has many details about the app. And you can talk about the… huh… company's inception. So you can start the marketing plan. I don't know if that's the right name."

"Yes, that's correct, marketing plan. But we need to talk about the app before, and then about mission, vision, and values."

"I don't know those things!"

"It's about the company purpose, Hailee. I can tell you it's not only profit and selling. We can meet Elle next weekend. What do you think?"

"Great! I'll send her a message."

Chapter Three – Version 3.1

The weekend came fast to the girls, and now we have three of them: the Ideas Girl or the Founder, the Designer and Ms. Marketing (now they have positions too). They are having a meeting at Elle's house.

"Hi!"

"Hi, Emma! Where is Hailee?"

"Oh, she's in a new date with a new guy."

"A boyfriend? So soon? She just broke up with her last boyfriend a few days ago!"

"Yeah, I told her that too… But she doesn't listen to me, Elle! It's okay, she's having fun with boys, that's all."

"Okay, please come in, Emma!"

"Thanks!"

They meet Charlie, Elle's father, as you know, at the living room.

"Good afternoon, Mr. Panning!"

"Hi, Emma, how are you doing?"

"I'm fine, thank you, Mr. Panning!"

"Emma is helping Hailee and me as the marketing specialist, Dad!"

"Oh, that's great, girls! Good luck!"

"Thank you, Mr. Panning!"

"We're in the bedroom, Dad!"

And then they go to the headquarters.

"Well, what we got here?"

"This is it: sometimes I have to go to the hospital to visit my father, that handsome man down there. And this visiting is on class time. But I can't leave the hospital because I have to talk to the doctor. Just to know if my father is fine or to have some recommendations, right? And so, I have to wait for a long time, sometimes over than two hours. I've waited for four hours once, because the doctors don't have a right time to come, they are always late. And, of course, teachers don't wait for me to begin the classes! Finally, if I had some way to talk to the doctors, it would be great!"

"Why not a phone call?"

"Jesus, this is the third time I'm listening this joke in this story!" Elle makes a gesture with his right hand.

"Story? What story?"

"This app's story, Emma!"

"It's just a suggestion, Elle, take it easy!" Emma laughs.

"Okay, a phone call is not a report. And a message is not a report too. That's what I need: a report about my father. Hailee and I have written some questions to put in this report."

"Let me see it, please."

Elle opens the file in the computer and Emma reads the questions.

"So short?"

"Yes, we wanted to make it simple. Because I think the doctors won't have time to answer ten questions or more. So it's simple questions, just to update me about my father. If the doctor has to say anything else, there will be a blank field."

"Fine, I liked it. It's brief and easy to fill out."

"Yes, that's the primary goal."

"And then what?"

"And then... we need to find who is gonna buy this. Wait. First we need to produce this. And that's Hailee's job. But she thinks she can't. Did she tell you that?"

"Yes, she did. She said something about front-end and back-end."

"Oh, I got that. She can do only front-end, right?"

"Right."

"Then we need a back-end developer. But, before that, we need a sketch. Oh, wait! We have a sketch already, I've scanned it, and it's in my computer. Check it out."

"Hmm... good. But how can we sell this?"

"Oh, no! We have to produce this first, I mean coding and all. This is just a sketch."

"And who's working on that?"

"Huh… Hailee, I guess."

"Isn't she the designer?"

"Oh… we are taking many roles here, Emma. You know, we don't have so many people working with us."

"Fine, so let's start with what we have now. Hailee told me about the story of the app name. We can use this like a touching story."

"Can we?"

"Completely, Elle! A great story is a very powerful approach in marketing. Especially if this story is connected to the company's beginning. We have a good chance here."

"Great! But how do we use this?"

"This is the deal: probably we'll have to present this to an audience, or to investors. And then you can tell the app's story. But you don't tell like a sad or melancholic story. You do this like an inspiring one, like a driving force in your life. We'll put that on a website too."

"I can see it! Wow, you are good!"

"That's why I'm 'Ms. Marketing'." Emma smiles.

"Oh, Hailee told you this nickname?"

"Yes, few days ago. Wait! Did you know about this nickname too?"

"Huh… no!" but Elle laughs forced.

"Oh, I'm really the last person in the world to know about this…"

They laugh a little to relax a little more. They have a touching story which explains the reason to make the app, to begin something, and that is a nice start – how many companies can tell an emotional true story? And now they can even think about a company, not only an app. However, this journey is not that easy.

A short time later, Charlie comes to the bedroom.

"Hey, Ms. Blonde, you have a visit."

"Hi, ladies!"

"Hailee? What a surprise! What happened?"

"Oh, the date is over. So I came here for business! Yes!" she makes a gesture.

The other girls look each other, they wait for a while.

"Huh… oh, forget it!" says Elle.

"What?" Hailee asks.

"Nothing. It's not important." Elle says.

"What?" she insists with some gestures.

"Did you break up with your new boyfriend already, sister?" Emma interferes.

"No! We're not together! We're still getting to know each other! It's just... just a talk. I didn't even kiss him!"

"Okay, understood." finishes Elle.

"Huh... does your father call you 'Ms. Blonde'?" asks Emma.

"Yes. When my mother died, I became the only blonde woman here. So, he started to call me like that."

"Okay. Good story."

"So, where were we? Did you get some progress?" asks Hailee.

"Yes, we've talked about the app and its story." answers Elle.

"Now we need to talk about the company." says Emma.

"Oh, mission, vision, and values?" remembers Hailee.

"And how do we start this?" wants to know Elle.

"Well, first, I'd like to explain why we are doing this, it's important. Mission, vision and values are the basics of any company, right? That's why we need to do this. Because later, when we'll be working, probably we'll forget to do this, or we'll have no time. But this will be the 'general lines', the principles of the company, and we must remember them every day. So, we need to think wisely before writing this. Okay?"

"Okay." Elle and Hailee say.

"So, the mission is our purpose, why this company exists. Anyone wants to start?"

"Elle?" asks Hailee.

"Hmm... we help people."

"Just like that? So simple?" asks Hailee.

"It's simple to say, but not so simple to do!" Elle laughs.

"Could you be more specific, Elle? You can help people in different ways: with money, love, a ride, a favor, maybe." Emma asks.

"Hmm... now it's hard to say..."

"We help people bringing them closer?"

"We bring people closer?"

"We help people and bring people closer?"

"We help people and their relatives?"

"We bring people and their relatives closer?"

"We help people and the marketplace?"

"We work to the people?"

"We solve problems in the marketplace?"

"We solve people's problems, maybe?"

"I think this is not working, ladies!" Hailee says.

"Hmm, everything we are saying is right!" says Elle.

"Yes, you both are right." completes Emma.

"So what?"

"Everything is right, but we can't have it all."

"So we go back to start."

"And that means…"

"That means…"

"We help people." says Emma.

"I don't get it. Why are we back?" Hailee says.

"Yes, why?" Elle says.

"People will understand when we show them the app. They will see what the company does. If they don't, you'll explain, Elle." Emma teaches.

"Why me?"

"Because you're the founder."

She agrees moving her head. Now everything is so different than before, few weeks ago. An idea, an app, a company (maybe a small business for now, but she likes to call it that way). It is all very different than classes, homework, and teachers. Is she in the adult world already? She told me nothing.

"What about the vision, Emma?" the sister asks.

"The vision statement is about our objectives and ideals. It's about where we want to be in the future and what we are doing to reach this. It must be inspiring and memorable, because the vision statement will give us a direction, it will guide us."

"I don't understand. Isn't 'Helping people' a vision statement?"

"No, it's different, Hailee. The mission statement is why the company exists; the vision statement is what we want."

"Well, we want to help people, right? So, it's the vision."

"No, that's why we are here: to help people. I know, it's confusing, but it's different. We are here to help people and we want…"

"Help people!" Hailee smiles.

"No, that's why the company exists! The vision statement could be… huh… 'we want to see people being helped'."

"Great, Emma! You just changed the verb tenses, the passive voice, and blah blah blah!"

"It's just an example with the same words, Hailee! Because I don't know what to say! Elle?"

"Huh… we want… we want a better world, where people don't have to wait for hours at hospitals…"

"Good one! That's a vision statement! Not a pretty one, but it's good!" says Emma.

"I still don't get that!"

"You'll understand when we finish it, Hailee, don't worry!" says the older sister.

"Okay, how about 'We want to see a world where people are closer'?" says Elle.

"Not bad."

"We want to bring people closer."

"That's a mission statement, Hailee."

"I didn't get that! It's all the same to me!" Hailee complains.

"Okay, so let's try like this: how do we want people see us? I mean target audience, marketplace and the other companies. So it should be something like 'We want to be viewed like a great company.' "

"Oh, now I'm starting to get that…" Hailee says.

"We want to be known as an inspiring company?"

"Yes, something like that, Elle! But that's too usual, I mean standard." advises Emma (and she is correct).

"We want to be seen like a company that helps people." and Hailee laughs.

"We want a world without distances."

"Wow, I'm impressed, Elle! But I think that's some company slogan or a song." Emma says.

"God, this is hard!" complains Elle.

"We want more hot boyfriends!"

"Great, Hailee! And no men will want to work with us!"

"Think about what you were feeling when you had the idea, Elle. All the events and the feelings before it." suggests Emma.

"We want to live in a world where people and their relatives are closer?" someone says.

"A world where there will be no distance between them?"

"We want to reduce distances between people?"

"We want a better world, where people are not so far away from each other?"

"We want to make easier the communication?"

"We'll have a lot of work with that…"

"We solve problems in the marketplace and we solve people's problems. Because we want to live in a better world, and we will build it." says the founder.

"Wow! What was that? Now I am impressed, Elle! Repeat, please, I'm writing!"

"Oh, didn't you get that, Hailee? Oh, God! What did I say? Wait,

wait! Huh... people's problems... and... Oh, my God! We should have a recorder here! Wait, I can remember! I can remember! Wait, don't say anything! I can get this!"

"Easy, easy! Just say it again! Think and say it again!" Emma smiles.

Elle says word for word while Hailee is typing and making a backup. That afternoon is being very useful and productive. And now they have almost all the company's statements.

"Okay, ladies, now we need our values." Emma directs.

"Values?"

"What values?"

"The values are our principles, our beliefs. They sustain the company and support the mission and vision statements."

"English, please."

"Like, huh... ethics. And moral or loyalty." teaches Emma.

"I get that! That's easier than the vision statement." says and points Hailee.

"If you're saying so..."

"What? This can't be hard, Emma! How many values do we need?"

"Enough values."

"How many is that?" asks Elle.

"I don't know! Enough is enough!" Emma smiles.

"Okay, so let's try two to each one of us. We'll have six values." starts Hailee.

"Fine, so what's yours?" says the older sister.

"I don't know. Let me think. Maybe knowledge and expertise?"

"Practical things."

"Is it wrong?"

"No, I'm just saying." Emma, huh... says.

"Okay, your turn."

"I could say... honesty and focus." suggests Emma.

"Elle?"

"I would say... charity and... collective well-being... And... fun!"

"Fun?" they doubt.

"Yeah, why not? We don't have to be serious all the time. Because even if we take the worst job ever, if we are having fun, it's worthwhile."

"The founder says..." laughs Hailee.

"Hey, it's not like that! I'm just placing my opinion! Everything we're doing now, if we don't even have fun... I don't think it's worthy, ladies. I'm not being irresponsible. It's just... how can I say... it's just... not thinking seriously all the time, like, huh... if you fail you're fired or you're dead. Not all the things must be like this. Does it sound irresponsible?"

"Not so much." says Emma.

"Okay, so we change this. We put 'a little fun sometimes'."

"Oh, that's much better!" says Hailee. "I'm serious, it's better."

"Yeah, why not? Good." agrees Emma.

"And put 'sometimes' between brackets. How about that?"

"Great, we are writing an art book now!"

"Okay, take off the brackets, Hailee!"

"Ha ha ha! I'm just saying, Elle! Don't worry, I'm putting your desired brackets!"

"Ha ha ha!" they laugh.

And now it is almost night at the headquarters (also known as bedroom). The girls are tired of talking about statements and reasons and jobs and all of this. Sometimes they just want some fun and it is not wrong. They are not irresponsible, they are humans. And even when you are doing what you love, what you were born for, you get tired. I cannot write for sixteen hours, thirty days in a month, for one year. Because I am human. Moreover, we do get tired. Anyway, I think they are having fun with all that unusual work – those girls are growing up.

Chapter Three – Version 3.2

"A company?"

"Yes, Lily, a company."

"You mean a start-up company?"

"A start-up? What is the difference?"

"It's different, Emma, and this concept is not very clear to all people. A company, most of times, is a traditional company like car, food or electronics maker. A start-up works in an uncertain market, sometimes a niche, and there is no assurance in its success. And, many times, a start-up means technology and that means internet, but this is not a fixed rule. However, as I said before, this definition isn't clear to everyone. If you ask to someone else, he or she will tell you different words."

"So we can call our company as a start-up, Lily?"

"According to what you've told me, yes. Let's think a start-up has some different features like age, growth, and stability. And, as I said, it works in an uncertain market, which means it can grow as fast as it can fail. There is more: the product must be scalable and repeatable.

I mean, you produce once, and you repeat forever, only with some improvements. Therefore, it's cheaper, and cheaper is good, right? Finally… scalable means you can replicate easily even in larger systems."

"I see, Lily. Oh, I didn't know those things! I mean, I knew a few about it, but not exactly as you told me now. Thank you!"

"You're welcome, Emma!"

"So are you in?"

"What? Is this a job interview?"

"Huh… not exactly, but it can be!"

"God, I'm not even dressed properly, Emma!"

"Ha ha ha! It's okay, I can't see you by a phone call! So are you in or not?"

"Oh, I don't know, Emma! I'm working so hard now! I don't think I'll have time for that!"

"You must be in, Lily! You're my best friend! And I think we're doing something here!"

"Oh, I'll think about it, okay? Don't be angry."

"Sure! But sooner or later we'll need you, Lily."

Lily has a graduation in Management, especially Finance. That allows her to say what a company can pay or not, and the most important: what a company must pay or not. And she loves that (I mean money). She used to say Finance was "above everything" in any company because "money rules" everywhere. She is not a consumerism victim, she is just being realistic. The girl with "the most perfect and powerful eyebrows ever" (according to Emma's speech) has dark brown hair (not so long) and hazel color eyes (yes, that hard to explain eye color). She is also 1.65 meters tall like her best friend Emma. And I cannot tell you how much they weight. Lily also can make an extremely meticulous financial control of her personal expenses. So accurate that she never delayed any payment and never asked anyone for money – in her life. That financial control is almost sick for ordinary people. A plenty of numbers, spreadsheets and calculations that could make a mathematician blushes. However, she has some usual likes as sushi and swimming – her thick dark eyebrows get wet three times every week.

Sooner or later, Emma, Elle and Hailee will need Lily and her skills, because, as the finance girl says, "money rules." And then, Emma will invite her best friend again, for an adventure called start-up. Actually, that will take less than forty-eight hours to happen. Then, Lily will join the team.

CHAPTER FOUR – VERSION 4.0 – HOW CAN WE ORGANIZE THIS MESS?

The Manager

"A contest?"

"Yeah! What do you think?"

"Huh... sure, why not? But... are we ready for that?" Hailee is afraid.

"I don't know! Are we?" Elle smiles.

"Don't you know? And are we going to take part in this?"

"Yes! It's only for students at college, so we don't have to worry, I guess. And it's an opportunity to have some feedback, especially from the teachers."

"Okay, let's do this!" Hailee agrees.

But they are not ready. They have to present an app, but where is it? They just have sketches on a paper. Any solution? Elle has read the rules of the competition, of course. If not, she would not call her friends (and now partners). And the rules are clear.

"Don't we need to demonstrate the app? I mean, it doesn't have to work?" asks Hailee.

"No, of course not! We just have to show the idea, the project. That's what we have for now."

"But what about the other teams?"

"I don't know! Maybe they'll do the same."

"What if everybody shows a working app? And only we show some sketches?"

"It's quite possible, Hailee. Well, at least we'll have the feedback. I think that's the most valuable."

"So you're not thinking in the first place?"

"Yes, I am! But I need to be realistic, Hailee. I have to see the other teams first. So I can tell you about the first place."

"Hey, Emma told me that! In a war, you need to go to the front to say if you can overcome the enemy."

"What?"

"It means you can't plan from the office. You need to go to the front. That's marketing, Elle!"

"Oh, that's too advanced to me, Hailee!"

"But you just said! Ha ha ha!"

"Ha ha ha!"

"So when do we start this?"

"Let's talk to Emma and Lily!"

Chapter Four – Version 4.1

When the night comes, the fantastic four are having a meeting at Elle's bedroom (the headquarters).

"I'd like to talk about the company first." Elle begins.

"What is it?" says Hailee.

"Well, should we present the company in the contest?"

"I don't know. Is it necessary?" says Emma.

"I think it would look like more professional."

"But how much time will we have?" Lily says.

"Huh... wait, let me see the rules...Huh... between five and ten minutes."

"What?" says Hailee.

"Five minutes? That's an elevator pitch, but longer." teaches Lily.

"Huh... English, please, Lily." asks Hailee.

"It's a speech you make about your business. And it must be fast like an elevator talk. That's why it's called elevator pitch. Ideally, an elevator pitch should take one minute, maybe less." the finance girl explains.

"What? A minute? It's impossible!"

"It's not impossible, Hailee! Many people do that!"

"What can we say in one minute? Only our names? And the company's name, maybe?" asks Emma.

"No, we say the problem and our solution; who is our target and who are our competitors, and those things are up to you, Emma; and then we say who we are. I would love if we could show some financial planning, but I think we'll have no time for this." explains Lily.

"In one minute? All of this? People do that?"

"Yes, Hailee."

"God, this is hard..."

"But we'll have up to ten minutes in this contest, Hailee. It'll be easier." Lily comforts her.

"Can we have a powerpoint or something, Lily?" asks Emma.

"Yes, I guess so. What's in the rules, Elle?"

"Just a second... Yes, we can!"

"How professional is this contest, Elle? Do you know anything about that?"

"Huh… well, it's a college contest, Lily. I don't know how professional it is."

"Better we get prepared, ladies." advises Emma.

"What about the judges? Any professionals or only teachers?"

"Hmm… wait, Hailee… Yes, there are professionals of the sector, huh… IT men. But I don't know any of them."

"Oh, so this is big." says Lily.

"Really?"

"Yes, they call some people from the marketplace to support, to give credibility to the contest. It looks like more important and, how can I say? 'Serious.' What if Bill Gates is in the jury?" Lily winks with a mouth snap.

"Wow, it would be awesome!" says Emma.

Now they are on a mission. It is not the homework or writing or some school project. And, as Elle said, they will have the feedback on what they are doing. But, is it enough? Why cannot they dream higher?

"So, I'll start to do the five minutes elevator pitch." starts the founder.

"Can you make the powerpoint, Hailee?"

"Oh, I hate powerpoint, Emma… I'm a designer… but I'll do it."

"Thanks! Because I'm writing the contents."

"I'll help Elle with the presentation then." finishes Lily.

They work until late at night. For all the time they think what they are building: maybe only an app for us, readers and watchers, but it is something else to them – what can they do? Where can they go?

When you start a dream – or a project, if you prefer – you can meet two sorts of people: the believers and the losers. The first kind will encourage you. These persons will boost your will and energy because… because they can dream too! Do not waste your time with the second group. This one will try to say what you must do or who you must be. Do not get angry with them, just feel sorry for these people – they do not know what they are doing. Only you can say who you are or what you can do. If people do not like you, they should walk away. Just be you. Those girls are being themselves. And they are growing up fast.

Chapter Four – Version 4.2

Elle and Lily.

"How long?"

"Hmm… eleven minutes and sixteen seconds."

"Oh, no…"

"It must be faster, Elle!"

"I'm trying, Lily!"

"What if you don't say anything about us? Let people think about and ask."

"Let's try!"

"It must be seven or eight minutes, Elle. So we'll have some spare time if something goes wrong."

"Okay, let's try it. I think I'm getting anxious, Lily."

"Don't worry, Elle, everything is gonna be okay. You'll make a great presentation and the audience will love it. And we're gonna get the first prize!" Lily encourages her.

"Oh, okay… I'm already sweating…"

"It's just ten minutes, Elle."

"I can live a life in ten minutes, Lily!"

Hailee and Emma.

"What exactly do you want to say with this, Emma?"

"What?"

"Huh… 'Our goal is try to communicate to patient's relatives that the patients are fine?' "

"What is wrong?"

"Too long. It doesn't fit in only one line in the slide."

"Is it a rule?"

"Yes, I've just created it, right now."

"Okay, how about 'Reporting'?"

"That's all?"

"Yeah, that's all."

"I didn't get that."

"What if we put only one word in every slide? And Elle will explain everything."

"Nice! But can she explain everything in ten minutes? And the slides will not help her?"

"They will."

"Okay, so why don't we put only an image in every slide?"

"Only a picture?"

"Yes. That's how people are doing the best presentations at present."

"How does it work?"

"Well, we put a picture to suggest what Elle is gonna explain. Like, huh… Elle is gonna speak about patients at hospitals, so we put a picture of a hospital. A pretty one, of course."

"I like it! Let's do like this then!"

Elle and Hailee.

"What is this?"

"It's the powerpoint slides."

"Where are the texts?"

"There are no texts."

"I can see that, Hailee! But why?"

"Huh… we chose not to use texts."

"And you didn't ask me about that! What if I forget the texts?"

"Will you?"

"I don't know! I don't know about tomorrow, Hailee!"

"But you are practicing, Elle! You won't forget it!"

"Huh… this powerpoint supposedly should help me in the presentation, Hailee."

"But, it's so beautiful, Elle! Check out this picture of happy people! I took half an hour to find this! Are you nervous?"

"Okay, okay, Hailee… I'm just getting stressed, I think! Oh, God! I'm collapsing here, Hailee!"

"Oh, God, Elle! Just breathe! Breathe!"

"Jesus, what if I forget everything during the presentation?"

"I don't know! Don't ask me! Well, that's why you're practicing, Elle!"

Lily and Emma.

"Don't you think we should put some numbers, Emma? I think it's not complete, I mean… fully loaded."

"I don't know, Lily. I don't know what a kind of contest this is. If we could ask to someone… we can get ready for everything, but it can be too much for a college contest. I mean, we can work hard and people just want to see an idea on a paper. In the other hand, we can write only the idea and other teams can come with a working app! We don't know…"

"So, what can we do?"

"We wait."

"And let's see what happens." Lily smiles.

"And let's see what happens." Emma agrees and moves her head.

"Okay, like the old times…"

"Yeah, like the old times, Lily." Emma smiles.

They had studied together. And, at the college, sometimes you have to choose between "done" and "perfect" – maybe you have to do that in all your life, by the way. Moreover, the twenty-four years old girls (fine, I will call them "young adults" then) had to make that choice many times. In the end, when you leave a few colleges, what remains is your knowledge, your degree and, now and then, your soul. Because some things are as they are: unchangeable. They could talk about learning and teaching, but they are not in a college anymore. And, at that moment, it does not matter to Lily and Emma whether the other girls are trying hard on studying.

However, is it right to forget what you have lived? Is it bad when you go back and think about your old troubles to help people? Or you just laugh and ignore them (the people and the troubles)?

Next weekend, the "First Entrepreneurship Contest – Design, Ideas and Mind-Blowing" will begin. Yes, the name is unusual (and fun).Two girls do not look concerned (but they are); one of them is stressed because of the last one. And this last one girl is almost having a syncope already.

Chapter Four – Version 4.3

"How do I look?"

"You look fine, Elle!" praises Hailee.

"I'm sweating!"

"Don't worry, everything is going to be fine!" says Emma. "You're the founder, remember? So, be the founder!"

"Nobody told me it would be so hard!"

"Nobody told you it would be easy." says Lily.

It is Saturday afternoon, and they are at the contest, the first entrepreneurship contest in that college. They are still seated at the auditorium chairs to watch the other groups. The most of the teaching staff was there, even from the other fields of knowledge (not Graphic Design or Information Technology). The first group to present is formed by three boys and one girl. They are saying something about sun's energy and how their project can improve its using. It is a nice presentation, with a good powerpoint slide show. They also have some brochures, and they deliver to the audience.

"We don't have any printed material…"

"We are digital, Hailee! Stop underestimating our work!" says Emma.

"I didn't! But can we have a few printed next time?"

"We're trying to finish this one, Hailee." laughs Lily.

The second team comes with a new approach to e-commerce. The five boys have an app, a working one.

"Is that working? Really?"

"Huh… yes, Hailee, it's working."

"And ours is not!"

"Don't worry, Hailee, everything is going to be fine!" Lily comforts her.

"Yes, stop comparing, you both!" warns Emma.

Now it is time to the third group. Two girls and two boys come with a new project to help people in disasters, especially children.

"What is that?"

"What?"

"The T-shirts!"

"Oh, my God! Are they wearing T-shirts with a logo? Their company's logo?"

"Huh… yes! It's a company logo!"

"We didn't even have a logo, Hailee! We forgot that!"

"Ladies, please! Just watch them!" asks Emma.

"Yes, please! Just be quiet for a moment!" asks Lily.

The fourth group of boys comes to show an app to provide a new payment way with fingers and numbers. They have a logo, a working app and brochures.

"Oh, it's getting harder…"

"How long do we wait here?"

"We are the next, Hailee! No, there is another group before us."

"Oh, I think I'll pass out here."

"Hey! Stop with this, you both!" asks Lily.

"Ladies, we got to go! The staff is calling us to get prepared!"

The girls go to the backstage: powerpoint slides, smiles, postures, gestures, and clothes, everything is ready to start. They still have time to see the other group of six boys. These boys present an app to help small business in marketing and finance.

"What do you think, Lily?"

"Not bad, but it's just regular, Emma."

"Oh, so you are judging now?"

"We are judging all the time, Elle!"

"But you say nothing!"

"We are watching before judging!" Lily laughs.

"You don't look girls! We do speak all the time!"

"And now, we'd like to call the next group." announces the host.

"Oh, God, it's happening… we don't have a name for our group!"

"Be quiet, Hailee!"

The girls come to stage and thank the audience with their best smiles. Cheers. Emma, Hailee and Lily stay one or two steps back while Elle comes to front. It is show time.

"My name is Elle, and these are my friends Hailee, Emma and Lily. Our project is about communication. Communication between doctors and patient's relatives. It's like a report from the doctors. Therefore, patient's relatives don't have to go to the hospital. They receive a message in their cell phones, which informs the patient's status. In this way, patient's relatives don't spend their time with visitations. They can be informed about their relatives."

"Hey, what if I want to see a relative at the hospital?" someone yells.

Elle lowers her head and thinks; she looks to the other girls. Does she have an answer?

"We can take questions after the presentation, mister! Thank you!" says Emma.

"Go on!" Lily says with a gesture.

"Huh... where was I? Oh, when I said people don't have to spend their time, I didn't mean people don't have to visit their relatives."

"So what did you say?" other person asks.

Elle stops speaking and looks to the girls again.

"Could you ask that after the presentation, mister, please?" says Lily.

"Huh... well, our objective is not splitting people, of course. Our objective is... is..." she starts to sweat.

"Hey, don't you know about your own project, young lady?" someone asks.

"She doesn't!" a person laughs in the audience.

"Mister, we are taking notes of all these questions, okay? Thank you!" says Lily.

Elle remembers her father. Why is she doing that? Fortune and glory? Self-protection? Self-assertion? She remembers her mother. What would she do in that case? How would she behave in front of approximately one hundred people at that auditorium? People asking and challenging her. Suddenly, she remembers.

"Our objective is..."–she takes a deep breath–"is helping people. Because people have relatives at hospital, but they still have their lives. We do not abandon our relatives because we are working for them, out of a hospital." her voice breaks and she almost starts to cry.

"Now, I'd like to talk about competitors and marketplace." Emma comes to front with an irresistible smile and interrupts Elle.

The blonde girl understands. She could not go on. Those questions, those people, what was that? They did not practice any of that. Furthermore, people did not ask so much to other groups, only a few questions after every presentation. Why?

Emma speaks comfortably while Elle is still thinking. Ms. Marketing speaks about rivals and market – she loves it. She is saying the app can be an alternative to phone calls and long and useless reports, which only doctors can read. Emma still says that maybe the marketplace can resist because the app is quite unusual – people can prefer visiting their relatives. In the other hand, sometimes these same people do not have time to visit – and she says this is exactly the opportunity they are trying to reach. Emma also emphasizes that the objective is not splitting people, but saving time when people have to wait for the doctors only to know a few things they can get in their cell phones. She says these things can be reported through the app they are planning. Ms. Marketing finishes the presentation and the audience applauds. Only one person asks about dates and scheduling and Emma says the team are still planning this. There are no more questions and we can listen the applauses again in the auditorium. The show is over. The girls thank and go to the backstage.

Almost an hour after all the presentations, they get the result.

"Wow, not so bad, huh?"

"Not so bad, Hailee? Eleventh place! What presentation have you seen?"

"Hey, it was the first time, Elle!"

"It was fine, Elle, come on!" says Lily.

"Fine? Emma?" Elle looks at Ms. Marketing.

"I think it was good for now. But we can improve, surely we can."

"God! Am I the only one who could see that disaster? An eleventh place?"

"Disaster, Elle? Come on, be reasonable!"

"I'm being, Lily!"

"What did you expect from this presentation, Elle? A perfect one? A hundred percent?"

"I just expected… oh, forget it, Lily!" she lowers the head and turns to the other side.

"What?"

"Nothing! It's not important!"

"Oh, I think it is! Come on! Just spit it out!"

"I didn't like a few things that happened over there, Lily…"

"Like what?"

"Things I saw."

"Things?"

"Yes! Things!"

"So?" Lily raises her opened hands.

"Huh… I'd like to say… I'd like to see… more engagement here."

"Excuse me? Engagement?" she opens her eyes widely.

"Yes! Engagement, Lily!"

"Why?"

"Because everything was fine to you and Emma, I mean all the time! Our presentation was going down and you were just saying 'it's okay, it's fine', 'don't worry'!"

"I'm sorry, I think I didn't get that!" she says almost indignant.

"The presentation was a mess, Lily! But you and Emma just said it was fine!"

"Huh… I'm not listening to this, Elle! We were just calming down you and Hailee! Because you both were freaking out back there! Emma and I were just trying to finish the presentation as well as we could! And you're saying we were not engaged?"

"That was what it looked like, Lily!"

"Oh, I'm not listening to this! Look, girl…" she raises a finger.

"Don't you call me 'girl'! I'm not a child!" she raises a finger too.

"Okay, sorry. Look, Elle, a presentation is not perfect all the time. We work hard for that, we fight for that, but sometimes you just can't perform a perfect one! And, many times, you are only trying to finish it, that's all! I had some very good experiences in presentations and a lot of 'not a hundred percent' of them! It happens! You just keep going with what you have and what you learned. You can't be perfect all the time!"

"I… agree with Lily." says Ms. Marketing.

"I agree with Elle!" the younger sister says almost outraged.

"Okay, so what now? We fight?" someone says (Lily).

The blonde girl lowers her head and thinks. How could she be wrong? She has tried so hard and for so many days… and the juries liked the idea. Maybe she is seeing Emma and Lily as strangers into that team, because all the time it was her and the best friend Hailee. Now it is so… unusual having different people with her. Did she work so much time only with Hailee that now she cannot work with other persons? That would be weird – and one more taught: grouping and working with different personalities.

"No, we don't. You're right, Lily. I was just stressed and anxious. I'm sorry."

The thick eyebrows girl smiles and hugs Elle (but she did not say 'It's alright'). And then they are all in a loving huge hug (so cute). There will be more contests, more chances, and they will be prepared, I guess. That night, they had enough to learn.

"I just went too far in what I said, Lily. I'm sorry."

"It's alright, Elle. I had some experiences you and Hailee didn't; as well as Emma. But, we are here to help. If not, I prefer to get back to my spreadsheets."

"Okay. I got that, Lily. Thank you." she smiles.

"Maybe someone can help us with this, huh... 'mess', as you said."

"Who?"

"I know a person, Elle. I'll keep you all in touch."

And, fortunately, Lily said 'It's alright'."

Chapter Four – Version 4.4

That same day, at night, Lily's home.

"Why didn't you tell me that, Lily? Oh, I could pay to watch that!"

"It's not funny, Anna!"

"Why not? You, those girls, sweating, stuttering, and all those college stuff? It's funny, Lily! It's pretty funny!"

"Ouch, Anna! Can you do this or not?"

"I'll meet the girls, then! But I'll make no promises, Lily! You know, I'm working, I have a boyfriend, and I have no time for this."

"Fine! I said exactly the same few days ago!"

Anna is Lily's sister, two years older sister. She works already at a company, and she is a manager. No, she is "the" manager, because she is very competent, almost a genius. Not only at work, but at home too. Anna used to manage all things in there: Lily makes the numbers work, Anna manages the tasks (and times and roles and all the rest). She can manage a team of twelve guys at work, therefore managing a house is a piece of cake.

They are living together in a small rented house because their parents live in other state. Sometimes, these parents come to see the little girls (Anna Kelly is only 1.57 meters tall). The girl with blue eyes and light brown hair color is loyal, intelligent, and courageous – as a manager must be, almost a lion. She shows some artistic flair sometimes – could she be an actress or a singer? Lily always says she could. Thus far, that taco and Lord of the Rings fan prefers to manage people and stuffs.

Certainly, she will say "yes" to her sister, Emma, Hailee and Elle, especially because Anna loves new challenges. As I said, she is courageous, because that will be a tough work – and with no return guarantees. Soon (on next chapter), the fantastic four will become "The breakfast club" – or not.

CHAPTER FIVE – VERSION 5.0 – LADY CODE.

Introducing Ellen

"What do you mean with 'a mess'?"

"What you've heard: 'a mess'."

"Please, define 'mess', Lily."

"Well, we've started very well, Anna. Elle is very committed and I think she has a great potential. Suddenly, a piece of shit just started to ask!"

"Language, Lily!"

"Sorry! Someone started to ask and Elle just panicked. In the first question, she did okay. But as the questions were increasing, she got nervous and fell down."

"Ouch! And what did you do?"

"Emma took the lead."

"Always Emma saving your ass, Lily…"

"Hey, watch your language, Anna!"

The older sister smiles. Emma used to help Lily many times at college – and Anna saw all the times. When they leaved the school, the opposite has happened: Lily started to help the best friend Emma at work, especially when Emma's mother divorced the second husband, few years ago. And, at that moment, Anna does not know what the little sister wants.

"So what, Lily? Do you want I join the 'special forces team'?"

"Why not, Anna? They have high expectations."

"I don't work with expectations, Lily. I work with 'right', 'correct', 'sure', 'true' and so on."

"I don't believe you're saying this to me! I work with numbers, Anna, not you! You work with people, so you should accept 'expectations'."

"Oh, it doesn't work that way, Lily, you know that! I can't deal with 'hope' anymore. Because if anything goes wrong, I know exactly who's gonna be fired. That's what you get when you're the manager. You need to deal with persons, personalities, moods, and bad days of all these. As much I work with people more I love dogs, cats, fishes, and birds."

"So you're in?"

"What? Haven't you heard what I've just said?"

"Yeah, I have. That's why I'm pretty sure you're in."

"Oh, fine, Lily…" she says and smiles. "Let's see this. What is it about?"

Lily starts to explain everything from the beginning. When Elle had the first idea, when she shared with Hailee and how Emma joined the team and called her. Lily does not take so long to say all this.

"Really? Who's is this Elle? Have we met already?"

"Huh... I don't think so. She's Hailee's friend. I think you know Hailee, she is Emma's little sister."

"Emma? Oh, long time no see! I'm so busy these days!"

"Everyone is busy all the time nowadays, Anna!"

"And?"

"And, don't you give me those lame excuses." she raises a finger nicely.

"Okay, Lily... The idea is good, I give you that. But you need to make more. If Elle just panicked with a few questions, it's because you still have doubts about the... huh... how are you calling this?"

"Business? Project, maybe."

"This project. When you go to a presentation, it's not just what you're wearing or your hairstyle. You must know all about what you're saying, and all about what people can ask. And, yes, you have to imagine all the questions people can make during the presentation. I don't think you were prepared for that..."

"No, we weren't."

"Really? And why did you get there?"

"Well, the girls called me, I just accepted. Emma was into the project, so it influenced me. I have a good feeling about this, Anna."

"A good feeling? Oh, that's you again, with your hunches and intuition, Lily..."

"What is the problem? Did you never use it?"

"The times I used it, it went wrong. That's why I just quit that."

"So what exactly do you need to get into this project?"

"Oh, are you trying to negotiate with me, Lily? What's the next question? Will you ask me about my wishes and dreams in the company? Where do I want to be in ten years working with you?"

"Come on, Anna! Emma is in because it's about her sister Hailee! You should do the same for me. I'm your sister, in case you don't know!"

"Oh, Lily, I wish I could work like that... It would be a dream, really..." the big sister says.

"Okay, I'll send a message to the girls that you're totally into the project, Anna."

"Oh, come on, Lily! Don't push me!"

It is complicate. Anna has a great job at a big information

technology enterprise. She has a good salary and an almost stable job. Why should she take a risk in an emerging business? And with college girls? She will have to teach them so much... Besides, Anna Kelly has a boyfriend too: a nice and loyal man, with a thick beard – that, according to Anna, is a very relevant part. She is already thinking about marriage and kids, not entrepreneurship or working eighteen hours in a day.

"Comfort zone, Lily. That's why I don't want it."

"Oh, you don't have to be so honest, Anna... Okay, we'll be waiting for you in the next meeting."

"Oh, God! Are you listening to me?" she laughs when she says. "I'm just saying 'no', Lily!"

"Okay, I'll call mommy." she threatens her.

"What? Don't you dare to do that, Lily Jane Davelman!"

"And daddy too."

"Ouch! Stop it! We are having an adult conversation here!"

"And they will say 'Anna Kelly Davelman, just help your little sister, for Christ's sake!' "

"This is not fair, Lily! Totally not fair!"

"Just see Elle telling the app's story, Anna. If you don't like, we're done here. I'll just ask you some advices later."

"Why do you want me seeing her? Is she special or something? Is she a superhero?"

"Huh... actually, we almost fought."

"Excuse me?"

"Yes, we almost fought."

"Oh, and now you're calling the big sister? To fight?"

"God, of course not, Anna!"

"I'd like to remember you that you are eight centimeters taller than me."

"It's not that! Oh, crap!"

"Watch your language, Lily!"

" 'Crap' is not a dirty word!"

"I'll call mommy and daddy to talk about that..."

"Oh, my God..."

"And that is a blasphemy."

In Davelman family, they used to say only good words and avoid curse words. This kind of education was very important to those girls: they have nice friends and relationships with everyone. Maybe it can seem a futile or an useless thing, but it works for them, at least.

As you get older, people start to listen carefully what you are saying. Just imagine a president – or a manager as Anna – saying curse words in a speech. I probably would lose respect for him or her.

"She faced up to me, Anna." reveals Lilly.

"Really? Why?"

"We were discussing, and I called her 'girl'."

"Then she said she is not a child."

"Yep! How do you know that?" Lily frowns.

"I just know. And it's not the first time you call someone like that, Lily. How old is she?"

"I don't know. She's in the last year in the college, so she's in her twenties."

"And she faced up to you?"

"Yep."

"Okay, I'll talk to her, I'll watch her speaking about the app, but I'm not gonna fight."

"Oh, it's nice to listen this last part!"

Lily is not used to take insults. She is aggressive sometimes, as you have read and imagined in the last chapter. If there is anything she must speak, she does, no matter who gets hurt – most of times, it is not her.

And Lily was impressed when Elle faced up to her – with a raised finger too. People did not do that when the thick eyebrows girl started to raise her lovely voice. She had a good feeling about that, despite the fact that she was in a heated discussion with Elle. They were just making a few and usual adjustments, in my opinion.

"And I know you want this, Anna."

"Do I?"

"Yes. How long can you hold this life?"

"My life is good, Lily! What are you talking about?"

"Really? I see you complaining almost every day, Anna."

"That's usual to human beings, Lily."

"I don't think so. I don't complain every day as you do. I just handle it."

Now Anna could see that her younger sister was right. She had a good job, a nice boyfriend, and all the blah blah blah that society wants to see us making. Everything in her life was planned already, like an engineering design. No emotions, no jumps ahead, no shocks, no detours, no distractions. Maybe Anna needs some of these things. Don't you?

"I'll listen to her, Lily."

"Okay, thank you, sister!"
"You're welcome!"

Chapter Five – Version 5.1

"That's all?"
"Yes. Anything else, Hailee?"
"No. That's all."
"Well, I can truly say it's very good."
"But?"
"But, it can be better."
"How?"

In that pleasant afternoon, Anna starts to speak about improvements. Not only in the app, but also in the presentation and, of course, in the project management. They are at Elle's home, headquarters. You know already I am talking about the blonde girl's bedroom.

"You must be a hundred percent ready, Elle."
"But what about that 'It's better done than perfect' stuff?"
"This works fine in theory, Elle. In real life, you need a minimal to start. You have it, I can see. But now you need to improve this 'minimum'." says the manager.

"Can you help us, Anna?"
"That's why I came here, Elle."
"It wasn't so hard to convince her, Elle."
"Really? Oh, no, that was hard, Lily! You wanted to call mom!"
"Did you, Lily?" laughs Hailee.
"Almost." she says and grins.

Then Anna listens to all the notes that Lily and Emma have written down at the contest. The working app from a group, the brochures from another, the T-shirts, and so on. Anna is thinking about all those "mistakes" the girls have made.

"Okay, ladies, let's see what we got here. I see Emma has finished the company's statements, right? This is good. And then we have the app. You have the purpose and a good story to tell about it. This is very good, too!"

" 'We' have the purpose and all, Anna. You're in."
"Oh, sorry, I didn't get used to that idea yet. Okay, so we have the app statements too. And who is coding the app?"

Silence for two seconds. The girls look each other. Still silence. Hailee says.

"Huh… I am. I mean, I'm trying to."

" 'Trying?' " says the manager.

"Well, I need to see that, actually."

" 'I need to see that.' This is a bad sign, Hailee. It means it's not done and someone maybe is trying to do. Anyway, nobody is doing anything about that." Anna says.

"It's because we didn't need a working app to that presentation, Anna. But, as we have seen, we need it. Finally, we are beginning to code and look for someone to help me." Hailee says.

"Can't you code, Hailee?" Anna asks.

"Nope. I'm just capable to code the interface, and how it will operate. I don't know how to make it communicate to a server and all that. Sorry, am I being clear? I mean, you know this code talk, right?"

"Yes, I work in an IT company; I manage twelve IT guys."

"Oops, sorry for that…"

"It's okay, I didn't give you my resume, ladies. Huh… well, we need a coder then."

"Don't you know anyone, Anna? A co-worker, maybe?

"Huh… just guys, Elle. If you don't mind, I can call someone."

"We do mind!"

"Really, Hailee? Why? Emma asks.

"We have a deal, Elle and I."

"English, please." Emma asks.

"I'm gonna tell you a story, but I think you all know it. No, it's not a story, it's a fact. When you work with guys in a project or something, and there is hard work like, huh… coding, people used to think all the hard work was made by the men. And we are just props. People think we do nothing."

"Agreed. That's why I work only with Hailee in the college." the blonde girl says.

"Huh… yes and no, Hailee." says Anna. "In some cases, yes. But this is changing. Slowly, but changing. We are getting into many areas nowadays. Coding, engineering, and all. But, okay, if you have this 'statement'. Everyone agrees on this? Emma, Lily?"

"Yes, sure." says Emma.

"Don't you think we need different opinions here, Anna? I mean, what if we need a man's perspective?" Lily asks.

"I see, Lily, but I don't think this is so critical at the moment. By the way, I think we have already different opinions here. Like you and Elle, for example."

"Did you tell her about our talk, Lily?" Elle smiles.

"Actually, I've told her about our heated discussion. Of course I've told her, Elle! She's my sister! Besides, I'm sure we need to be clear. We are beginning a company and we don't want any intrigues here. What we have to say, we say it. Don't you hide anything, even the bad things. No, especially the bad things!"

"Okay, deal." says Emma, and the other girls agree.

Elle is just seeing that a company is a very serious thing. It is not a school project anymore. She can see how Lily and the girls are engaged in the project – and now they have even a manager! Elle does not feel like losing power and authority – she is not the lead anymore. However, as her father said in chapter two, "Everyone in the team has his own task." At the moment, every girl has her own task. Then, Elle is not concerned about other people in charge. She is learning, and, the most important: she is growing up.

"I know a coder, a girl." says Anna. "She's a very close friend. But I think she's gonna say a resounding 'no'. Maybe a 'thanks' too."

"Ellen?"

"Yes, Lily. She's not coming, she has thousands of jobs. And, as you know, the best coders usually choose their jobs. And I don't think Ellen is gonna come here."

"I said the same, just like you, Anna. And we are here." smiles Lily.

"And there is one more thing: she's outspoken. More than you, Lily, in fact." advises Anna.

"Am I outspoken?"

Emma lowers her head and says nothing, just smiles. Elle looks at Hailee and smiles too.

"Okay, sometimes, I am. But, not all the time."

The girls do not stop smiling, especially Emma, who spends more time with Lily.

"Okay, I'll call her then."

"Can you call her today, Anna? I mean, now?" asks Elle.

"I think she's sleeping because she codes at night. At this time, she's unavailable, totally out of service. Oh, she has those crazy schedules too. We need to get used to this."

Chapter Five – Version 5.2

"I'm in."

"Really?"

"Yeah!"

"So easy like that?"

"Yeah, why?"

"I thought you would refuse."

"It's a so simple app that I can code it in the break times, Anna." says Ellen.

"The girls will not believe me, Ellen!"

"Oh, that's none of my business…"

"Now it's, Ellen. Welcome aboard!"

"Huh… do I have to meet those girls?"

"Of course, Ellen! You're in!"

"What do you mean?"

"It's not a part-time job or a simple one, Ellen! It's a partnership!"

"Okay, just give me ten percent of the company, I'm good. Wait. How many girls? Just share the company between all the partners and give me my stake."

"Oh, wait, you didn't get this, Ellen… It's a full-time job, it's a partnership as I said. You must BE there."

"You know exactly what I think about working with people, right, Anna? That's why I work alone, here, with my computer. I don't need to be with people. It's boring and troublesome."

"Oh, God… I don't know how many times I've heard that, Ellen…"

"And why you keep coming here, Anna? I'm fine, I'm good. I mean, I have my jobs, a lot of them, by the way, and I'm living so well like this. And you're trying to take me to the, huh… how do you call it? 'Real world?' "

"It's not 'normal' living here alone, Ellen!"

"I don't live alone, Anna! I live with Jennifer."

"See? You don't even call your mother as 'mom'!"

"She's almost my age, Anna! And this is just a detail."

"Almost your age? Jesus, Ellen! She is sixteen years older than you! She's not almost your age!"

"I talk to her like my older sister, Anna, she's my friend. I live fine with her, not fighting like other families. In the end, that's what matters: living well with your relatives. And I do live well here."

"Okay, I know I can't change your mind, Ellen! I'm not here for that. But, sooner or later, you'll have to come and meet the girls. We're not a job from some place in Asia or Africa! This is not crowdsourcing!"

"Fine, Anna! When the time comes, I'll be there. Just don't ask me to be with you all the time, because I have my jobs here. And, this is more important. Besides, why are you in this, huh… project? I don't know how you are calling this."

"You can call a project. I'm in because… huh… Lily is in, and she's my sister."

"And you think you need to be there too? Because she's your sister? And you need to help your little sister? Come on, Anna, show me something!"

"Not only that, Ellen…"

"What else? Tell me."

"She has a hunch."

"Oh, God! A hunch from your sister? One more reason for not being there! Huh… I don't get along with her, Anna, you know that."

"But you can do that, Ellen! She's not a bad person! Maybe it's a chance to you both!"

"Oh, my God, Anna! Now we are talking about what? Reconciliation? Peacemaking? We're not enemies, Anna! I just don't like to work with her. Sometimes she's… she's inattentive!"

"She's not inattentive, Ellen! She is the finance girl! She deals with money!"

"She's fast with numbers, Anna, I give you that. Okay, this is the problem: she speaks too much!"

"Oh, come on, Ellen! Don't be so cruel!"

"Okay, my friend, let's do this! And I'm just doing it because you're my best friend, right? And don't be so full of yourself with that."

"Thanks, Ellen! There will be a meeting on Saturday, after lunch, Elle's house. Call me, I'll show you the way."

"Fine."

"And, please, take off these pajamas! It's almost noon, Ellen!"

"I'm home, Anna!"

They have begun the story as dynamic duo. Emma came into it and they became the three musketeers or the trinity. With Lily, they could be called fantastic four. Then, these became the breakfast club or fab five, and now, huh… suicide squad?

CHAPTER SIX – VERSION 6.0 – THE DINNER.

About marketing, leadership, design, team work, friendship, ice cream and pizza

Ellen is 1.55 meters tall. Dark brown hair, always tied with a hair band (she changes the colors). Light brown eyes. Favorite color: green; favorite food: sushi (as Lily). She is very outspoken, but it seems very natural for her. I mean, it does not look forced and she does not look angry or sarcastic. Ellen prefers to be honest, and she likes to get the same back from the people. The coder girl does not like to work with people, as you have read before. Most of times, she likes to be alone. Not because any disappointment. Because she likes it – it is just her option. Ellen Fage likes to talk to smart people, but she thinks a work is more productive in solitude. No, it is not about feeling, it is about a quiet place. The tiny girl likes comics, computer hardware, and games. She is straight when she talks, like this paragraph.

"Hi, Anna, I'm coming."

"Where are you?"

"I'm at your door."

"Oh, wait a second!"

Anna comes quickly to the front door and Ellen is sitting down at it, typing on cell phone.

"About time." she says.

"Actually, you should call me BEFORE you get here, Ellen! When you leave your home is a good moment."

"Okay, next time I'll remember that. Should we go now?"

"Just a second, I have to grab my purse. Come in!"

"Thanks. Where is Lily?"

"She's there already."

Anna drives for few minutes. It is her first car, a small and very powerful one. It is not a pink or purple vehicle, it is black with silver five rims wheels with car wrapping – that is a little out of date, but she likes it (and it protects the paintwork). Besides, it looks like a ghost or something from the shadows – according to Anna's thinking. The car seats are blue (she loves this color); and the stereo plays some Beastie Boys song. Anna Kelly loves all that: cars, parts, tuning, driving at night or maybe at afternoon on a nice and silence road, piloting against other driver (this last one only on videogames, of course).

She is a gearhead! And that car, her first one, is very special – she has worked for almost a year to buy it. Soon, they get to Elle's house.

"Hi!"

"Hi, Anna! How you doing? And you must be Ellen!"

"Hi, Elle, nice to meet you!"

They come in and meet Charlie.

"Good afternoon, Mr. Panning!"

"I'm glad to meet you, Mr. Panning!"

"Hey, girls, how are you?"

"Fine, thank you, Mr. Panning!"

They go to the headquarters. It is almost full of girls: Lily, Emma, Hailee, and counting.

"Hey!"

"Hi, Anna!"

"Hi, everyone! This is Ellen, the code girl. These are Emma, Hailee, and you have met already Lily."

"Hi, everyone!" Ellen tries to be nice.

"Hi, Ellen."

"Hi, Lily."

"Huh… shall we begin? Elle, would you like to tell about the app to Ellen, please?" asks Anna.

"Sure! Huh… sit here, Ellen, please! We need a larger place, maybe!"

Ellen sits down at a chair and Elle starts to tell her story. From the beginning, when she was at the hospital (waiting for hours to talk to the doctor), until the first presentation and the disaster – according to her.

"And that's all, Ellen. Now we are going to make this app and change the world!"

"Do you want to change the world?" asks Ellen.

"Yeah, why not?" answers Elle.

"It's a lot of work, Elle."

"Don't you want to change it?" asks Hailee.

"Huh… not all the things. It's working to me… the biggest part, at least."

The girls look each other and they are surprised. Doesn't she want to change the world?

"Huh… Ellen, be nice, please." Anna asks and smiles.

"Oh, sorry, I'm just being honest, girls. I've tried to change the world when I was younger, and I just found out that I couldn't. I'm living fine with that. If I want to change, I change myself. It's easier, and it works."

"It's just a way of speaking, Ellen. Like an inspiring thing to say when you are building a company." Lily says.

"Thanks for explaining, Lily. I really appreciated that." she says nicely – or she shows some sarcasm.

Silence for two seconds.

"Huh… okay, ladies, let's talk about business, please! How can we produce this app? It's a good beginning for today!" says Anna.

Elle and Hailee talk to Ellen about the app: what they want, what they have planned, and the design. In the meanwhile, Anna, Lily and Emma make the rest: management, finance and marketing. I can feel a combination of perfumes floating in the air because there are six girls in here. However, the mixture is not unpleasant, as you could think, it smells good. Maybe those girls fit when they are together, that means they are compatible – maybe.

Soon, the night comes, and someone shows up at the bedroom's door.

"Hi, girls! Is Ms. Panning working here?"

"Hi, Dad!" Elle stands up and smiles.

"Well, I'm going to meet some buddies. I would invite you, but I'm sure you are busy with your enterprise, right?"

"Yes, Dad, we're just starting here!"

"Okay, I'll let some money to buy pizzas. And I bought some ice cream to you, girls, I hope you like chocolate. There is cookies and cream flavor too, if you prefer. Please, enjoy it!"

"Oh, thanks, Dad! We're starving!"

Some moments later, at the table, they are having a, huh… nice, but not so healthy dinner. It is Saturday night, and they do not bother about shapes or balanced diets. At that time, girls just want to have fun.

"Could you give me mayonnaise, please?"

"Where are you going to put mayonnaise, Lily?"

"On the pizza, of course, Hailee!"

"Yuck!"

"Better than putting mustard and ketchup! This is not a hot-dog! And this mayonnaise is a 'gourmet edition'! It's not a regular mayonnaise!"

"I'm putting just a little on the crust, Lily!"

"The crust is like a signature, it's the differential."

"But I like with mustard and ketchup, Lily, ha ha ha!"

"By the way, you are making design, right, Hailee?"

"Yep. Why?"

"Because design is a very important feature nowadays, as you know."

"Sure, Lily! Elle is helping me with that."

"I read some surveys about design, and listened to some friends. They really buy apps only because of a good design. People do that, not only with apps, but with all the rest: cell phones, cars, wearing, and so on."

"Yes, we need an impressive design to our app, I mean a stunning one. People say they don't care, but that's not what really happens."

"Exactly, Hailee."

"What about money, Lily?"

"What is it?"

"How can you calculate how much we're going to spend?"

"It's not 'spend', Hailee; it's an investment."

"Okay, how can you calculate our investment?"

"First we need to know what Emma will create in marketing. For now, we need the money for domain registration, website hosting. You already have all software to create design, right?"

"Yes, sure. I'm using free software and tools."

"And the software tests can be made locally, in our home computers. I don't have much work for now, so I'm taking care of these small details about start-up universe you still don't know. But I need to be here for the moment when you'll say 'So much money?' or 'It's too expensive!' Because everything is fine and cool when you're working with friends – it's enjoyable. But once people ask you to get your purse and give money… this is when you see who is committed or not."

"Do you think we'll do that?"

"I don't know, Hailee! We need to talk about stakes as soon as possible. It's important to agree to this before the business gets serious."

"But we are serious already, Lily!"

"No, Hailee, we're just warming up, believe me… you get know a person only when you give money and power to him or her. For now, we are just playing business. I know it's not a game, and we have good intentions here, but we'll talk seriously only when we begin to talk about money, profit, stakes and, maybe, loss."

"Loss?"

"Loss. It happens."

"Oh… I was so excited that I didn't think about that."

"Welcome to real world, Hailee."

"Well, then I'll be happy if I don't waste my time, Lily. I still need to finish the college."

"You should want more, Hailee. We are in the business now, and there is no easy restart button in this game."

Meanwhile, on the left side of the table:

"Can I have the olive oil, Emma?"

"Sure, Ellen, it's here."

"Don't you like it?"

"No, I prefer plain pizza, Ellen, thanks! I think I gained some grams in the last few days."

"Oh, sure you did, Emma." she smiles.

"Did you call me fat?"

"No! I'm just agreeing with you!"

"Hmm... Anna told me you're, huh... outspoken. Am I being impolite saying that?"

"A little."

"Okay, sorry. But you've started." Emma smiles.

"Oh, so you don't like people agreeing with you?" Ellen smiles too.

"Did I say that in any moment?"

"You almost did."

"Well, 'almost did' is not 'I did', Ellen."

"Okay, understood, Emma.

"Hey, are you fighting?" asks Anna.

"No, we're just having a nice talk here! Right, Ellen?"

"Yeah, just a nice talk! You see fight everywhere, Anna! Please, enjoy your pizza, Emma!"

"You too, Ellen!"

Emma starts to eat her pizza using hands (she washed them before) while Ellen prefers fork and knife.

"I was wondering, Emma. What exactly is your role here?" Ellen cuts a piece of pizza.

"I'm the marketing girl, Ellen." Emma takes the food in her hand.

"She's Ms. Marketing!" says Hailee.

"Oh, you have a title? And what is it? I'm not doubting about your skills, please, don't think that. I'm just curious."

"Marketing is a process." Emma bites a chunk.

"A process? Like a software process?" Ellen holds the pizza in front of her mouth.

"Hmm... no, I don't think so. I don't know software process, actually." Emma smiles and keeps chewing.

"So, what is it?" Ellen bites.

"It's a... Marketing is the process to make our company and our product indispensable in the life of the consumer." she says.

"Now in English, please!" asks Ellen.

"It's everything involved in making our product, the app, indispensable to the consumer, Ellen. They must think they really need our app, they can't live without it. Like our business. The consumers need to think our enterprise, our brand, is part of their lives. It's not about social standing or luxury, it's about necessity. Our company must be a basic requirement to the consumers like food, water, and, huh… Wi-Fi hotspot!"

"Oh, I got it! And how are you going to do that?"

"Here comes the tools, Ellen, the marketing tools like internet, social network, advertisement; we can even make an event to promote our app."

"That sounds expensive." Ellen chews.

"Sure it is. But it's just an example, Ellen."

"And what tool will you use?"

"In fact, I still don't know, I'm studying. Probably, we'll use the direct contact with the clients."

"And that means?" Ellen makes a gesture.

"We make contact with a potential client, and here we can use e-mail or phone. Then we visit this client and present our product. The best shot would be a friend who could be a client. If you know someone, tell us, please. In our case, this is the cheapest option, especially because we don't have a large budget. We're just beginning, Ellen."

"It sounds good to me, Emma. I mean, all this story about Ellen and her father, and how she has started. I think you have something here."

"WE have, Ellen. You're with us, right?"

"Huh… yeah, I think I am. Anna told me it's not a part-time job, it's a kind of partnership. Indeed, I'm still thinking, Emma."

"Well, you're eating the pizza and probably you'll have some ice cream, so I think you are in, Ellen…"

"Hey, nobody told me about this rule!" Ellen laughs.

"Too late, Ellen…" Emma winks.

In the other side of the table:

"Someone could give me mustard, please?"

"Are you going to put on pizza, Anna?"

"Yeah, I'm trying, Lily. We all are trying here, actually."

"Now you're talking about business, right?"

"Right, Elle!"

"Can I have the ketchup, Hailee?"

"What? Are you trying out this too, Anna?"

"Yep! I'm going crazy tonight, ladies! We're all here, working, Saturday night, and my boyfriend is sending messages every minute! But it's fine! I'm happy, I'm very happy!" she shouts.

"Is she okay, Lily?" asks Elle.

"Huh… yes, I think."

"How long are you dating, Anna?"

"Long enough, Elle. We're almost engaged!"

"Oh, that's lovely!"

"But he doesn't know yet, Elle…" warns Lily.

"Oh, that's awful…"

"I'll tell him soon, Lily! He almost knows!"

"Sure, Anna! Keep repeating that, every day…" says Anna's little sister.

"That's a good beginning, Elle, communication." Anna puts some mustard and ketchup on the pizza.

"What is it?" Elle stops the fork with a piece of pizza on the plate.

"As the company leader, you must communicate very well. In all events, people will ask you, not us, because you have started this business." she finishes putting mustard and she drops the spoon inside the glass pot.

"But I guess I'm the youngest here, Anna. Hailee, when is your birthday? December?" Elle puts the piece of pizza in her mouth.

"Yes, December."

"I was born on April, in the following year. Should I take this leader role?"

"No matter the age, Elle. It's your story, that's what matters."

"It's a great responsibility, Anna." she does not bite another piece of pizza.

"Yes, it is. Are you prepared?" Anna smiles and tastes pizza with mustard and ketchup.

"I think I am…" Elle stops eating.

"We'll support you, Elle! Don't worry!" says the manager.

"Thanks, Anna!"

"And you must improve your speech. I was talking to Lily again about the last presentation. You can practice with us."

"You mean, speaking to you?"

"Yeah, why not?"

"I think it's weird!"

"But that's how it works! Do you want to practice your speeches in the contests? To investors?"

"Okay, I got it, Anna. Huh… sometimes I get nervous… especially when people ask me things. I think I'm not ready yet."

"You will, Elle, don't worry. We'll achieve that! Hey, it's not that bad with mustard and ketchup!" Anna smiles.

"Freaks!" Lily says.

"Do we have to talk to investors too, Anna? Why?" Elle starts eating again.

"Well, there will be a moment when the company will raise, I hope. And if we don't have money enough to expand the business, we'll need investors. We can even sell the company. There are companies which are created only to be sold."

"I don't think I want to sell our company, Anna. We didn't even create it yet!"

"Oh, I'm talking about faraway places, Elle, don't worry! Just telling you. There are other important things you must know for now."

"What is it?"

"Leadership, for example."

"I think I am a good leader, Anna. I mean, I've convinced Hailee to start all this!"

"Yes, that's a good beginning, Elle! You can assemble the people to start a business!"

"And I think I can manage people too, Anna. Well, I, huh…"

"Cough, cough!"

"Oh, come on, Lily! I can do it!" Elle laughs and shows her bright teeth.

"I said nothing, Elle!" Lily has bright teeth too.

"There is a difference between being a leader and just a chief or someone in charge, Elle. You obey people in charge because of hierarchy, but many times, you don't agree with them; sometimes you don't even trust them. In the other hand, it's not the same with the leaders: you blindly FOLLOW them; you BELIEVE in what they are saying to you; you don't discuss because you are all ears to their promises; you could even give your life when they speak – that's very different. Then, Elle, be the leader."

"What if I can't?"

"Just imagine King Theoden in the Battle of the Pelennor Fields! 'Spears shall be shaken, shields shall be splintered'! Got it?"

"Huh… I think I don't remember 'Star Wars' very well…"

"Oh, God, Elle! Forget it!" Anna says outraged.

" 'Lord of the Rings', Elle!" says Lily.

"Oh, I watched this movie a long time ago, Anna…"

"How can't you remember that scene? Well, you must be the leader, Elle! Because people are counting on you now!"

"You mean, you all? It's a great responsibility, Anna."

"Yes, it is. Are you ready?"

"I think so. But what if I'm not?"

"Well, so be a good person in charge, at least. However, don't wait that we follow you. We'll just obey you."

"That looks so dramatic, Anna! You're scaring me!"

"Yes, it's dramatic, I know! I'm just trying you out, Elle!"

"Oh, is it a test then?"

"It's a full-time test from now on, Elle!"

"But you can help me, right?"

"Sure we will! We're here for that! This is the second lesson."

"What?"

"Team work."

"Oh, I like this one! If I wanted to decide everything by myself, I wouldn't have called you here."

"Yes, team work. That's how it happens. Because I can see we have complementing skills. This is the best way to start a business, you know? Huh… well, many times a few people, three or four, play all roles, but I'm happy each one of us has a clear role."

"When Hailee and I started, we were doing all the jobs here, Anna. In some moment, we didn't know where to go. Then we've talked to Mr. Johnson, a professor. He has advised us about business and marketing. So we called Emma to help us. Emma called Lily and now we're all here."

"There is another important thing. We know our roles, right? We know you're the leader, the head, because you're the founder, Elle. So, I don't want to see any kind of envy here, okay? I don't want to see people trying to get noticed. We're all the same. We all have talents, expertise, and skills to be here. So, don't tell me someone is more important than the others. It's not. We're in this because we're good enough. No one is better than anyone else here. Is that clear, ladies?" establishes Anna.

"Yes, sir!" Hailee salutes.

"Okay!" says Elle.

"Totally agreed!" Emma says.

"Yep!" says Ellen.

"Sure! Good point, sister!" Lily says.

"One more thing: no matter what happens, we are all together in this."

They agree again. Anna has many experiences in managing people. And she knows everything can go down if the team does not work as a real team. Those girls are not a group of people doing a job together. Now they have an agreement. Not any signed paper, but maybe they do not need that – they have honor.

"Let's make a deal, ladies." says Anna.

"What?"

"We are 'all in' in this business, okay?"

"Is it a poker game, Anna?"

"Yes, it is, Ellen."

"Nobody folds?"

"Nobody folds, Emma."

"Deal."

"Deal."

"Deal."

"Deal."

"Deal."

"Okay, so now we have a deal, ladies. Don't you ever think in giving up."

"Yes, sir!" salutes again Hailee.

"And give me more mustard, please!"

"Oh, my gosh, Anna! I don't believe that…" Lily says.

"So you finally get into this, Ellen?" says Emma.

"Yeah, I didn't even realize that…"

"Just let it go, Ellen…" she completes.

"Welcome aboard again, Ellen!" says Anna.

"Thanks, Anna! Well, now I think I'm in."

"Why did you take so long, Ellen?" Lily asks.

"I don't know… I'm just a little busy the last days. So I'm not listening to new projects. And I…"

"And you…"

"Well, Anna called me here; she told me this is a kind of a special job. No, sorry! Actually she didn't tell me that. She's in because Lily's in. Right, Anna?"

"Yep. I don't know why I'm here! I think it's because you need me. I mean, not because I'm a special girl in the world and you need me. Because when I came here and I listened to Elle's story… I just felt I would must be here."

"Well, your story is moving mountains, Elle!" says Lily.

"Good! And the best thing is the story is true! Well, no, this is not the best thing, because my father...you know... at a hospital..."

"Yeah, it's the best and the worst at the same time..." says Hailee.

"Well, what now?" asks Lily.

"Now, Hailee and Elle will begin the app design while Ellen will start coding. Emma, you need to choose the marketing strategy and give me a budget, right?" asks Anna.

"Right!"

"Finally, Lily and I have to make some contacts with potential clients. We'll also search for some contests around here, in the state. What do you think, ladies?" Anna asks again.

"Awesome!" says Hailee. "I want to try this again! I'm sure we can do better next time! Right, Elle?"

"Sure we can! I can't wait!"

"Yes, but for now, we need the app, I mean a working one." advises Anna. "A prototype, at least."

"Can we have brochures, Anna? Please, please, please!" asks Hailee.

"Yeah, and T-shirts! We need T-shirts!" says Elle.

"Oh, these things are not for free, ladies, just remember that!" advises Lily.

"You're always pouring cold water, Lily! Come on!" complains Hailee.

"I'm just doing my job, Hailee! I'm controlling the money!"

"Okay, so we can't have brochures and T-shirts because Lily doesn't want. What else?"

"I didn't say that, Hailee!" Lily laughs.

"Ladies, let's think about that later! The priority is design, coding, and marketing." says Anna.

"Huh... do we have a name, Anna? Like a 'team something'?"

"No, we don't. Good question, Ellen." remembers Emma.

"Do we need one?" says Elle.

"Yeah, totally! Maybe 'Team Bellas' or anything like that!"

"I think someone is using that already, Hailee..." says Anna.

"Oh, crap! Maybe we can use the app name for now. What do you think, Elle?" suggests Hailee.

"Yeah, why not? Until we find out a good name."

" 'Dad's Home Team'? It doesn't look cool or wild."

"But it's cute and mysterious, Ellen. That's worthwhile for us now." says Emma.

"I forgot! We're ladies, right?"

"Right!" Emma answers.

"Anything else? Any rule?" asks Ellen.

"We don't say dirty words here, Ellen." says Lily.

"What? Are you kidding to me? Is this a convent or what? Are you nuns?"

"Anna's words, Ellen, not mine." Lily winks with a mouth snap.

"Well, it's our family's words, Lily. But we can perfectly use this. Why not? We don't say 'hey, guys!' It's our differential." Anna says.

"Competitive advantage." says Emma.

"What?" asks Hailee.

"In business, especially marketing, it's a nice way to say: our product has something the others haven't."

"Who wants ice cream?" offers Elle.

"Oh, about time!" Emma says.

"I didn't finish the pizza yet! You both eat too fast!" Lily complains. "You don't even taste it!"

"Put some ice cream on the pizza, Lily! How about that?" says Ellen.

"Gross…"

"Chocolate, Emma?" offers Hailee.

"Thanks, little sister! I love it!"

"Hmm… there is a theory about loving chocolate, Emma." suggests Ellen.

"Really? What is that?" asks Emma.

"Lonely people."

"Huh… she's never alone, Ellen…" smiles Hailee.

"Why not?"

"Huh… didn't you tell her, Emma?"

"Nope."

"Because Emma has… huh… she kisses boys and girls."

"Oh, really? Wow! But you look a normal person, Emma!"

"I AM a normal person, Ellen!"

"Oh, sorry! I didn't mean that!" Ellen puts the hand on the mouth.

"No, of course not! You and half the world didn't mean that!" Emma laughs.

"I'm sorry! Really!" Ellen says.

"It's alright, Ellen! I hear that all the time!"

"Well, anyone else wants to tell some secret? Anyone else is shocked like me?" says Elle.

"Why shocked, Elle?" asks Lily.

"Because... huh... Emma looks... you know... a 'normal' person! Sorry for that, Emma!"

"Okay, okay, Elle! People used to say that, I don't care anymore!"

"Does anyone want to share secrets about sex, ladies?" says Ellen. "This is the time. I mean, now."

Anna looks to Lily. The little sister looks back, but no one says anything. They keep going.

"Hmm... Any questions about roles or tasks, ladies? I mean, we're back to business talk."

"No, Anna, I think it's clear." says Emma.

"I have a question. When do we start? Now? After dinner?"

"Yes, we need a deadline, Lily. How about two weeks? Is it okay to everyone?" Anna asks.

"Fine to me, but I'll wait for Elle and Hailee finish the design." says Ellen.

"Emma?" asks the manager.

"Yes, fine. When I finish, I can help you and Lily."

"Great! Thank you, Emma!" Anna says.

"Does anyone know a place to start selling the app?" asks Anna. "Maybe a friend or something."

"Hey, I think I know a person!" reminds Elle.

"Who?"

"The hospital my father used to go, Hailee! Remember? And I know a person, Doctor Alice!"

"Could you get in touch with her, Elle?" asks Anna.

"Huh... my father didn't go to the hospital in the last days, I don't know..."

"Yes, you can, Elle! We need to use business network. Anyone, anywhere, anytime." says Emma.

"But there are a few days I don't talk to her..."

"Did she give you a phone number or e-mail?" asks Lily.

"Oh, yes! Now I've just remembered! She said I could call her anytime to talk about my father's disease!"

"So it's time, Elle!" says Emma.

"Yeah, we can go over there! Oh, everything is starting to work now!"

"So, can you call her and make an appointment, Elle?"

"Yes, sure! I'll do it on Monday, Anna! Cookies and cream, anyone?"

"Oh, can I have it, Elle?"

"Sure, Lily!"

"Don't forget mayonnaise, Lily." suggests Ellen.

"Okay, Ellen, I'll smile to look nice to you! Okay?" she shows a very forced and funny smile.

"You don't have to be so aggressive, Lily!"

"I'm not being aggressive, Anna!"

"And stop fighting again, you both!"

"Again? This is the first time we're talking, Anna! And we're not fighting, by the way." Ellen informs.

"Oh, sure! The first time was you and Emma." Anna reminds.

"We were not fighting, Anna! We were just talking!" says Emma.

"You see people fighting anytime, Anna! Are you okay?" says Ellen.

"Oh, God, I'm sorry, ladies! I've been so stressed last days!"

"Troubles at work?"

"Yes, Ellen, always…"

"Please, don't take your stress out on us, Anna! We didn't do anything to you." asks Ellen. "You should take care of that. We don't want a mad manager here."

"Okay, Ellen, you're right, totally right. I don't know… everything is happening so fast… Sometimes I think I'm not ready for all this."

"You're not alone, Anna…" says Elle. "We all here, with all this… sometimes I think I'm not prepared too."

"But you are younger, Elle! You're still at college. I'm already working, I'm a manager, people expect…"

"Oh, and you are, huh… how old are you, Anna? Twenty-five?"

"Twenty-six."

"Oh, four years older… that's a huge difference, Anna, for sure…" Elle says with irony.

"But I feel people expect more from me, Elle! Even you, ladies! Because I'm the manager! I need to do this and that! And this must be in its place, and that must be there, and so on…"

"Can I disagree with you, Anna?" asks Emma. "People expect too much from anyone nowadays."

"Emma is right, Anna." says Lily. "People don't do their own things and they expect you do. And, yes, you're stressed. I agree with Ellen."

"Oh, that's new!"

"Huh… I don't have anything against you, Ellen! Please, don't see like that!"

"Me neither, Lily!"

"Hey, both of you, stop fighting! Oh, here we go again…" says the stressed girl (Anna).

"Okay, so let's make this clear. If you have anything to tell me, Ellen, just do it."

"I don't have anything to tell you, Lily!" she smiles.

"I'm waiting, Ellen." Lily doubts.

"Fine, I'll tell you if you want. I don't like when you play, huh... the boss. I don't like to see you giving orders."

"Why not?"

"Because you look a dictator."

"Excuse me?"

"Yes, when you say something, you look a tyrant."

"I don't think all people agree on this, Ellen."

"Really? Just ask it."

"Okay, we'll vote. Am I look a, huh... tyrant, as Ellen said?"

They vote. Anna and Emma vote for Lily, Elle and Hailee vote for Ellen.

"See? Two votes each side."

"That means something, Lily, definitely! It means half of the people think you're a tyrant!"

"That means nothing, Ellen! It means half of the people agree with me! Maybe it's just you."

"It's not just me, Lily, it's half of the people!"

"How long do they know me? Elle and Hailee? Two weeks? Three? This is between you and me, Ellen!"

"Okay. So, I don't like when you are very accurate with numbers. Sometimes we need speed, not accuracy."

"Huh... this is my job, Ellen! Numbers! I don't have to be meticulous with numbers? Oh, so don't be so accurate with code. Just forget some brackets and semicolons, how about that?"

"Okay, I'm done here."

"No, don't be done! Let's talk! We need everything clear here! We're making business, there is no time for little games!"

"See? That's another thing I hate when you do! You can't stop! I said I'm done, but you're still fighting!"

"I'm not fighting, Ellen! I'm just talking to you!"

"You take things too seriously, Lily!"

"May I, Ellen? May I take things seriously?" she says outraged.

"See? There you go again... I'm done, Lily, really. That's why I like to work by myself."

"Oh, maybe the problem is you, not me! Because you work alone all the time, Ellen! Maybe you're not ready for this!"

"I'm done, Lily, really. I'll not answer."

"You should, Ellen! I'm still talking to you!"

"I'm not answering."

"You are! You just answered!"

"Hey, you both! We're done now. And now it's not my stress, you ARE fighting!" says Anna. "Okay, we've said and we've listened everything we could. Are we good?" says Anna.

"I'm not a tyrant." says Lily.

"Maybe." teases Ellen.

"Hey, you, Lily and Ellen! I think we have much more work here!" says Elle. "I mean, we don't know each other! I just know Hailee, and when I met Lily and we discussed... I just realized I don't know people! I don't know you!"

"Yes, and even if you know someone for a long time, as Lily and Ellen, it looks worse!" Hailee completes and smiles. "Look these girls, they are ready to attack!"

"How long do you know each other? And you're fighting like that?" asks Elle.

"And what will happen in few years? How will we be in this company?" says Hailee. "Fighting like this? Even worse?"

Silence for three seconds. The girls look each other, some of them lower the head. Maybe they need only one word: tolerance. Or maybe another one: patience.

"I'm sorry, Lily. I was hard on you, I've gone too far."

"It's alright, Ellen. Sometimes, I do that too. Maybe more times than I should. I'm sorry."

"I just don't know who you are, Lily. Or what you want. I've worked with so many people I didn't know... It looks strange to me. That's why I've started to work alone. I like to talk, and, you know, sometimes coders don't talk to you. But I'm not like that. I'm a normal girl. I just work by myself, at home. That's just an option, it's not my way of life."

"If you don't know me, Ellen, you just have to ask me. I'm not a bad person. And I could say the same about you. I know you're my sister's friend, that's all. Hmm... I'll ask you from now on, if you don't mind." Lily smiles.

"Hey, sometimes we work for a long time with co-workers, but we don't even know their full names. That's usual. But, we don't have to do the same. We're more than co-workers, we're partners. And we can be friends. We're relatives already, as Lily and I, Hailee and Emma."

"Anna is right! We're building a company, we must be more than co-workers or partners! I don't want to see those dirty things that happen in some huge and famous companies, like stealing, betrayal, or power struggle."

"I agree, Emma! We can do better! We can make a better world, right, Elle?" says Hailee.

"Wait a second, I'll be back soon. Hailee, we have chocolate syrup in the fridge. I forgot that!"

Elle goes to the bedroom and takes her backpack. She gets a notebook and leaves. The blonde girl is bringing her writing (see chapter one) and then she reads.

"Check this out, ladies."

She reads the entire text to the girls. They listen carefully with no talk. In the end, Elle says.

"We can't ask men to do something for us if we don't do anything for us before. We can't claim anything about men before we start to tolerate ourselves. What do you say? How can we require anything from men if we don't agree with each other first? I mean, between us. We're just fighting here, for small reasons! Because we don't talk! Isn't it strange to you?"

"We can't change the world if we can't change ourselves, ladies! We begin this change here, between us, not out there." says Hailee. "How can I ask you anything if I'm not doing my own job? It's weird! And give me more chocolate ice cream, please! I'm feeling anxious already!"

"Can I have a little more too?" Emma bites the lips.

"Okay, ladies, it's up to us now." says Anna.

"Yeah, let's change!" Lily says.

"We can do this together!" Elle says.

"Let's do this!" says Hailee while she is taking more ice cream.

"Why didn't we take so long to talk about this?" Emma asks.

"Next time, tell me about the self-help meeting, please. I'll bring some tissues." says Ellen. "Not to me, to Lily, of course!"

"Oh, she has just started again!" Lily laughs and shows her bright teeth.

Everyone laughs. It is a nice Saturday night. They could be at a club or a bar, filling their bodies with alcohol or something worse. However, Anna, Elle, Ellen, Emma, Hailee and Lily preferred to be there, changing things. Now they are saying a few things I cannot listen and then they smile and laugh again and again. They do not have to begin so big or fast as a teenager rush – because they are not teens anymore. They do not have to change everything, like a revolution, with violence and victims. They are just girls; girls changing their own world. And they are really growing up.

CHAPTER SEVEN – VERSION 7.0 – ONE CHANCE.

Climbing

"When?"

"In three weeks."

"Is it enough?"

"Huh… we have already an almost working app; we have a good story to tell, Elle is improving her speech. I think we are almost ready, Anna."

"I've heard two 'almost', Emma."

"Well, we still need to finish some stuff, Anna."

"Do we have time for this?"

"Yes, if we really want it."

"Okay, we're in!"

Few days ago, Emma has found out a new competition. Not at a college anymore, this one is a state tournament. Of course it is important. Those contests are a chance to show up in the start-up scene. It enables entrepreneurs to introduce their products and companies to possible investors – the angel investors. They are called like that because they act like angels to the start-ups: these people (or groups) bring money, knowledge, experiences, and network contacts. I could not say which one of these is the most important; it depends on what stage your company is. In the case of my girls in this story, I could say they need all of them.

"Did Ellen finish the app already?" wants to know Anna.

"Yes, I think she did. The most part, at least." answers Emma.

"Did she test it?"

"Oh, I couldn't say that, I have to ask her."

"Okay, let me text her. Did you call the girls?"

"Not yet, but I'll call them."

"Fine, tell them we have a meeting on next Saturday, morning, seven o'clock. I'll call Lily."

"So, huh… early?"

"We're in a hurry, Emma! Three weeks go by too fast! And we have the weekends only, because we have our jobs."

The girls have much work before the contest named "Entrepreneurs in the House: Meet Innovation, Creativity and Smart People" – I do not know who is creating those names. Elle have to practice her speech: telling the app's story, presenting the company and the team, answering questions. Hailee has to explain the design, if it is necessary. In most of these contests, the team has only a few minutes to tell the whole story. Emma, of course, will explain marketing strategies – these are very important to investors. Lily has to tell about money and numbers, and how they expect to get money in this business. Anna will say how they are organized as a team; what they are planning, and schedules. Finally and very importantly, if they have time, Ellen will explain code. Not variables and constants, but how they build the app: programming language, available systems on release, and so on. The most probable is only Elle and Anna will speak. As I said, they will have a few minutes, and the other girls will answer only if someone in the audience asks. In any event, all of them must be prepared.

"Can we have brochures, Anna? Please, please!"

"Lily?"

"Huh… what will you put in these brochures, Hailee?"

"I don't know! This is the problem number two!"

"So forget it for now, Hailee; let's focus on the presentation, okay?"

"Aw…" Hailee does a pout.

Ellen has to finish the app. It is a hard job because she is alone, but the code girl can handle that. Anna is managing the team. They work at home, because no one have time for meetings during the week – the girls have jobs, college, homework, and lives. On Saturday, the Dad's Home Team can talk about the details. For now, they talk through the internet, telephone, instant messengers or even smoke signals – what they have in hands.

"How is the app development?"

"It's happening, Anna."

"Huh… you didn't convince me, Ellen."

"It's… going."

"Going where?"

"I didn't make all the tests I wanted. Some bugs here and there, but we don't need to present the entire app. We just show some parts."

"Okay, so tell Elle what parts we can show up. We don't want any embarrassment like some E3 presentations or something alike, okay?"

"Roger that!"

They also have incomplete things. The team does not have a logo for the app – this is very important. And where is the powerpoint presentation? Probably Hailee will do that (she will complain); the other designer (Elle) is practicing the speech.

"Why do I have to do this dirty job, Emma?"

"Because you're the only available designer, Hailee."

"Oh, next time, I want another role in the company…"

"It's just a few slides, Hailee!"

"I hate powerpoint… Why don't we make a short movie?"

"Because we don't have such time. The clock is ticking, little sister!"

"Who came up with the idea of get in this competition, Emma? We're in a hurry for days and days! We don't have time for this! I'm not even studying at college!"

"Huh… I don't remember… I'll ask someone later…"

Some details can make points at a presentation. A pretty logo, a brochure, a different way to present your company like a short movie or even a song – why not? However, firstly, check out who the jury is, please.

"Can we have T-shirts, at least, Lily?"

"Why do you want T-shirts, Hailee?"

"Because we're a team!"

"We are a team anyway, Hailee!"

"But people don't know that!"

"Do you have the team logo already?"

"Huh… nope! I'm still working on that!"

"And what will you put on the T-shirts? Our pictures? Not cool, Hailee."

"I didn't finish that yet… work, work, work… and when you finish, there is more work."

"Welcome to adult life, Hailee!"

The most important thing is: do you have something relevant to say? The second is: can you explain that in few minutes? And the third: will people believe in your skills to make that happen? If there is a fourth: will people spend money and time on you?

"How are we, Lily?"

"You mean money or time, Emma?"

"Both."

"We are good in money, we are bad in time."

"Jesus, can we finish this? How are the other girls?"

"I don't know. Anna does. Hailee is still wanting some brochures and T-shirts, what do you think?"

"It can be useful, Lily. But what will we put on these brochures? The app's story? We don't know how many people will be there. We don't know how many copies we'll need."

"I just said we can't, Emma. We have no time for writing stories, designing, and printing. And I need to work earlier tomorrow. Oh, this week is being the worst one ever!"

"Don't worry, Lily! It can get worse; you'll see next week."

"Oh, my gosh!"

"But in the end is so rewarding, Lily! You'll see!"

"I can't wait…"

Then we have the speech. Some people judge your group based on your leader. However, I do not think they believe in that. People just like to judge you and complain all the time.

"Is it good, Anna?"

"Huh… you must believe in what you're saying, Elle." Anna makes a gesture with closed fists.

"I am!"

"Really? It's not convincing me!"

"Okay, let's try again!"

"Watch out for your posture, Elle. You are, huh… almost curved. And show me some attitude too."

"I'm not showing? Oh, then we need to begin again! I mean, from the beginning!"

"We have no time for begin again, Elle! Just show me more attitude!"

"Okay, let's do it!"

"Wait, wait! What are you doing, Elle?"

"I'm walking!"

"Are you in a hurry?"

"Huh… no!"

"And why are you walking with so large footsteps?"

"My footsteps?"

"Yes! You're walking like a man! A man in a hurry, by the way!"

"I think I'm eager!"

"Larger footsteps mean you're in a hurry. We're ladies, we don't do that when we're speaking. So, just walk smoothly, in a small area, but don't forget to look to everyone in the crowd. You can make eye contact, but don't get nervous for that. People will laugh or they will ignore you, just don't bother and keep saying what you have to say."

"Okay, here we go!"

"Wait, wait, wait! What are you doing now?"

"I'm speaking!"

"No, you're not! You're opening your arms too much! Are you going to hug someone? You're not Tony Stark speaking!"

"I can't open?"

"No, definitely not like that!"

"Okay, I got it! Jesus, this is so hard!"

"Wait! What are you doing now, Elle?"

"I'm not opening my arms!"

"And what are these? Wings? Look your elbows! Bend your arms slightly and keep your elbows close to your body. Like this, okay?"

"Okay, now I can do it!"

"Wait, wait! Look your gestures too! Don't open your arms so widely! Take care of your footsteps! And don't forget your elbows! And look to the crowd!"

"Oh, my gosh! Let's do it again!"

"Oh, no, wait!"

"What now?"

"Your hands! You're moving them too much! Are you a... what are you? A magician?"

"Okay, I will not move my hands, Anna!" Elle laughs.

"No! You can move your hands, but lovely. Like a lovely and cute girl."

"I got it!"

"You can even use your fingers, in a cute gesture. Like this. Yes, just use this. And don't clench your fists at the same time. It looks like you're nervous or angry. And don't snap your fingers! I mean, never! And don't make any repetitive movement with your hands. People will think you're anxious."

"But I am!"

"They don't have to know that!"

"Fine, let's do it!"

"Wait a minute, Elle! Didn't you paint your nails?"

"I, huh... oh!"

Chapter Seven – Version 7.1

The day is coming and the girls are almost ready. On Saturday before the competition, they meet at Anna and Lily's house – the new headquarters.

"Hi, Anna!"

"Hi, Emma! Hi, Hailee!"

"Where's Lily?"

"She's in her bedroom. She's still sleeping, actually."

"What? Just wake up her!"

"She's coming, Emma, don't worry."

"What about Ellen?"

"She's on her way. Where is Elle?"

"Oh, she was supposed to be here already. I'll call her."

"Please, come in!"

Hailee and Emma go to the living room. It is not a big place, but the house has a cozy atmosphere. You can easily say that two girls live here. There are flowers and "cute stuff" everywhere. The indoor paint is salmon (not pink); the furniture is clear; the sofa is comfortable and smooth instead of traditional and dark. There is a wide window in the front, and a curtain with blue and orange drawings blocks the rays of sun.

"Nice place, Anna! So warm!"

"Thanks, Hailee! Please, be my guest, you both! I'll call Lily."

Anna comes back in few minutes; Lily comes with her. The little sister is still wearing pajamas.

"Hello, lazy!" says Emma.

"Hello, sleeper!" says Hailee.

"Oh, don't tell me! I'm having a bad week, ladies!"

"Why? We're almost there, Lily!"

"Oh, troubles at work, Emma… don't worry, I'll be fine."

"You must be, Lily! The event is tomorrow! Oh, my gosh, it's so exciting!"

"Yes, it is, Hailee…"

"Wait! Do you sleep wearing teal fish pajamas?" asks Hailee.

"Yes… I'm a pisces. And guess who gave me these pajamas."

"Anna, of course!" answers Emma.

"Why not? It's cute! Look at her! She looks like a big fish queen of the seas! And she gave me a blue lions pajamas!"

"Because you're a lion? I loved it!" Hailee says.

"Oh, wake me up tomorrow morning, please!"

"No, Lily! We have so much to do today!" says Emma.

"Yes, we need to adjust the final details!" Hailee says.

"Okay, where are Ellen and Elle?" asks Lily.

"Elle is coming. I've talked to her." says Hailee.

"Ellen is coming too." Anna says.

They keep talking about amenities and daily life while Lily is changing clothes. Soon, she comes back just to meet Ellen and Elle coming.

"Hey!"

"Hello, Elle! Did you come together?" asks Lily.

"No, I've just met Ellen at the door!"

"Hi, Lily!"

"Hi, Ellen! Come in!"

They go to the new headquarters, the living room.

"Tell me everything, Ellen! Did you finish the tests? Are we good?"

"Huh... yes and no, Anna!"

"Oh... what happened, Ellen?"

"I had to work yesterday, a new client..." says Ellen. "I had no time to finish this... I'm so sorry, ladies..."

"Okay, Ellen, don't bother! We'll work with what we got here. What about you, Elle? Did you practice in front of the mirror?"

"Oh, Anna, it was a little weird to me, but I did. My dad helped me too."

"Hey, is your father coming to see us at the competition?"

"Yes, I think he's coming, Emma! Last time he went out with a lady. I don't know who she is. But this time, he's coming."

"Your father? A date? Oh, my God!" says Hailee.

"Yes... he had a date... he's still young, actually. He's forty years old."

"And the dad's little girl is jealous... ha ha ha!" says Hailee.

"I'm not! Oh, come on, Hailee! It's just... weird! But he's young, he can date anyone! I don't care... so much..."

"Ha ha ha!" laughs Hailee. "And he's handsome!"

"WHAT?"

"He is, Elle! Brittany showed me some pictures of your father!"

"Who's Brittany?" asks Lily.

"She's a girl from college." says Emma.

"What pictures?" asks Elle.

"From the time he was a football player!"

"Oh, I don't believe you're saying this, Hailee!"

"I'm just saying, Elle! It's not a big deal!"

"Have you heard what you just said, Hailee? Imagine you as my stepmother!"

"Oh, that's weird!" Hailee stops laughing.

"Agreed!" says Emma.

"Agreed, but it can get worse." says Ellen. "Just imagine your stepmother, huh... pregnant."

"Oh, awkward, completely awkward!" Emma says again.

"But it happens, Elle! You can't control people's lives! It's unusual, but it can happen!" says Ellen.

"Stop looking my father, Hailee!" but she laughs.

"I wasn't!" she laughs too.

"Huh... ladies, I think we're fine, then." says Anna. "We have the app, or a prototype, but it's working, or half working properly. Powerpoint? Hailee?"

"Done, Anna! It's in my laptop, in two flash drives, in my cell phone; and if we have an internet link there, we have a copy in the cloud. We have all the backup."

"Awesome, Hailee! Thank you!"

"Working app, check; powerpoint, check; speech, check. Anything else I could have forgotten?" asks Anna.

The girls look each other and say nothing. Silence for three seconds (this is usual only in awkward moments).

"So? Anyone? Nothing?" says Anna.

"No, we're ready, Anna!" says Lily.

"Yes, we are!" says Elle.

"Just waiting for tomorrow afternoon!" says Hailee.

"What about now?" Ellen asks.

"Huh... clothing?"

"Good point, Emma! I need a new dress!" Anna says.

"Excuse me?"

"I need a new dress for this event, Lily!"

"Huh... do you have money for that, Anna?"

"I have a credit card, Lily!"

"I don't believe you're saying this, Anna!"

"Actually, WE need new dresses!" says Ellen.

"Yeah, we do!" says Elle.

"So, let's go shopping!" says Emma.

"Huh... wait a second! Do we really need this?"

"Don't you need a new dress, Lily? I mean, we always need a new dress!" says Anna.

"Huh... no! I always have a new dress for these special occasions. I save things, actually. Because if I have no money, at least I have a new dress to wear." Lily teaches.

"Let's go shopping!" says Hailee.

"Yeah, let's go, Lily, come on!" says Elle.

"Oh, no! Wait, wait!"

They GRAB Lily and put her inside Anna's car. Then, the girls go shopping. I am not sure if that was the best reward for the hard work in the last days. However, they just did it without listening to me or anyone else. I think they deserve that.

"Did you see my ring, Lily?"

"What ring?"

"My 'AK ring'."

"I didn't, Anna. Have you seen inside the car?"

"No, I'll check that later."

"Hey, girls! Blue?"

"Better than pink."

"Why not pink?"

"Because there are only girls in our team."

"And?"

"And people will think we're not serious."

"Will they?"

"I have a friend, a guy. He told me when he sees a girl in pink at office, he doesn't take her seriously."

"Really?"

"Yes, that's prejudice! But we can't change it for now. Let's focus on what we can change, ladies."

"Okay."

"Not even salmon? Salmon is not pink."

"Nope. Salmon is almost pink, Elle!"

"I like white! Anyone?"

"No, only you like white, Emma."

"Fine, I just have chosen my color!"

"Good for you, Emma."

"What about this skirt?"

"Above your knees? No way!"

"It's just a few centimeters!"

"It's not a club, Hailee!"

"Yes, it's a business meeting!"

"Accessories?"

"Only the conservatives and discreet."

"Why?"

"Because the accessories can't draw attention more than your face does!"

"Wow, that's a very good tip! Thanks! My self esteem just improved now!"

"What about necklines? V Neck? I like turtleneck!"

"Yeah, it fits you, Elle! I like that!"

"Do you prefer green or blue?"

"I like... blue! No, bright teal, by the way. I don't think they have

109

bright things here. Actually, I have already a bright teal dress; I don't know why I'm here!"

"We're having fun, Lily!"

"There are many stores to go, ladies!"

"I like the black one! Is it too showy?"

"Hmm… yes and no. You're very tall, that's too showy!"

"I like this blue, what do you think?"

"Huh… everyone is choosing blue? What is that? Working clothes? Football kit?

"How about casual style?"

"Yeah, casual, but still business style."

"What? Where did you get that?"

"Not so formal, I mean."

"Not jeans and T-shirt, but not a long dress."

"Yes, it's not an Oscar's night!"

"But it's not a Saturday night too!"

"Bingo!"

"I'm not following you, ladies!"

"Oh, just pick a color, then! We choose for you!"

"No, I want to choose my own dress!"

"You can pick a skirt too, or a blazer. It fits you, I think."

"Wait! Who's choosing dress and who's choosing pants?"

"Dress, totally!"

"Pants and blazer for me!"

"I don't know yet! Sorry…"

"I like jumpsuit…"

"It fits you, Anna, but not for this event. Or flare pants. Yes, definitely, flare pants to you."

"Necklaces or not? Look this!"

"Not that one, Elle; it's too expensive!"

"Oh, it's genuine diamond! Oops!"

"Yes, it is! Pick another one, please!"

"How will the other teams wear?"

"We don't know!"

"We don't know anyone there!"

"Yes, we should get know someone! That could help."

"We don't know anything about the other teams!"

"Forget it! Let's focus on ours!"

"But what about that rivals strategy talk?"

"It's just a business talk, Hailee! They are not rivals!"

"They are! They can take the first place!"

"Whatever! We'll be happy in a second position!"

"No way! I want the top!"

"Have you worked for the top?"

"Huh… I don't know, maybe…"

"Do you remember that conversation about being in the front in a battle? That you can't make choices inside an office?"

"Yep!"

"So, let's see the competitors first. Then I can tell you if we can reach the top."

"Deal!"

"Totally agreed!"

"Did you choose colors already, ladies? I'll pick this light blue."

"Light green for me."

"This black one, with some textures. I like the feel and look."

"White for me."

"Teal, bright, very bright."

"Oh, I'll pick this blue pants then. And that blazer, I don't know. Black?"

"Okay, so Anna has chosen. What about you all?"

"I'll take that white dress." says Elle.

"White blazer and pants for me." chooses Emma.

"Blue dress, with discreet neckline because Emma doesn't want a low-cut dress."

"I'm just taking care of you, little sister!"

"This one, as I said before, light green dress with square neckline, please." says Ellen.

"You like green, right, Ellen?"

"Yep!"

"Huh… that black dress with V neck to me." picks up Lily.

"Hmm! Mysterious black woman in a taller and longer silhouette!" says Emma.

"Black fits anything. I can wear this basic dress again and again, actually. And it's a balanced look."

"Oh, that's just like you, Lily! Give me the numbers and percentages of this choice later, please!" says Ellen.

"This is a rational purchase! It's not an impulsive one like you're doing! Watch and learn, ladies!"

"Gosh! Is she a girl?" Hailee asks.

"WHAT?"

"Ha ha ha!"

"Ha ha ha!"

"Ha ha ha!"

"Ha ha ha!"

Then, after four hours and twenty-two minutes, they finally leave the clothing department. I truly do not know how long they were at shoes stores.

The girls spend all the afternoon shopping. They have free time, and their job is done. After many hours at stores, the girls come back home (the headquarters or Anna and Lily's house). They are, of course, trying on new clothes, new accessories, and new shoes – they like that (I think all people do). Anna brings some beers, but not everyone drinks alcohol. Elle and Ellen do not, and then they are having some sugar-free juice.

"Check it out!"

"Oh, so lovely, Hailee!"

"Ellen, try this one!"

"Thanks, Elle!"

"Hey, you look good in white! Great choice!"

"Loose hair or tied back?"

"Hmm... loose for you."

"Thanks, Lily! I'll not ask you why, because you'll probably give me some numbers, ha ha ha!"

"I'm not listening to you, Hailee..."

"Hey, ladies! What if we get the first prize? Have you imagined that?"

"Wow! It would be awesome!"

"It's a bigger competition, Elle! People from all over the state will come."

"We can dream for free, Anna!"

"Yes, you're right! I'm just warning you, you know? Sometimes you dream too high, and the fall is painful..."

"Have you ever fallen, Anna?"

"Oh, don't tell me... a lot of times..."

"Too many dreams, Anna?"

"As always, when you're younger, Emma."

"And then you become adult, and you forget all your dreams... right, Anna?"

"Unfortunately, yes, Ellen..."

"Wait! You don't have to forget your dreams! What are you talking about?"

"Sometimes, things don't happen the way you want, Elle!"

"And you begin your life with taxes, debts and headaches."

"But you told us you have a life, Anna! I mean, a good boyfriend, a good job and so on…"

"Oh, sometimes this, huh… 'perfect life' is not so perfect, Emma."

"Why not? I've seen your posts. You're always happy in them!"

"Oh, forget social networks, Emma! That's not real life! Not really! People post only the nice moments! Do you know the between the panels in comics? Where superheroes are taking a shower or healing injuries, or maybe peeing? People don't post those moments in social networks."

"But, Anna, you have a nice life! Good job, boyfriend and blah, blah, blah…"

"I don't know! What's a nice life, Elle? What's a nice life to you?"

"Hmm… my father, healthy, this is the most important. Finish college, get a good job. I don't know! A boyfriend, kids, family… I don't know!"

"If this is your 'perfect life', Elle, why are you here? Why are you standing here, with us, in this entrepreneurship adventure?"

"I don't know, Anna... maybe I want more, just like you. I'm not expecting my father lives forever. He can die anytime, doctor told me that… If I can help him while he's alive, I'm grateful! He's everything to me! In the other hand, I need to watch my life too. If he dies, I don't even have a job!"

"Ouch…"

"Hey, if you need anything, you can count on us, Elle!"

"Thanks, Lily!"

"You're welcome!"

"Not everyone has a perfect life, Elle, don't worry!"

"Yes, people show these 'perfect moments', and that's all. Sometimes they don't have anything inside them to show."

"But you look good, Ellen. I mean, I don't see you complaining or anything."

"I have my troubles too, Emma. Don't get me wrong…"

"You say nothing!"

"It doesn't mean I don't have! I just don't share."

"So share it, Ellen! Do you want to talk about?"

"We're all ears, Ellen."

"Huh… okay… my mother… she is dating a guy and I've never met him. And I'm concerned about that, of course. My mom is forty-two years old. We always share those things about men and boys, but not this time. I mean, we used to share these experiences, because she's not so much older than me. She got pregnant when she was only sixteen years old."

"Oh, so young! I can't imagine myself in her place!" says Lily.

"Yes, she had a bad time, you know? In the beginning, my grandfather didn't support her, but my grandmother did, at least. Jennifer is a great mother and I can talk to her about everything straightly."

"Why don't you ask her about this, huh... dating situation?"

"I do, but she doesn't talk. She changes the subject."

"Why?"

"I don't know! She changes!"

"What about you, Emma? You look fine! I mean, you're a pretty girl, smart, nice job..."

"Well, despite the fact that I'm, you know, kissing boys and girls... I'm fine."

"This is not a problem, Emma!"

"When you live in a prejudiced world, it's a problem, Ellen. People think I'm abnormal! If I were gay, it could be worse, I think. I mean, I date guys, and people say nothing. But when I'm with a girl... this is when the troubles start... Why can't I have some peace?"

"Sorry, can I ask you something, sister? I'm just curious! Do you prefer boys or girls?"

"It depends, Hailee! Do you prefer the older guys or the younger ones? Dark hair or blond? Or maybe bald?"

"Oh, not bald, please!"

"Beer? Someone?"

"I'll have one more, please, Lily!"

"You're not talking so much, Lily."

"I just want to finish this job, Elle."

"We'll finish tomorrow, Lily!"

"And then? What happens next?"

"Wait, are you eager, Lily?" says Ellen.

"No! I'm... I just don't know where I'm going to. I think I'm just tired..."

"Where do you want to go?" Emma asks.

"Huh... I don't think these things about family, kids, and mortgage are the best options for girls, you know?"

"But that's what we have! Show me your way, please!" says Hailee.

"We can live fine without all those things. We can have a career, a company, maybe changing the world in the break time of these jobs. Why not? Why do we need kids? To be, huh... 'complete'? I don't believe that! No way!" she makes a gesture and frowns.

"That's what people expect from us, Lily!"

"I do expect too much more from people, Hailee, but they don't show me anything!"

"Okay, so what is your 'perfect life', Lily?"

"Huh... running a huge company; teaching young girls to be themselves, encouraging them, this is important; maybe speaking about money and finances to people who can't go to college. I think family and kids are not in my perfect life, ladies!"

"That's not a problem, Lily!" says Emma. "Not at all!"

"Isn't it?"

"Totally not, Hailee!"

"Sorry, but I disagree!"

"Really? Why?"

"Well, I really want to get married! Why not? And I want kids, maybe ten!"

"Ten children? Jesus!"

"Okay, maybe three or four! But I want kids, definitely!"

"But you'll get fat, Hailee!" Emma says.

"Agreed!" says Anna.

"What's wrong with that? I'll probably be fat when I'll get old! We can't be young forever! It's... it's life! Why should I be skinny all the time?"

"She's right!" says Ellen. "But I don't want to get fat so soon, actually." she completes.

"But it's a consequence of life, my life! I want kids, I get fat, it happens! You know? Omelet, eggs, breaking?"

"I'm getting hungry here..."

"That's why I call her 'Bahamas'..." Elle reveals (and laughs).

"What? Why?" Ellen wants to know.

"Hailee 'Bahamas'. It's her nickname."

"Why 'Bahamas'?" asks Emma. "Tell me all your nicknames, little sister, right now! Because you created a nickname to me and you didn't tell me!"

"Because she's planning to get married in Bahamas!" Elle says and smiles.

"What? It's a nice place! You should see some pictures!" says Bahamas, oops, Hailee.

"Wait! Are you planning your wedding already?" Anna asks.

"Of course, I am!"

"But you're still, huh… how old are you, Hailee?" asks Anna.

"Twenty-two, just like Elle!"

"Okay, okay, I will not discuss, Hailee!" says Emma.

"In fact, she's correct, ladies." says Lily. "Planning is everything. I hope you're saving money for that too, Hailee. Not only dreaming, but planning and saving money. That's very good."

"I am, Lily! I'm saving money already! Not so much every month, but I am!"

"You just surprised me, Hailee! I didn't know you were a dreamer!"

"Just one thing I don't understand: if you dream with wedding and all these conventional things, why do you date so many guys, Hailee?"

"She's testing them, Lily; that's what she says." reveals Elle.

"What's wrong? I'm having fun! And I want to choose wisely, that's why I date guys. And it's not so many, by the way!"

"Surely not, Hailee. She changes boyfriends every month, that's all." says Emma.

"Oh, God, sister! Not every month! That happened only for five months last year!"

"Jesus, five boyfriends in one year? That's an achievement, Hailee! You'll get a card or a badge for that! You just increased your level now!" says Ellen.

"Hey, don't judge me, ladies! No one is normal here! Ha ha ha!" she raises the index finger.

The night comes as always (and at the same time), and they have to leave. Anna gives a ride to Ellen, Elle and Hailee.

"Oops!"

"Are you drunk, Hailee?" asks Ellen.

"No! I just stood up too fast!"

"Uh-huh… sure you did!" says Elle.

"I'm fine… luckily, I won't drive."

Emma's house is near from there, so she stays for a while. She is helping Lily to clean the living room. It is not so messy or dirty, only cups and (many) bottles on the table. Emma takes the cups to the kitchen while Lily turns on the stereo system. Soon, Ms. Marketing comes back to living room.

"I just don't want a hangover tomorrow…"

"Me too…"

The stereo starts to play "Just a girl."

"What are you doing?"

"Oh, I just need some dancing to take off this stress!"

"Really? Are you drunk?"

"Almost... I'm stressed, eager and almost drunk... and I just want to dance now. Come on! Come here!"

"Oh, I can't be standing for now..."

"Yes, you can, come on!"

"No, wait!"

"Come on, show me what you got!"

"Oh, is this a competition?"

"Yeah, any problem?"

"Fine, look this!"

"Wow, I didn't know you were a stripper!"

"I'm just starting, lady!"

"Oh, yeah? So check this out!"

"Belly dancing? Nice move!"

Now playing "Underneath it all."

"Oh, that's just like me..."

"I like this one too... more rhythm, less rush..."

"More sexy too..."

"And alluring..."

"Are you seducing me?"

"No, you're not my type, I think..."

"Why not?"

"I don't know..."

"Okay..."

"What's your type?"

"Hmm... I don't remember..."

"Don't you?"

"I don't remember anything... who are you?"

"I'm your friend..."

"Just a friend?"

"Until now..."

Finally, the stereo plays "Don't speak."

"Oh, this is the time when girls and boys dance together!"

"Yeah..."

"Shall we?"

"Why not? I don't see any boy here."

"Hmm... the girl can dance..."

"Yes, I can. You?"

"I can dance cheek to cheek too."

"Okay, show me."

"Check this out."

"Hmm… you smell good. What is it?"

"I don't remember; something expensive from France."

"Hmm…"

"You smell good too. What is it?"

"Huh… Midnight something… I don't remember…"

"Smells good… you smell good… by the way…"

"Thanks… you too…"

They stop dancing and look each other.

"Are you taller than me?"

"No, we're the same height. Why are you shorter?"

"Oh, I'm falling!"

"Don't pull me!"

They fall down at the right side of the sofa. They are clumsy half on the sofa, half on the ground. Fifty-fifty between both of places. I do not think that is the right thing to happen in the story, but it is happening.

"Ouch! Are you okay?"

"Oh, I'm stressed, Emma! I'm just stressed and drunk!"

"Don't be…"

She gets close to her best friend and touches her face.

"Hey, you scared me! I thought you were going to kiss me!"

"So I think you'll freak out…"

Kiss. One. Quickly. However…

"Oh, I'm sorry, Lily! I didn't want to… that was awkward…"

"Really? I don't think so. Come here…" she whispers.

"No, wait, Lily!"

Kiss. Another one. Longer. Emma did not want in the beginning. However, she did not refuse or oppose in few seconds. Someone is a good kisser here… They are just playing, having some fun before the job next day. I think I told them not to drink so much alcohol.

CHAPTER EIGHT – VERSION 8.0 – CONSEQUENCES.

Why didn't you tell me?

"Fourteenth."

"Yes, Lily, fourteenth."

"I don't believe that!"

"Why not? We did our best."

"Our best, Elle? Did you do your best?"

"Huh… yes. I think yes."

"And what if your best isn't enough?"

The competition has ended, and the girls have gotten a fourteenth position. Now, Elle and Lily are, huh… talking.

"I don't know, Lily, you tell me."

"I think we should have worked harder."

"Didn't you work harder? We all did!"

"I did! But if we got a fourteenth place, we need to try even harder."

"I think we're improving, Lily. I mean, fine, we got an eleventh place before; and now a fourteenth. But this one was a bigger competition. People from all over the state came into it. The last contest was for college students only. I think we're improving here, Lily, really."

"Really?"

"Yes, really. And, by the way, you told me we can't be perfect all the time, remember?"

The thick dark eyebrows girl looks at the long blonde hair girl and agrees. Maybe their best is not enough, so what? They have done their best, and that what matters. Elle has learned that when she does her best is already a reward. Maybe it is only Lily thinking she could do better.

In the end, everyone has their own thought, their own conclusion, and it is not different to them. They are girls building a company, and they are humans too. As we could see (or read), they have troubles and concerns, just like you and me. They are not extraordinary, they are just… unique – like you and me.

"What should we do now?"

"It's not the end of the world, Hailee!"

"No?"

"No, of course not! It's just a contest, it's like a thermometer."

"Oh, so I think our temperature is not so good…"

"How many teams were there, Hailee? Thirty? Forty?"

"Thirty-five. I've read on the website."

"And we're in the top half of the table!"

"Yeah, Emma... you're right. But it hurts to be so far from the first place..."

"There will be other contests, and other chances, Hailee, don't worry!" the older sister encourages her.

"Okay..." she finally smiles.

The girls are trying to rebuild their own universe. Because each one of them has done the best; or that is what they are thinking. Maybe people expect too much from prizes and positions, and they do not care so much about the effort, the experience. Could Lily do better? Or maybe Emma? What about Elle or Hailee? Ellen? Anna?

"Next step, captain?"

"Yeah, Ellen, next step... I think we're still pulling ourselves together. Let's give some rest to the girls."

"How many seconds, Anna?"

"Oh, okay, Ellen... maybe a few seconds before we restart." she smiles.

"I don't know why they are crying, actually. That was just a competition. There are thousands of these out there. The real deal is the marketplace, not a contest."

"I think you should tell them that, Ellen. Because... I don't know! Each one, in her own way, will understand this result. You can understand you could have worked harder, or not."

"We should move on, Anna. Marketplace doesn't stop. It doesn't wait for us, here, crying like babies. Emma should know that."

"Oh, she's not crying. She's comforting Hailee, I think."

"Just schedule a meeting, Anna. We should talk about this. It's not normal. I know the girls are disappointed, but we don't have to be like that every time we lose something. It's just an event, as I said."

"They are not guys, Ellen. I know you usually work with guys, and I know they are not like us. But I need to respect this moment. Let them think and talk for a moment. They'll learn by themselves, I hope."

"Okay, you're the boss, Anna. And, yeah, you're right. I used to work only with men... Jesus! I'm becoming a guy!"

"But I'll schedule a meeting, Ellen. Don't worry."

The manager Anna goes to the team; Ellen comes together.

"Ladies? Everyone? I know we're all disappointed about this. And I know we could do better. We CAN do better. But this is not the only contest in the city, not the only in our lives. So, we are moving on. We came here, so far, not to give up. We came here to learn, and we did. Every moment we have lived here, good or bad, was worthwhile. There will be another day, and when this day comes, I'll be counting on each one of you. Who will be with me?"

Elle looks at Lily and smiles only with her mouth, not showing the bright teeth. Emma smiles to Hailee, who is smiling too. Hailee shows her lovely smile almost all the time, by the way.

"Do we have options?"

"Yes, Hailee. You can stay here crying for… forever! And your boyfriends will forget you in few days."

"My boyfriends? It's only one, Anna! Oh, come on! Not this talk again!"

"Your ex-boyfriends will also forget you, Hailee!"

"I don't care, I already forgot them!"

"Jesus! I'm not listening to this!" says an outraged Elle.

"Okay, ladies, so we are having a meeting tomorrow night."

"Tomorrow night? So soon?"

"Yes, so soon, Emma. I know you have jobs and homework, so we'll chat, right? Be online at eight o'clock; at night, of course. Questions?"

"Nope."

They all agree and then the team leaves the theater. It was the first time the girls speak to so many people, three hundred, at least. The last time was very different: they have met less than one hundred people at college. Elle and Hailee were surprised; Emma and Lily, not so much, but they were a little. Ellen and Anna used to talk to many different persons at work, and they have seen bigger presentations for business. The more experienced girls were not so impressed with the large hall or the audience size. Anna and Ellen were impressed with the fact they were speaking to that public. All the girls are improving and growing up.

Chapter Eight – Version 8.1

At night, Ellen's house.

"Why didn't you tell me?"

"I wanted, Ellen."

"But you didn't, Mom."

"Yes, I didn't…"

"We've always talked about that."

"This time is different."

"What is so different, Mom?"

"Well, he's a young guy, Ellen."

"And?" she makes a gesture with one hand.

"I was afraid of what you could say…"

"Huh… what could I say?"

"That I'm old for him."

"Jesus, Mom! Really?"

"Yes, really."

"I do care about who you're dating, Mom; if he is a nice guy or not. I don't care about ages, I do about love. I care about your happiness, not what people will say. I don't give a damn to people!"

"Ellen!"

"Oh, sorry for that, Mom…"

"Are you okay?"

"Yeah, I am… I think I am…"

"I know this face, Ellen Fage. What happened?"

"It's the girls, Mom."

"What girls? Are you dating girls?"

"NO! MOM! I'm in this new business with the girls! And… huh… we didn't do so well today."

"Are you talking to girls, now? Oh, this is new! This is good!"

"Oh, come on, Mom! I always talk to girls!"

"Yes, sure! You talk to Anna, and… Anna, and Anna too!" Jennifer smiles.

"No, I have more women friends! You just don't know them."

"Okay! So what is this about? This business?"

"We're creating an app, as you could see at the competition. But I think the girls are not ready for that."

"Why do you think that, Ellen?"

"I'm not sure. I think they are not quite mature for this business."

"And why not?"

"Oh, they still care about T-shirts and dresses, and these cosmetic stuff. And they were too much concerned with our fourteenth position."

"And what would you do at their age, Ellen? Something different?"

"I don't know… I think I just grew up too fast, Mom."

"Are you grown up already, Ellen?" Jennifer doubts.

"Huh… yes. I think…" Ellen doubts too.

The coder puts a hand over the head. Ellen can see she is not so tall. She looks to Jennifer again.

"Okay, not so much…"

"And why are you running out of patience with your friends?"

"I don't know…"

"You should, if you are an adult, Ellen. Adults have the responsibility when they talk to kids. Because adults are mature already, kids aren't. There are no excuses for adults."

Ellen lowers her head and thinks. Yes, Jennifer is right. Adults, most of times, have patience when they must deal with kids. The code girl thinks and realizes that she is still a girl – or a young adult. That is not bad, it is just usual – Ellen is still twenty-six years old. Particularly, I think she is just impatient.

"What do you suggest, Mom?"

"Well, you tell me! You're the adult here, right? I'm hiding my relationships and so on…"

"Oh, come on, Mom! Don't do that! Just say something!"

"Well, I've liked what I've seen there."

"But?"

"There is no 'but', Ellen. I think you have a good team, and you look friends. The girls look committed, at least. You all were well dressed too, this is important."

"Why is this so important, Mom? It's just dresses…"

"Because, you know, when we are doing anything, especially those 'men things' like business, we need to be well dressed, we need to speak carefully, and we need to look perfect. People expect that from us."

"Girls are doing business for years, Mom!"

"But men still don't take that! We'll be doing business for thousands years, and they still won't accept it! This is the world we live, Ellen! We can't change it!"

"Well, my friends don't agree on that. They want to change the world."

"What do YOU want, Ellen?"

"I don't know… I want to do my job, get my money, buy my stuff… live…"

"Is this enough to you, Ellen? Working, buying, working, buying… How old are you? Maybe you're three hundred years old and you're tired of this world. I got it."

"I just want to live in a better place, Mom. No! I want to live in a normal place."

"And what are you doing to get that?"

"Huh… not so much…"

"And?"

"I don't know… I'm asking you."

"I think you have a great chance to do something, Ellen. I mean, with those girls. They are nice ones! I could invest on your business, why not? I liked it."

"What about the other people, Mom?"

"They could invest too! You don't know!"

"That's the problem: we don't know."

"Ellen, all the businesses are doubtful when you start. You can make researches, you can consult people, but you never know how is gonna be. So, just start it."

"What if we fail?"

"You start again and again, until you get success. That's what entrepreneurs do."

"I don't feel like an entrepreneur, Mom…"

"You don't have to, this is just a title. The most important is what you do. The title is just a label; that's for outside people."

"Anything else, Mom? Any magic advice?"

"Huh… sorry for not saying I'm dating your friend's father."

"That's okay, Mom! We were surprised! When Elle's father came to introduce you… I didn't know what to say… I didn't know if I should laugh or not! That was weird!"

"Sorry for that, Ellen…"

"The girls were surprised too! I think Elle was the most. She cares about her father; this app, this business is all about her and Mr. Panning."

"One more reason to keep going, Ellen! Your friend has a good reason: her father. Take that to you!"

"Yes, you're right, Mom. I think I need to grow up too."

"Hey, don't be sad! Everything is gonna be fine, as always. You can make a good app, create a great business, change the world!"

"I don't know if I want to change this 'men world', Mom…"

"You should, Ellen. You all have a good reason now. And I think you like those girls."

"Okay, Mom."

"Oh, one last thing: that boy, your friend Michael, he came here to ask you something. He said he couldn't send you a message; he needed to talk privately."

"Oh, I think I know what he wants. He wants some money, I mean, borrowed."

"Why?"

"It's his birthday, and he wants to go to Vegas. He has some unreleased money from insurance company. He needs some money for one weekend only."

"Insurance?"

"Yes, he had a car accident few days ago. The insurance company didn't refund him yet."

"Take care about money, Ellen."

Chapter Eight – Version 8.2

In the meanwhile, at Elle's house.

"Why didn't you tell me?"

"I was waiting for the right moment!"

"I don't believe it, Dad! What a coincidence!"

"It should be a surprise, Ms. Blonde!"

"It WAS, Dad! Completely!" she laughs.

"Huh… I saw the girls… they looked sad…"

"Yeah, Dad… fourteenth place is not so encouraging…"

"Oh, come on, Ms. Blonde! There will be other chances!"

"Yeah… Anna told me that too…"

"She's the leader, right?"

"Huh… no, actually… she said I'm the leader, she's the manager."

"And why aren't you leading?"

"I'm trying, Dad, really… but it's so hard… sometimes I think all the world is against me and the girls…"

"And do you think it's easy to everyone?"

"I think it's not easy to me and the girls."

"Leading people is not easy, Mary Elle. Never. Do you remember when I used to play football? When I was the captain?"

"Yes, sure."

"I remember a game, one of the last games I've played. In the halftime, my team was losing for eight points. And… God! The other team was playing so nicely! They were crushing us down! They were almost perfect! Then, in the break time, a buddy, Jones, do you remember him?"

"Yes, I do! Mr. Jones has named you 'The Fox'." she smiles.

"He came to me and he asked 'Can we change this game, Fox?' I said 'Is there any other score for us, Jones?' "

"Wow…" the blonde girl opens her eyes widely for a while.

"And we did it. We changed that game, we won! We got the championship that year, and that game was the most important of all the season. Later, Jones came to me again with those gestures, grimaces and twists he used to do, remember?"

"Yeah, he is funny!" she laughs.

"He asked me with that unusual voice: 'Hey, Fox, how could you be so sure about this win?' "

"What did you say?" she smiles and waits for a great reply.

"I said 'I'm the captain of this team, Jones. I do lead people here. To me, there is no such 'impossible' word; I can't work with that.' "

"Wow…" she says again. "I wish I could be like that, Dad…"

"You can! You can be anyone! It's your choice, Elle! Every day, you pick a card. This card is who you will be in that day. What card do you want today?"

Elle lowers her head and thinks. It is so easy when you are a confident adult… She is a young adult already, but is she confident? Finally, she thinks the "adult world" is not so interesting as her best friend Hailee used to say. Sometimes it is complicated and hard. When will it be a wonderful world, as the songs she has listened?

"It's all about choices, Elle, your choices. Remember that."

"Okay, Dad… thanks!"

She smiles with her bright teeth and hugs him kindly. It is a nice night at that family's home.

Chapter Eight – Version 8.3

In the same time, some sisters are talking.

"Why didn't you tell me?"

"I wanted to, but we were so busy and rushed, Emma…"

"God! That's a discrimination, Hailee! That should be a federal crime! A world crime!"

"And what should I do? Nobody would believe me!"

"Did you see who they were?"

"No, they didn't know I was listening to them."

"Were you sneaking?"

"No! I was looking for the toilet on backstage! Then I heard some people talking about us."

"What exactly did they say?"

"They said, huh… do you want to listen all the words?"

"Yes, I do!"

"Okay, they said 'A group of girls? Here? No chance! We can't give the first prize to a group of little girls playing business here.' "

"God! I hate that! Was it a man voice?"

"Yes, both of them."

"Jesus, Hailee! You should have told me that!"

"And what would it happen? It's my word against their word, Emma! And we... we are no one there. If they were the organizers, that would be even worse! We could be disqualified!"

"It's not about prizes, Hailee! It's about being correct or not!"

"I didn't see them, Emma! What could I do?"

"Okay, I got it! But next time, tell me, please! We'll figure it out! Those things can't happen at a state competition!"

"I think that's how this world works, Emma! It's not only that competition!"

"That is discrimination against us, women! We can't allow that!"

"But it would be a mess! A scandal at the contest!"

"I don't care, Hailee! It would be an example to the other organizations!" she is outraged.

"But, think about it, Emma. In the next competition, we would be known as 'that group of girls who likes a scandal.' What do you think?"

"Yes, you're right... but people forget all that quickly. Just look all the scandals on internet. Do you remember any name or place?"

"Huh... nope."

"In few months, everyone forgets everything. And we're in the marketplace again."

"Don't worry, sister. We'll be successful in the enemy camp, in a clear victory."

"Are you sure?"

"Yeah, I'm pretty sure."

"But if you see anything wrong, tell me, Hailee."

"Fine, next time I'll tell you. I promise."

Chapter Eight – Version 8.4

Finally, at Davelman sister's home, we can listen to a conversation.

"Why didn't you tell me?"

"You should know that, Anna. You're the manager."

"Oh, now, I'm the manager?"

"Yes!"

"It's hard to check everything, Lily! Especially at those events! It's too rushed!"

"Well, I'm telling you now. So, just take actions."

"Fine, but next time, you tell me, please, Lily."

"Okay."

Lily has reminded that the company does not have any client yet. And she has heard that is relevant to the competitors, especially at a state contest. Unfortunately, she forgot to tell Anna about that.

"And what now?"

"Now, we're gonna get buyers, Lily."

"Really? You mean, money, real money?"

"Yeah, real money, Lily! I know you like it!"

"Of course I like it! Everyone does!"

"Okay, huh... Elle told us something about a client, remember?"

"Yes, the hospital Mr. Panning used to, huh... attend."

"Oh, Christ, Lily! He doesn't attend the hospital!"

"Just a little joke, Anna!"

"Okay, so we're going to that hospital this week, okay?"

"As visitors?"

"No, as patients, Lily! What is the matter with you? Why so many jokes?"

"Oh, that was a messy weekend, Anna! We go shopping on Saturday, we got drunk; and on Sunday, we met Elle's father with... ha ha ha! Oh, my gosh! With Ellen's mother! That was so confusing, so weirdo and... so funny! I just want to laugh a little, Anna! Because we did it, not so well, but it's done! I want some rest now!"

"We can't rest, Lily!"

"Oh, there you go with this 'manager talk'! Why don't you get some rest too, Anna? It's Sunday!"

"Because we're improving, little sister! We can't stop now! That's how the companies go down! Because the heads don't go harder every day! They think only one effort, once a month, is enough for a year! We must keep going, Lily!"

"Okay, okay... so tell me your plans, Anna."

"We'll plan this visit, I mean to that hospital; we make an official logo, some brochures, we get our best dresses and we go there. We need a powerpoint too. And some sketches, not the prototype."

"Why not a prototype? The app is almost working."

"Because customers don't need to see a prototype. When they see something on the screen, on a laptop or a cell phone, they think it's fully working. They don't understand what a prototype is."

"Are they so stupid?"

"Yes, they are, Lily! They don't understand that prototypes are just a not yet finished version of a software. If they see a screen, with beautiful colors, cool buttons and blinking lights, it's working. That's how regular people think. Yes, it's depressing."

"Don't tell me..."

"We make an appointment, I'm calling Elle right now. And we can finish the logo and all the stuff during this week! We can't lose much time, Lily!"

"Okay..."

"Are you listening to me, Lily?"

"Yeah..."

"Oh, God! Am I talking to myself for ten minutes here?"

"Eight. Eight minutes..."

"Gosh, Lily! Wake up! Just take a shower before sleeping, at least!"

"Okay, tomorrow... good night, Anna."

CHAPTER NINE – VERSION 9.0 – THE FINANCE GIRL.

Girls triumphant

"This is the deal, ladies: now we are really making a company. I mean, it's time to put some money here. I'm not talking about buying some paper clips or staplers. It's time to level up."

That is how Lily has started the conversation. They are going to visit a potential client, and they need to buy things and invest money. There is no time for excuses as "Oh, next month, maybe" or anything else. Now they must increase the business.

"How much money, Lily?"

The thick eyebrows girl opens a spreadsheet – she loves it – in the laptop and explains every detail on it.

"We need to purchase a domain, for our website; we need some software licenses, as Ellen told me; we need an accountant and a bank account. There are some taxes in opening a company too. And we need to register the mark as soon as possible. These are the final numbers. For now, I mean."

The girls see the red cell in the spreadsheet and they look each other.

"Okay, it's not so much money." Ellen says.

"Phew! I thought I would have to sell my body for that!"

"Is it on sale, Hailee?"

"No! It is not, Elle!"

"Just checking…" she smiles.

"Okay, Lily, so how can we do that? We give the money to you?" Emma asks.

"We'll make a contract first. It's an articles of incorporation and bylaws. The accountant will take care of this, and this means more cost. Oh, we need a corporate bank account."

"Corporate? Oh, my God! We're making business!"

"Yes, Hailee! Now it's the real deal!" says Anna.

"What about this corporate bank account, Lily?" asks Elle. "Who's empowered to administer it?"

"You, Anna and I, Elle."

"Why not everyone?"

"Because not everyone needs to administer it, Emma." says Lily. "Does everyone agree on that? If you don't, it's time to talk."

"Jesus, you're so quiet now! Are you afraid or what?"

"I think we're just nervous because it's the real deal, Anna!"

"This is how it works, Elle. It's time to grow up, ladies." Anna answers.

"I told you things would get serious when we would talk about money, didn't I, Hailee?"

"Yes, totally, Lily…"

"It's fine to me! I'll send the money to you, Lily."

"Fine, Ellen."

"Me too. I'll send Hailee's money too, Lily."

"Thanks, Emma."

"I'll give you the money tomorrow, Lily."

"Okay, Anna. I can remind you, if you forget."

"I'll ask my father to send to you, okay?"

"Fine, Elle, thanks. So, we're officially starting this company, ladies! Now it's time to make real business!" Lily says.

"Huh… weren't we doing yet?"

"No, we were just warming up, Emma." Lily answers.

"Yeah, we were playing contests until now!"

"Yeah, something like that, Hailee!" Lily says.

"Fine, so where were we? Elle, did you talk to that doctor? What is her name?" Anna asks.

"Alice, Doctor Alice. I've talked to her."

"And?" says Anna.

"She can meet us on Friday, afternoon, two o'clock. Don't be late, she said. She has crazy schedules, as I said before."

"What exactly is her job there, Elle?"

"She is a director, Emma; one of the directors, actually. I think it's a high position. I mean, I've heard her name many times over the P.A. system while I was talking to her at the hospital. And many people came to call her. She looks very important over there."

"Well, that's a good chance, then!"

"Anna is right, we need to make our best, ladies!"

"Agreed, Lily. Everything must be working; this time, there are no excuses."

"Sure, Emma. But what exactly will we present to her?"

"The sketches, Ellen."

"Wait a second, Anna! Sketches? Seriously?"

"Yes, Hailee. We present our idea, we talk to her about what she really needs in this app. Then we build it."

"I don't get it, Anna. Why don't we show the prototype?"

"Because people don't understand prototypes, Elle. They think it's all working already. And, in fact, we should talk to a medical professional before making the app, not after. That's how it works. But we were making the app for the contests, then…"

"Huh… did we start in the wrong way, then?"

"No, absolutely not, Elle! You and Hailee have begun right! An idea, some sketches, talking to a professor; that was very good. Now, we are making a fine tuning, an adjustment. First, we need to know what the client needs; I mean what exactly Doctor Alice needs. And we still don't know if there are legal complications on this app."

"Legal complications, Anna?"

"Yes, Hailee. Because it's a report about a patient. And what if a patient dies? This report can be used like evidence. Have you thought about that already?"

"Wow… things are getting serious here…"

"Yes, Ellen, this is very serious. And what if a doctor doesn't want to share everything? It happens. In case of terminal patients, this is usual. Doctors don't want to take the hope away from people."

"And in those cases, our app is useless, right, Anna?"

"I'm afraid so, Emma."

"So, we have just started and now we are finishing this?"

"No, Hailee, we'll figure it out! We'll think about it!"

"How, Anna?"

"Huh… I don't know. But we'll find out. I'm pretty sure about this."

"Yeah, we can create something."

"You're the ideas girl, Elle. Do something!"

"Oh, now I am everything in this company!"

"And you're the leader too! Don't forget that!"

"Ouch, Lily! Wait a second, please!"

"And don't panic, please!"

Elle lowers her head and soon she raises it. Her fingertips start to sweat and she rubs them with the thumb. She looks at Emma and asks.

"What did you just say, Emma?"

"Don't panic, don't freak out."

"That's it!"

"What? Panic? Wait, I'll bring some fresh water first."

"Yes, Hailee! Panic!"

"Excuse me?" say Ellen, Emma, Lily and Anna.

"What for?" Hailee frowns.

"When we'll have a terminal patient, there will be a 'panic button' in the app!"

"I'm not following you, Elle."

"Me neither."

"I didn't get it too."

"Is she okay?"

"I don't know!"

"Wait, wait! I'm thinking!"

"Oh, bring some fresh water, Hailee..." says Lily.

"Stop kidding! I'm speaking seriously! Just a second!"

The girls stop talking and joking while the blonde young lady thinks. They look each other and make some grimaces, but they do not interrupt Elle.

"Yes! That's it! A panic button!"

"Huh... English, please!" asks Ellen.

"This is it: in terminal patient cases, the doctor will push the panic button. This means it's better the family comes to the hospital to talk personally. Because it's a serious case, it's terminal! And the doctor can't send any messages. That would be irresponsible."

"I like her!" Ellen smiles.

"That's amazing, Elle! You mean, in some special cases, serious cases, the doctor has the option to call the family to talk, right?"

"Yes, Anna! And when someone gets this 'panic button message', the family will be ready for the bad news! Wow, she's good!"

"I told you she was the ideas girl, Lily!"

"Thanks, Hailee! And thanks to Emma for the panic! Ha ha ha!"

"I didn't panic yet! This time I'm just listening and learning! Congrats, Elle, you did good!"

"Okay, ladies, now we're back on business!" says Anna.

"Huh... did we leave the business?"

"Just a way of speaking, Hailee!" Lily says.

"And now we have a panic button!" says Ellen.

Chapter Nine – Version 9.1

They are visiting Doctor Alice.

"Good afternoon, Doctor Alice!"

"Hi, Elle! How are you doing? How is your father?" she smiles.

"I'm fine, thank you! My father is fine too, thank you! Oh, I'd like to introduce some ladies. These are Anna, Emma, Lily and Ellen; I think you remember Hailee. Ladies, this is Doctor Alice!"

"Hi, Anna! Hi, Emma! Oh, so many names! Hi, Lily! Hi, Ellen! Of course I remember you, Hailee! Hi!"

"Hi, Doctor Alice!"

"Hmm… please, follow me. We have a meeting room right there."

"Okay."

They go to the room and they have a sit. Alice is sitting down at the head of the table; it is a large table, with at least twelve chairs. The room is very clean, with creamy walls, and clear, with a wide light blue windows. Through these windows, the girls can see a beautiful garden with white and orange flowers.

"Nice place, Doctor Alice!"

"Thank you, Elle! Well, you said you'd like to talk to me about an app, right?"

"Yes, Doctor Alice. Huh… this story has started with my father. Sometimes I waited here for a long time to talk to a doctor."

"Yes, we have some hard schedules, sorry for that, Elle. I remember once, I got here and you were sleeping at the patient's room. I remember your father was looking better than you."

"Oh… I remember that; how embarrassing!"

"Don't bother; it happens, Elle."

"So the app is exactly about this: waiting or saving time. Doctors can send a message to the patient's relatives. It works like a report."

"Really? What happened to the phone calls?"

Hailee laughs a little.

"Oh… I thought I wouldn't listen this joke in this story anymore."

"Excuse me?"

"Huh… Well, this is an alternative to phone call, Doctor Alice. Because, as you know, people can be busy even for phone calls. So, this app will work with few questions like patient's status and discharge dates. I think, huh… I mean, we think this can be useful. Because patient's relatives don't have to wait here for a long time. When the diagnosis sounds good, of course. And the doctors won't spend so much time talking to people about a good and stable diagnosis."

"What if we have a complicate case, Elle?"

The girls smile.

"Oh, then we have a panic button, Doctor Alice."

"Panic button? Like a 911 call?"

"No! It's a 'less serious' button. The doctor can push it when he or she needs to talk personally to the patient's family. Because, in some cases, it's better talking in person, not through messages, right?"

"Yes, that's very clever!"

"Thank you!"

"Did you take too much time to create that?"

"Huh… we have made some meetings to find out this… feature."

"Very inventive, really! And what more do you have?"

"We'd like to listen to you, Doctor Alice." Anna says. "We'd like to talk to a sector professional to improve this app. Then we can produce and sell it. But first we need to improve it."

"Oh, I think I'm the right person, Anna. I have many ideas to that. And, huh… sometimes people don't listen to me here, you know?"

"Really? Oh…"

"Yes, you say over and over, and people want to work like they always have worked, I mean in their entire lives. Nothing changes. But I think I can help you as much as you can help me."

"And what do you need, Doctor Alice?" Emma says.

"Well, first of all, the app needs to be easy to use. I mean, very, very easy. Because people don't like to learn new things anymore. They want to see a known design; they want large buttons, intuitive features and easy to set options. I know that because some people here can only run Internet Explorer and access Facebook. In this order, by the way."

"They don't even know if Control Panel exists, right?"

"Yes, Ellen; unfortunately, yes. So, the first thing is: easy to use. Sorry, are these sketches?"

Hailee shows the papers she has.

"Oh, this is good! And you have some questions already!"

"Yes, Doctor Alice. We didn't want to put too many questions. Because it's a report, not a book about the patient."

"This is completely right, Hailee. We don't have much time to fill long questionnaires. And people don't like to fill long questionnaires too."

"Few days ago, Doctor Alice, we were talking about a question. In some cases, more severe cases, do the doctors talk straight to the families? I mean, do they say everything they need to say?"

"That is a complicate question, Anna. I think not all the doctors say what they should. It's hard to them too. And I know the relatives just want an opinion, not a guarantee. But, unfortunately, not all the professionals are ready to sensitive conversations like that."

"And what if the doctors don't want to use the app?"

"This could be a problem, Lily. But I think this, huh... 'panic button', as you call it, can solve that. Because when the doctor push it, he or she will have to talk straightly, not clam up. This feature can be very useful."

"Will they use the panic button?"

"Hmm... I don't know, Emma, really. This must be the last option. I mean, in a real 'panic' case. You have to explain this very clearly."

"We'll put a confirmation message when someone hits the button, Doctor Alice. Because the doctors must know this is very important. They will have a serious talk to the patient's family when this button will be pushed. The doctors must know this is absolutely not for play."

"Great idea, Ellen! Yes, you definitely should do this!"

"We have also a blank field, Doctor Alice. Look at this, please."

"Hmm... this is very good! We'll have a virtual keyboard, right?"

"Yes, sure. And there is an option to record a voice message, if the doctors don't want to type or if they are too busy."

"It's a very good feature, Hailee! And what about operating systems? Will you release this app for all cell phones?"

"Oh, you're a heavy user, Doctor Alice! I mean, you really know about this! It's good to talk to someone who understands what we are saying!"

"Thanks, Ellen! People used to call me 'G Doc' here. It's for 'Geek Doctor'... Last week I had to fix the laptop of the secretary, a Windows trouble. It's embarrassing."

"Wow, you're one of us, Doctor Alice!"

"Really, Ellen? Because you look, huh... 'normal' girls... no offenses!"

"No, we're not! We play games, we read comics, we like computer hardware." Ellen says. "I don't think we're 'normal'."

"I don't like hardware, I like cars." says Anna.

"And I like food!" Lily says. "I mean, good food, not pizza with mustard and ketchup."

"Oh, that's interesting! Well, I realized you were different when you just arrived here. Because you don't call yourselves 'dudes' or 'guys'. Ellen has introduced you as 'ladies'. I like that. I hope you also use those words when you're not in a business meeting."

"Yes, we do, Doctor Alice! And we don't say curse words too." smiles Anna.

"Really? Oh, that's rare! I think I'll get along with you, ladies! We'll work fine together!"

"It's our pleasure, Doctor Alice!" Anna smiles again.

"So, could you make a prototype? How much time do you need?"

"Ellen?" Anna asks.

"Huh… maybe one or two weeks, I think."

"Fine, I'll talk to the board in the meanwhile. But I can assure you, we'll use this app. It's time to update this place, you know? We need this modernization. We still use too much paper here. And paper means archives, which means large rooms to store, which means hard ways to search for. It's a waste of time! And we can talk about prices, of course. Because I think you're not doing this for charity, right?"

"Yes, Doctor Alice! For now, we'll charge it only for maintenance costs, and a small profit." Lily says.

"Are you sure?"

"Yes, because we're working like partners for now, right?" suggests Lily.

"Well, if you say so, it's fine to me. I need to take care of costs too, by the way. So, please, send me a message when you'll have final numbers, right?"

"Okay, Doctor Alice, thank you!" they say.

"I'll be waiting for the next meeting, huh… ladies!"

The "more than thirty years old" doctor smiles to the girls. Alice Bragan is busy today, as she is all the time. Her long dark brown hair is tied up – a green and yellow hair clip helps the doctor. The dark brown eyes are big, and the mouth is made by thin lips which become in a large smile – when she is happy. This does not happen all the time at that hospital. The place insists in working the old way. The Aries doctor, born on April, needs patience to work in there. Most of the board is formed by men, and most of them do not listen to her. The doctor thanks the ladies and they leave. Now the girls have a precious client and partner.

CHAPTER TEN – VERSION 10.0 – WHERE IS THE MONEY?

Bills and yells

Almost one month later.

"We need to improve design."

"Really? How much?"

"Much."

"Why?"

"Because Doctor Alice liked the features, but not so much the design." says the founder.

"She said nothing, Elle."

"But she did an… huh… unusual face."

"Now you are reading faces?"

"I've always read faces, Hailee, especially yours. You make a lot of funny faces!"

"I don't!" she pulls a face.

"You do! You're doing now."

"I'm not!"

Three weeks ago, the girls have talked to Doctor Alice. She liked the app, and then she started to use it as a tester – and as a business partner. The girls had their first win. Now they are working to improve design and solve some software bugs.

"Sometimes, I don't know why we need to work so hard in design."

"Because people like beautiful things, Lily."

"Really?"

"Yes, I've talked to some experienced coders. They make two apps with exactly the same features. The colorful and cute app has much more downloads."

"How much more? Do you have a percentage?"

"No, I don't, Lily." Ellen smiles. "I don't have this number for you, sorry. But I can assure you, they are correct."

"Well, fortunately, we have two designers here. Or… huh… maybe trainees."

"No, they are doing good! Hailee and Elle are talented. Elle has other roles here, but Hailee can perfectly handle this." the brunette coder completes.

"Do we have a deadline? I didn't hear Anna saying anything."

"Huh… wait a second… next delivery will be on the next week.

I think Doctor Alice is not so hurried about design. Because the app is working, actually."

"Did you solve that last bug? The send button fails sometimes. You need to push it harder. It's funny."

"I think that's caused by some screen error, Lily. But I'll check that."

"Okay, thanks, Ellen."

Design is a very important feature nowadays. You can say it does not matter, but how do you choose your clothes? Only because you like the colors? Luckily, the girls are working correctly.

"Anna, did you confirm those values to Lily?"

"Yes, Emma, I did."

"Huh… I know this is not my responsibility, Anna, but how is our account?"

"It's good to hear you asking this, Emma. Accounts should be everyone's job, actually. Don't be afraid of asking that, okay?"

"Okay."

"Huh… we're doing well. I mean, not bad."

"You are not convincing me, Anna."

"Huh… in fact, we're not doing so well, Emma. Because we have many bills to pay, or I should call them 'investments'. It's perfectly normal in the beginning. And the problem is that we're not making so much money as we thought we could do."

"Why not?"

"Well, the hospital, it's not paying so much money. It covers some costs, but this is not enough, of course."

"I'm afraid to ask you… 'and?' "

"And… we need more clients. Soon. I mean, when the girls finish design, we need to release this quickly. Is the website online?"

"Not yet. They didn't build it."

"Who?"

"Huh… design and code. They are still working in the app. I think we're late, Anna."

"Yes, we are, Emma. I think we should shorten the deadlines."

"Girls will go crazy, Anna."

"Or we go down. They need to study, to work, to finish this. Pick one, Emma."

"Oh…"

"Sometimes, I don't understand why people like design so much. Is it to flaunt?"

"Yes, totally, Anna! This is how the world works nowadays."

"Even if I don't agree on that?"

"Yes, the world doesn't care about what you agree or not."

"Oh, this is sad…"

"Welcome to the 'men world', Anna. They built it this way."

"What if we don't improve design? I mean, it doesn't have to be perfect. What if we make a so-so app? Just for a faster release, maybe?"

"Do you want to go down consciously, Anna? Design is still very important. Ask Apple about that." Emma blinks an eye with a mouth snap.

Chapter Ten – Version 10.1

Friday at Anna and Lily's house – the headquarters. A phone call.

"Hello? Elle?"

"Hello, Ellen! What's up?"

"Huh… I need to talk to someone. Where is Anna?"

"She didn't come back from work yet. Lily didn't too."

"Are you alone?"

"No, Hailee is here. We are working. Are you coming?"

"Yes, I'm almost there. A few meters."

Ellen arrives and knocks the door.

"Hi. Did they come already?"

"No, they didn't, Ellen! You just came too fast! In three minutes! What's going on?"

"Huh… it's a hard talk…"

"Just say it, Ellen!"

"I need some money."

"Money? What for?"

"A friend of mine is asking for. And I have promised to him I would borrow it. He's a very close friend, don't worry."

"But you need it now?"

"Yes, he's going to Vegas this weekend. He's leaving tonight, by the way."

"Vegas?"

"Yes, it's his birthday. He's planning this trip with some buddies for months. Sadly, he had some, huh… unforeseen events… and he is asking me for money."

"Why doesn't he ask to his father?"

"Huh… because he's not, huh… eight years old. Me neither."

"Hi, Ellen! What's up?"

"Hi, Hailee!"

"We're having a serious talk here, Hailee."

"What is it?"

"I'm asking for money, because, actually, I was saving the money to borrow to my friend. So, Lily came with this, huh... investment. I was not planning that so soon. This money would be borrowed, it shouldn't be here, I mean, in the company. That's why I'm asking."

"Is he a good friend? Is he hot?"

"He's not bad, Hailee. He's tall. I mean, taller than you, not me."

"I don't know..." says Elle.

"And, by the way, I owe him."

"You owe him?" Hailee says.

"Yes, he helps me in some jobs when the deadlines are killing me. Not to mention while we were at college. He's a very good friend."

"When will he return the money, Ellen?"

"On Monday or Tuesday, Hailee. He comes back from Vegas and he gets some money from insurance company."

"Insurance?" distrusts Elle.

"Yes, he has some money to get from insurance company."

"What for?" the blonde girl asks.

"Car accident."

"And how is he going to Vegas? By car?" now the brunette girl asks.

"Yes."

"Huh... I don't think this is a good idea, Ellen..." Elle says. She feels some fingertips sweating.

"But it was not his fault in the car accident. He was stopped at traffic light and the other guy just crashed it."

"Oh, that sounds better!" Hailee smiles.

"Well, okay, so how do we do this? A bank transfer?"

"Yes, we can make that online. And... I'm so sorry for asking you this, ladies, really... I wouldn't ask you if it was not important!"

"Don't worry, Ellen! We're here to help each other! We're friends and partners, remember?"

"Thanks, Elle! On Monday, the money will be back in the right place."

Chapter Ten – Version 10.2

Anna got home few minutes ago. Emma is there too, as well as Ellen, Elle and Hailee. Lily is arriving right now; she is putting her purse on the sofa. Anna is sitting at the laptop, checking accounts. The girls are around Anna. Lily comes closer.

"They what?"

"They got some money from the company account." says the concerned manager.

"WHAT?"

"It's not forever, Lily; it's for a while."

"A while? How long, Anna?"

"Only this weekend. Why?"

"We have four bills to pay on Monday! Accountant, for example! Monday, at morning, until ten o'clock!"

"Oh…" Anna looks at the other girls.

"I don't believe you did that!"

"It's a friend of mine, Lily."

"I don't care, Ellen! You don't take money from the company account! I mean, never!"

"Why not? It was for a good reason, Lily."

"I don't care whether it's a good reason, Elle! You never touch the company account! It's something sacred! Who's this guy?" Lily wants to know, and she starts to change her tone of voice. She will be angry in few seconds (you will read that soon).

"He's a very close friend of mine, Lily! It's his birthday, and he's going to Vegas. And I owe him that! He helped me many times when we have studied together!"

"I don't care about what you owe, Ellen! And then he wants to go to Vegas and you just borrowed the company's money?" she shows some disdain, irony, sarcasm and hatred (do not ask me how).

"We borrowed the money, Lily. I did that too." says Elle.

"Yeah, he looks a nice guy, Lily. And hot. I saw some pictures." Hailee tries to calm down the finance girl.

"God! We are not having this conversation! I don't believe you did that! Where is he going to? Vegas? Really? What if this guy dies? Does he have a life insurance? Do you have a borrower's note? Anything written on any paper? How can you prove he borrowed our money? HUH?"

"Lily, you… you are shouting…"

"I'M NOT SHOUTING, ANNA! THIS IS HOW I HAVE TO SPEAK WHEN YOU TOUCH THE COMPANY'S MONEY! IT'S NOT CORRECT! AND YOU DIDN'T HAVE THE RIGHT OR THE AUTHORITY TO DO THAT!"

"We… we have the right, Lily. We are partners in this business." says Elle.

"BUT THIS GUY IS NOT! THIS IS NOT FOR FUN! IT'S REAL MONEY HERE! DON'T YOU GET THAT?"

"Lily, please!" asks Emma.

"You should have called someone! Just a God damn phone call! Just a God damn message!"

"Lily, please! You're a lady!" Emma asks again.

"I'M NOT A LADY!"

"Just calm down, Lily!"

"HOW? WE'RE RUNNING OUT OF MONEY, ANNA!"

"It's done, Lily! Take it easy!"

"That was my job, Emma! My responsibility! They couldn't do that! I don't know what she is doing here!" Lily uses the index finger.

"What?"

"Yes, you heard me, Ellen!"

"Wait a second, Lily! Do you want to get back to this? Really? Were you pretending all this time?"

"No, I wasn't! I'm just regretting right now!"

"Regretting for what?"

"You know what, Ellen! Don't be a fool!"

"Oh, I'm a fool, Lily! Tell me why you're regretting! Because of me? Because I'm here? Is it? Just spit it out! I'd like to remember you that if I leave this place, the source code of the app leaves too!"

"Take whatever you want, Ellen! You've just messed up everything!"

"Oh, really? That's how is gonna be?"

"Ladies, ladies! Please! We've already overcome that, right? Right? I'm talking to you, Lily and Ellen!"

Silence. For three seconds.

"Look at me when I talk to you! I'm tired of these little fights! You and you, just say whatever you want to say and finish this childishness!"

Silence. For two seconds.

"Nothing? Fine! I don't want to see any fights here, anymore! I don't care if you don't like each other! I don't care if you're regretting or not! I don't care if you're doing this or that! I don't want to see this crappy talk anymore! This waste of time, money and patience! Did you get that?"

Silence. For one second.

"DID YOU GET THAT? Where do you think you are? At an amusement park? At a children's playground? You've signed a contract!

This is a commitment! Not only with yourself, but with ourselves! This is not for children! If there is any child here, please, leave now! Because if you stay, if you all stay here, I want to see some adult women! Not these little kids playing business! What about Elle's speech about tolerance? HUH? Can you change the world like that? Tell me! Because I'm here for almost two months, and I didn't see any change yet! And I think I'm being very straight with you all, ladies! Is that clear?"

Silence. For less than one second.

"IS THAT CLEAR?"

"Yes, Anna."

"Yes, Anna."

"Jesus Christ! We're more than this, ladies, really! And I know we can do, we can be better! I'm counting on you because I trust you. I expect so much from you because I know you can give me that."

The girls remain silence.

"Let's have a break." asks Anna. "Please."

Ellen, Elle and Hailee leave the room and go outside to get some fresh air.

"Nothing is gonna break this business, Emma. Nothing!" says Anna.

"It's done, Anna. We can't do anything except waiting for this guy."

"Oh, God! I have a bad feeling about that, Emma…"

"Anyway, it's done, Lily…"

Out of the house.

"She couldn't say that."

"I agree with you, Ellen."

"Thanks, Hailee."

"But it's done, ladies. I think we all missed today."

"I don't know why she does that."

"We don't know many things here, Ellen."

"But, it's fine, I'll comply with Anna's orders."

"Anna got so angry! She yelled! Can you believe that?"

"Don't make Anna angry, Hailee. You wouldn't like her when she's angry."

Chapter Ten – Version 10.3

Monday, at morning, ten o'clock. Two girls are still at home.

"So?"

"I don't know. Where is Ellen?"

"She's coming."

"How long?"

"I don't know. She doesn't answer my messages."

"Call her."

"She's not answering the phone too, Lily."

"What can we do, Anna? Any options?"

"Huh… we wait. Until everything blows up."

"Okay."

"You look calm, Lily."

"What can I do, Anna?"

"I don't know, it's strange seeing you like that. I mean, so peaceful."

"I think I'm here for something else, Anna. Not only for finance. I think I must learn more than marketing, coding, design and so on."

"And what is that?"

"I don't know; I'm still looking for. I'm learning to be peaceful, for now. I don't want wrinkles so soon."

"Good for you, Lily."

Midday.

"Hello!"

"Ellen?"

"Yeah, it's me, Anna! We have a situation here…"

"Oh, God… what is it?"

"My friend, the guy, he's at a hospital."

"Oh, no! How bad is it? Is he alive? What happened?"

"It was a car accident. Yes, again. He's unconscious, but stable. Yes, you've warned me."

"Where are you, Ellen?"

"I'm here, at hospital where Doctor Alice works. Huh… could you tell Lily, please? Tell her I'm sorry."

"She's here. Do you want to talk to her?"

"Yes."

"Hello? Ellen?"

"Hello, Lily. You were right, I was wrong. I'm sorry."

"Don't be, Ellen."

"No, I really shouldn't take the company's money! You were right! I'll promise you I'll fix this. I'm so sorry, Lily, really!"

"It's done, Ellen. We don't have to fight." Lilly takes a deep breath.

"It was my fault, Lily. If there is anything I can do to help, please tell me. I'm all ears."

"Huh… I'll talk to Anna here. I'll call you. Please, just take care of yourself, Ellen. And I wish your friend gets well soon."

"Thanks, Lily."

Lily hangs up the phone. She puts both of her hands on the face and lowers the head.

"You okay?"

"Yeah, I'll be fine, Anna, thanks."

"This is not you, Lily. I mean, so calm."

"I think I'm just changing, Anna. I don't know if I'm improving, but I'm changing."

"Good luck, sister."

"Thanks."

Lily starts to remind the bills and dates they have to pay. She has a photographic memory. That allows her to remind the exactly cells that point to values and then to dates. These cells are claiming attention right now, and the thick eyebrows girl is thinking about some quick solution – and feasible. She starts to swing legs, she is impatience. She opens the spreadsheet on her laptop.

"Can we extend payment deadline, Lily?"

"I don't think so, Anna. Maybe for a few days."

"But Ellen's friend is unconscious."

"Yes."

"And we don't know until when."

"Yes."

"And even if we can extend the payment deadline, we don't know if it's enough."

"Yes."

"Because the boy is unconscious."

"Yes." Lily says swinging her head nicely. She is folding arms too.

"How much money, Lily?"

"Huh…"

Lily shows the eye-popping value on the spreadsheet, Anna opens widely her eyes.

"Oh, my God!"

"Yes. Oh, my God. See why I just freaked out before?"

Anna stands up and goes to the wide window in the living room. She takes a breath and lowers the head. "How I let this happens?" she says to herself. Anna is the manager, she thinks all that is her responsibility. However, it was not her fault. It was a communication problem, maybe a permission problem – which became a money trouble.

Anna raises the head, her eyes look at the front of the house. There is something there, on the street. A black and very powerful thing – not pink or purple. It has silver five rims wheels and it is wrapping – that is a little out of date, but she likes it (and it protects the paintwork, by the way). This thing looks like a ghost or something from the shadows – according to Anna's thinking. Inside this, the manager can see blue seats – because that girl loves the color. She has worked for almost one year to buy it. Anna Kelly sees her very special first car and she knows its value is higher than the money they need at that moment. She turns the head to her sister:

"I think I have a solution, Lily."

CHAPTER ELEVEN – VERSION 11.0 – ANOTHER COMPETITION.

Hiring

The sisters are at a car shop.

"It was your first car, Anna."

"I know, Lily."

"And you love cars."

"I know, Lily."

"And I think we had no choice…"

"I know, Lily."

"And…"

"I know, Lily!" she turns to the sister. "I know!"

"Sorry!"

"At least, we're back, Lily. All the bills are paid; we'll have some slack in the budget, I hope. Did you update your spreadsheets?"

"Yes, yesterday."

"Well, let's call the girls. Emma has some news, she said."

"Really? What is it?"

"I'm not sure, but I think it's another competition."

"Another one? Aren't we spending too much time with those events, Anna?"

"It's a double-edged sword, Lily. We are spending time and money with it, I give you that; but we can introduce our company to many people. Emma told me there are three moments at a competition: before the event, when we get prepared and people can read about us on the contest website; during the contest, when we show our business; and after, when we strengthen the contacts made during the event. It's a showcase, Lily. Ms. Marketing knows how to introduce the company."

"Do you know this nickname too?"

"Sure! Everybody knows that!"

Chapter Eleven – Version 11.1

Later.

"She what?"

"She's pregnant!"

"Pregnant?"

"Yes, pregnant, Lily. You know… people used to…" she does some gestures.

"I know how it happens, Anna! I just don't believe it! Did she make, huh… unsafe? Maybe the condom came off inside her… huh… oh, forget it!"

"I don't know so many details, Lily! Ask Emma. She's freaking out, by the way. Ask and comfort her, please."

"What about the contest?"

"Good question, Lily."

"Can Elle handle this? I mean all design stuff and powerpoint slides? What more? Emma has some design jobs too."

"I don't know. Probably, Elle will get eager and she'll not handle with all those demands."

"God! Elle should be prepared already. It's not the first time!"

"But she's not, Lily."

"Hailee said this is time to make brochures and T-shirts; Emma agrees on that, but she said we can make more. What do you think?

"What did Emma say?"

"We should make an app to present our company to the people."

"An app to introduce another app?"

"Yes. And people will download the app during the presentation. There will be a QR code on the big screen. The audience will take a picture and they will be redirected to our website."

"That's a very good idea! But do we have time for this? How much time do we have until the round one?"

"Three weeks. Emma has talked to Ellen already."

"And?"

"And Ellen said 'Cool! Let's do this!' "

"But we still need someone to create design. And this 'app of the app' is one more design work, Lily."

"Yep! But now we have some money, at least. We can hire someone, a freelancer."

"Good. Do you know anyone who can help us?"

"No, but I'll ask Elle. She should know someone because she's studying design, right?"

"Yes. Please, do that, Lily."

Chapter Eleven – Version 11.2

Much later.

"His name is, huh… Tyler. Yes, it's Tyler."

"Is he good?"

"Huh, he's not my cup of tea; I don't like long hair and earrings, not even sandals!"

"I'm talking about skills, Lily!"

"Oh, sorry, Anna! Elle told me he got an 'F' once, but he's good. And he's not so expensive too."

"Not expensive? That means crap work?"

"I don't know, Anna. But, Elle has recommended only this boy. She doesn't have many friends at college. Did you know that?"

"Yes, we're all freaks and nerds, Lily. No one in this story has many friends."

"Story? What story?" Lily frowns.

"Our company's story."

"So can I call this boy for an interview?"

"Yes, sure. But we'll probably take him."

Chapter Eleven – Version 11.3

The following day.

"Huh… hi! You're Tyler, right?"

"Yes! And you're… Lily? Then you must be Anna."

"Yes, nice to meet you, Tyler." says Lily.

"Nice to meet you. Huh… you're tall!" says Anna.

"Oh, yeah. I'm in the basketball team."

"Nice! Huh… Can we start the interview, Tyler? Please, tell me about your experiences as a graphic designer."

"Well, I don't have so many professional experiences, Anna. But I really want to help you. And I have many skills in any graphic software."

"Like what?"

"From Photoshop to Freehand."

"Freehand is no longer available. The company doesn't exist anymore." says Anna.

"Yes, I know! But I have knowledge of it."

"But, why do you learn a, huh… about extinct software, Tyler?" asks Lily.

"Because it's important to get know every software; you don't know what to expect when you get into a new company, right?"

"Good point, Tyler. Huh… we don't use extinct software here, by the way."

"Okay, Lily! I got that!"

"We are hiring you for a freelance, right? It's just for a specific job. Because one of us is not available at the moment. Is this a problem to you?"

"No, absolutely, Anna! I really want to work. And it would be perfect if I could work at a start-up company."

"How do you know this is a start-up company?"

"Huh... because the interview is at your home, Lily. Well, I think this is your home, I can see a mug with your name right there, actually."

"Oh, we can bring some mugs with names to the office. It's a company policy."

"There are pictures on the wall too. I can see some of them. Is that picture in a Faith no More live concert?"

"You're a good observant, Tyler! You look like a girl!"

"Thanks, Anna! Huh... I don't know if this is a compliment, but thank you, anyway."

"Well, tell me more about you, Tyler. What do you expect in this company?"

"Huh... I'd like to make a good job, so you can call me more times. I really need to work, guys, huh... I mean, girls."

"Okay, and what do you expect from your life?"

"I want to finish the college this year. So, I want to work in some great company, I don't know yet. I don't make plans for long periods. Because the world is always changing. I like going with the flow."

"Okay, Tyler. You must dance to our tune here. What about your pastimes?" asks the manager.

"I like to play basketball. And... music, internet, friends... I think that's all."

"Do you have any huge regret in your life, Tyler?" says Anna.

"No, I don't think so."

"None? Nothing?" Lily says.

"Nothing. I would remember if I would have a huge one."

"Okay." Lily wonders.

"Huh... why so many questions for a freelance, guys? I mean, girls! Sorry!"

"Because we have a high level of expectation here, Tyler." says Lily.

"That's good! Sorry for asking this, Lily, by the way."

"It's alright, Tyler."

"Well, Tyler, you're in! You can work with us! Congratulations!" says Anna.

"Oh, thank you, guys! Huh… I'm sorry, I mean, girls! Sorry for that! Thank you, girls. Thank you very much!"

"It's alright! Tonight I'll send you some previous work, okay? We're in a hurry!"

"Okay, Anna! I'll be waiting for! Thank you again!"

Chapter Eleven – Version 11.4

Few moments later.

"So?"

"I don't know, Lily. What do you think?"

"Hmm… he called us 'guys' for three times."

"That counts?"

"Yes, that counts a lot, Anna! I'm not a guy!"

"Anything else, Lily?"

"Yes, he has bad breath too."

"Oh, that's bad!"

"And he was sweaty. Who go sweaty to a job interview?"

"Maybe he was coming from the basketball practice."

"And he has no regrets in his life! That's totally weird!"

"Really? Do you have any?"

"I have thousands, Anna! I'm human! But I don't tell that to anyone!" the little sister almost yells.

"Well, maybe he just didn't tell us, Lily."

"And I think he's a bully."

"Why? Because he's tall?"

"I just know, it's a hunch. And I also think it's stupid to learn discontinued software."

"Well, well, well! Good old Lily is back! Lily's in the house, people!"

"Ouch! I heard that, Anna!"

"Anyway, he's hired. I'm sending some jobs right now, actually."

"Okay. Tell him about deadlines, please. Wait! Cut one or two days in the deadlines."

"Why? Do you think he can't handle this?"

"Just in case, Anna."

"Fine. Did you tell the girls about this?"

"Yes, I've sent a message to everyone, but Hailee."

"Why not to Hailee?"

"She's at hospital, Anna."

"Why?"

"Emma didn't tell you? Oh, you're not reading the messages in the group!"

"No, I'm not! I can't read five hundred messages from you every day!"

"She was pregnant, but she's not anymore."

"What?"

"She thought she was pregnant, but she's not. And now Hailee is at hospital because of some menstruation complications and hormones and headaches and pukes and nauseas and all the rest of those bad things in our woman lives."

"Oh, my God! How old is she? Thirteen?"

"Twenty-two. Don't ask me, I don't know much more."

"What hospital is she hospitalized, Lily?"

"The same hospital where... Elle's father used to go, Anna! Hey! That's it! We can test the app by ourselves now! I mean, we can make any tests we need! Because we don't know how Doctor Alice is testing; she didn't call us anymore, right?"

"We have a meeting next week."

"But we definitely need to test the app, Anna! I'll notify the girls! This is the best news of the month! We have a client and it's us! Wow! We're our own clients now, Anna!" she looks very excited.

"Are you okay, Lily?"

Chapter Eleven – Version 11.5

"Well, this is the plan: the QR code on the screen directs people to our website, right?"

"Right."

"On the website, we introduce our company. The website must be made for mobile, right?"

"Right."

"And if the people in the audience want, they can download the app. This new app will tell the company's story, right?"

"Wrong."

"Why?"

"An app to tell a story of the app?"

"No, it will tell the company's story, Ellen."

"But this story is the app's story, Emma."

"No, it's not! There are two stories here!"

"Huh... do you have all the content already? I mean texts and images?"

"Huh… a half."

"So… we can't plan this, Emma. I need everything before starting. Because if I have to change screen sizes, images fields, and texts fields in the middle of the project… it's not gonna work. Probably I'll delay it. And we don't want further delays, right?"

"Right, Ellen. What can we do for now?"

"I don't know. Maybe you can think in other stuff. Because, you know, build an app only for this contest… it's not worthwhile. I mean, cost-benefit. It will take too much time and work."

"We can use it in other events, Ellen. And we can even use to really promote our product."

"I think the idea is very good, Emma. But there is no time for this next competition. How long until there?"

"Two weeks. I can finish text and images next weekend, maybe before it."

"And you give me ten days to finish this app to promote the other app? Wow… you really love me, thanks!"

"We should try, Ellen!"

"This contest, this next one, it's in two stages, right?"

"Right."

"And the finals are on…"

"Almost one month."

"Oh, now we can talk about this app to promote the other app! There is enough time for that, if you give me texts, images, and the entire plan, of course."

"Okay, Ellen! Huh… What if we don't go to finals?"

"An app to promote other app and our company? I've never seen this before. I think it's still a good idea, Emma. We can do it."

"So… can we start something?"

"Huh… this is how it works, Emma. When we build software, there are different ways to do it. We can build it in separate phases. This is the 'Waterfall Model'. Imagine when you have to make up. First you wash your face, then you apply concealer, and foundation, highlighter and so on, right?"

"Right."

"Then, there is the 'Incremental Development'. We break the project in smaller parts, so we can change those parts easily, right? It's when you make up your eyes, then your face, then your mouth, separately. But the final result is the same. Right?"

"Right."

"Are you really getting this, Emma? Or you're just saying 'right'?"

"I do understand, Ellen! I'm not stupid!"

"Okay, sorry! It's a little hard to see the entire process if you're not from this area. I know because I've tried to explain this to some clients, and they don't understand in the first time. Not even in the tenth time!"

"I can get that, Ellen. You're doing good as a teacher, by the way."

"Well, so there is the 'Spiral Model'. Imagine a spiral; we begin in the center. So, we move clockwise and we go round. Every round is a stage, and in every stage, we end something in the software. It's when you start to make up from your eye, you wash it. Then you wash your mouth, nose, another eye and so on. When you finish this first spiral, you have washed all your face. I don't think this works in real life, I mean in makeup, right?"

"Right, I got that. But why are you telling me this, Ellen?"

"Because sometimes I think you don't understand my job. Anna works with IT, so she knows it; Hailee can get this too, because she can code. But you, Lily and Elle come here with your ideas, and you want I start to develop something. You want me to type here, and you want to see screens, buttons, and colors quickly. It doesn't work that way, Emma, unfortunately. The magic is not on the buttons, but in what happens inside them. Most of times, I need the entire project to begin. Because, most of times, it's not easy or even cheap to change everything during the process. It's when you make up for an Oscar night, a showy and shining dress included, then, in the middle, you realize it's just a children's party. I mean, you can't change it in the midway. Right?"

"Totally right, Ellen!" Emma smiles. "You should be a teacher!"

"Oh, I can consider that!"

"Just tell me, Ellen: do you really like this? All those letters and specific rules? Only one single letter and it's all messed up, right? I mean, is it worthwhile?"

"Coding is like writing a good story: you can change places, if you want, and the code might work, as the story might be good. But when everything is in its right place, it's glorious. And when you see all this working, and you know you have built it… that's priceless, Emma!"

Chapter Eleven – Version 11.6

At hospital. Visiting hours. Hailee is lying on the bed.

"You hired who?"

"Tyler. He's a friend of yours; I mean, he studies with you and Elle."

"He's a jerk."

"What? Why?"

"Because he is."

"I didn't get that! Why?"

"Because he is, Emma!"

"I don't know what to say, Hailee! Anna and Lily hired him for a freelance job."

"He is a jerk, Emma! He'll not make anything!"

"But I think he is working fine; Ellen has some design already. Powerpoint! Yes, she got some powerpoint slides!"

"That's the only thing he can do, Emma! Powerpoint! We're wasting time and money with this guy!"

"Did you talk to Anna or Lily?"

"I don't have my cell phone, Emma! They confiscated it! I'm out of the universe! I'm almost sick because of it!"

"Oh, I'll ask to Anna or Lily call you."

"Why don't they come here to visit me?"

"They are working, Hailee!"

"I feel lonely here, Emma! I just have this stupid TV, stuck in the same channel all the day! And they don't give me the remote control! I've asked that for five times already! I don't think our app is a good idea, because patients need to see people! It's boring here!"

"Our app is about saving time, Hailee! We're not replacing visitation! Moreover, this is an unique experience you are having! We can greatly improve our app with that!"

"I hope I survive to see this, Emma! I'm getting sick here! And I don't want to be guinea pig anymore!"

"Oh, the doctor said you can be discharged in the weekend, maybe earlier."

"Really? How much time will we have to the contest?"

"Huh… a short time."

"Oh, God! This is not happening, this is not happening!"

"Calm down, Hailee! Everything will be fine! We're concluding the arrangements to the contest. Elle is improving her new speech; Lily and I are preparing some stuff about marketing and finance, because the judges can ask us about that. Ellen is fixing bugs. Anna is freaking out and so on. Everything is fine."

"Is it a national one? The contest?"

"Yeah, now it's the top of the tops, Hailee! This is as far as we can go!"

"And we need to show something, Emma! We really need!"

"We will!"

"But not with that guy, Emma! No way!"

"Just take easy and get well soon, Hailee!"

"I'm getting sick here, Emma! You don't understand! Oh, my God! That guy is trouble! Trust me! I need to warn the girls! I need to get out of here!"

Hailee sees a doctor through the little window on the door.

"Hey, doctor! Could you come here, please?" she yells.

"Yes? Huh... Hailee, right? Hailee Steamfield." he sees the medical record.

"Yes, it's me."

"How can I help you, Hailee?"

"Huh... that app you have in your tablet, doctor."

"What app?" he shows the tablet.

"That blue and orange icon. Dad's Home. Run it, please."

"Yes. What for?"

"Huh... I made this app, doctor. I mean, my team made it!"

"Hailee, what are you doing?"

"Do not interrupt me, Emma! There is a button... no, no! There is a field, a blank field below. Can you see it?"

"Yes, I can."

"Touch it and you'll see a virtual keyboard, right?"

"Right."

"Now, please, type the following message."

"I'm listening." the doctor says.

"Type 'The guy is a jerk!' Use caps lock key, please!"

"Hailee! What are you doing?" Emma smiles.

"And push the send button, doctor, please! The first registered phone number is of my sister, this lady right here. I'm talking to her, but she is not listening to me!"

"Huh... I'm afraid I'm not understanding you, Hailee." the doctor smiles.

"Don't worry, doc! I know what I'm doing! The second registered phone number belongs to some friends! They will receive the same message exactly at the same time! So, please, push the send button!"

"Hailee! Please!"

"Huh... is this for serious? Do you need something? Are you feeling okay, Hailee? Do you have any remedy to take at this time?" he checks his watch. "I'll call the nurse."

"I feel so much better, doc! Did you send the message already?"

"I don't think so." he smiles.

"Oh, and do me a favor, doc! If they don't come here in few minutes, just push this panic button! It's the red one! Okay?"

"Hailee, please! Stop that! I'm sorry, doctor! She is not feeling well today!"

"I'm fine, Emma! And this guy is gonna ruin everything!"

Chapter Eleven – Version 11.7

"Have you talked to him?"

"No, he doesn't answer my messages."

"Do you know where he lives, Elle?"

"No, I meet him only at college, Anna."

"Does anyone here know anything about this boy? Home address, Facebook, Twitter, Instagram, or anything useful?"

"You have his cell phone number, Anna."

"But he doesn't answer my calls, Lily. Did you talk to him, Ellen?"

"I just got the powerpoint, Anna. I have his e-mail."

"God! Who still uses e-mail?"

"Huh… old people? Companies? Professional contacts?"

"Okay, ladies! We need to finish some jobs this boy didn't. Design jobs. Elle?"

"I can do it, Anna. But I'm not so good as Hailee is. I prefer concepts, ideas, projects, those things. Hailee is the designer."

"Elle, it's highly important that you do what you have to do, right?"

"I got that, Anna! I'm just saying maybe the final result can be not so good."

"The contest is next weekend, Elle! We have no time for perfection!"

"I know, Lily! And I know we have to meet Doctor Alice the day after tomorrow! We're in a hurry! I know!"

"So, can you do that?"

"Yes, sure, Ellen! Just tell me what you need."

"Okay, I'm sending you the link with all your new homework, Elle. Enjoy it!"

"Where is Emma?"

"Emma's at hospital with her mother, Lily. Hailee will be discharged today."

"Really? Nice! She can help me!"

"Huh… I wouldn't count on that, Elle! We don't know how she is!"

"But we've received a message from her, Ellen!"

"What message, Lily?"

"Huh… 'The guy is a jerk.' That's the message."

"Is that all? What that means?"

"I don't know, Anna! Maybe some bug! Ellen?"

"No way! Somebody is making jokes over there! This couldn't have been typed by itself!"

"Only doctors have access to the app, right, Ellen?"

"Yes, Anna. Wait! Actually, anybody with access to the tablet could do that."

"Oh, we need to improve this… security issue. Maybe a password to open the app. Or to send messages."

"Noted, Anna. It will be on next delivery. Maybe the next of the next…" Ellen shows a forced smile.

"What about the boy? The freelancer?"

"We don't know, Lily! We need to focus on what we don't have at this moment."

"Have we paid him for the job? Please, say 'no'!"

"Yes! He has asked a half, Ellen."

"And did you pay, Lily?"

"I didn't want to. But Anna said yes."

"One more mistake in the list, ladies! No more advance payments. Wait! Two things: no more freelancers or young people here."

"We're all still young, Anna, actually."

"No, we're not, Ellen! We're adults already! I feel like a hundred years old person right now!"

"Have we spent money for only a powerpoint?"

"Yes, Ellen! We have!"

"God! I could have asked that to my eleven years old neighbor!"

"It's done, Ellen! We can't trust people anymore! It's us against the world!"

"Thanks for talking my language, Anna! And welcome to my world!"

Chapter Eleven – Version 11.8

"I TOLD YOU HE WAS A JERK!"

"How could we know that, Hailee?"

"I told you we were wasting time and money with this guy, Emma!"

"But we needed him, Hailee!"

"We didn't, Ellen! That was my job, my position!"

"But you were not here, Hailee!"

"I was coming, Elle! I was at the hospital, but I was coming!"

"We thought it was envy because he took your job, Hailee!"

"Jesus! I'm not a child, Lily!"

"We know you're not, Hailee!"

"And I told you he would ruin everything, Emma!"

"But Elle has recommended him! He studies with you both!"

"That means nothing, Lily! There are thousands of jerks at college!"

"Okay, Hailee! We didn't listen to you! Fine! It's done!" says Anna.

"And I've sent you a message! Didn't you get that? I just used our app, ladies! This is for communication, right?"

"We got your message, Hailee! But we didn't understand you!" says Lily.

"The guy is a jerk! What word didn't you understand?"

"We didn't, Hailee!" says Ellen. "Was it an encrypted message? Coded, maybe?"

"But how could we know he was a jerk, Hailee? How could you know?" asks Elle.

"Yes, how could you know something about that sandals and long hair boy, Hailee?" asks Emma.

"Yeah! How? Do you know anything about that sweaty and bad breath boy?" Anna asks.

"Don't forget discontinued software, Anna. And no regrets too. And he called us 'guys'. For three times." Lily reminds.

Ellen, at the table with your laptop, turns and stares Hailee. She is doing a "So?" face, and waiting for answers.

Silence. For three seconds.

"Because I dated him."

Emma and Lily, seated beside Hailee, open their eyes and mouths (very) widely, but they have no words. Anna, standing in front of Hailee, just opens her mouth – with no words too – and sits down (better than falling down). Elle, beside Anna, just says "Oh…" and she frowns. And, finally, Ellen, seated, tries to say something, but she realizes it is better turning back to her laptop and starting to type – anything.

"Okay, ladies, I think we're done here…" says Anna.

"Yeah, let's work to fix our scheduling." Elle says.

CHAPTER TWELVE – VERSION 12.0 – HOPE AND GLORY.

Fail

"So, this is the first stage, right?"

"Right!"

"And how this is gonna be?"

"Didn't you read the rules, Hailee?"

"No! I was at a hospital, Emma; isolated from the world!"

"Okay, okay! Sorry! This is it: the first stage is an elevator pitch. It's a short summary about us. I mean, the company, product, process and value."

"How long? Twenty minutes?"

"Are you kidding? There are almost one hundred teams to introduce their products, Hailee! We would be here for a month! It's only ten minutes for everything! I mean, ten minutes to get ready with powerpoint, cables, laptop, and all the rest! And we still need to make the presentation, of course! If we fail on cables and powerpoint, it counts on our time! Our score will decrease!"

"Oh, my gosh! Is this Army or something?"

"No, Hailee; welcome to the real marketplace!"

"What comes next?"

"It's two days for teams presentations; today and tomorrow. They will announce the finalists tomorrow in the late afternoon."

"And the finals are on next weekend, right?"

"Right. On Sunday afternoon, ten teams will come, only one will win."

In other place, the girls are walking.

"What about these finals, Anna?"

"It will be on Sunday. We'll have more time, thirty minutes. We can explain the entire project with details. That's good and bad, Elle."

"Why?"

"Do we have so much to say? Sometimes, you're for so long inside a project, that you think you don't need to say all the things. You think people will guess what you'll say. That's a trap."

"What can we do, Anna?"

"We'll start from the beginning, Elle: your story."

"That's good! I still remember when I got started."

"But we need to go to the finals first, Elle. We can't plan now."

In the meanwhile, somewhere else.

"Will we have a party?"

"Yes, Lily, a costume party! Can you believe that? In an entrepreneurship competition?"

"That's unusual, Ellen! Almost strange! Can you imagine all those nerds in a party?"

"Next weekend. Don't forget to put that on your schedule."

"But will it be for everyone? Or only for finalists?"

"Everyone, of course! The goal is interaction, networking, and maybe something else between the teams. It's a good intention, I think."

"I can bet anything, Ellen, there will be thousands of Darth Vaders and stormtroopers there!"

"Yep! And video games characters! Like us!"

"Have we chosen already? Video games?"

"What do you want? Stormtroopers?"

"I don't know! Maybe something like, huh… princesses? Zombie horde? Manga characters? Business girls?"

"Definitely not business girls! It would not be a costume, Lilly!"

"This is hard to choose, Ellen! Better we vote!"

"Okay, we'll vote. Good point!"

"And we need to choose quickly; it's next week already!"

"Yes, but we have the presentation before this party."

"Oh, I almost forgot that!"

Few minutes later, on backstage, the girls are waiting for. Laptop, cables, files, smiles and dresses are ready when the host announces the "Dad's Home Team." Six girls come up and meet the audience. It is a wide stage, with at least fifteen meters in length. The screen looks like a movie screen – it is very large, maybe two hundred inches wide. The girls are growing up, as the buildings they are going to. Elle, Hailee, Emma, Lily, Anna and Ellen are impressed. That is the place where they will get fame and glory – they expect. But before this, the girls have to go to the finals – they need to show what they got. The girls need an ace in the hole, but I think they do not play cards. They prefer video games or even board games.

"Good afternoon, everyone! My name is Elle, and these ladies are my partners and friends: Anna, Ellen, Emma, Hailee and Lily. I'd like to present you our business."

Most of people listen to, some people do not (they take their cell phones).

"Few months ago, I had a problem: I had to wait for long periods at hospitals, only to talk to doctors. And, as you know, doctors can have hard schedules. And, most of times, the doctors didn't have so urgent things to tell me. They could send me a message. The solution? An app to send a simple report. This is our product."

People stop checking cell phones. Elle takes the tablet and hit the orange and blue icon.

"You can easily access the system, as you can send this report. A login is necessary to avoid not authorized people access the system. As you can see on this, wow, huge screen"–she smiles–"it's only five elementary questions."

The audience smiles too.

"And you have a blank field to type any personal message, if you wish. When you push the send button, you will see a confirmation message. And that's all. A simple way to send a report about patient status, possible discharge dates and remedies." she smiles again.

Some people in the audience are whispering now.

"Our clients? The hospitals, of course. They will pay the bill, monthly, for our service. Patient's relatives will use the app in your cell phones for free. The families have someone at a hospital, then, we believe they have enough to worry about."

Some people go back to your cell phones. Some of them start to record.

"Why should you choose our app? This is very important, ladies and gentlemen. People don't have so much time to learn nowadays. Our app is easy to use, it's very intuitive. You don't have thousands of options in tons of pull-down menus. Because, as you all already know, doctors are very busy persons. The design is clean, as you can see on the screen over there. However, it's not just clean: you can see it's beautiful too. It's pleasant to use! By the way, how many apps you quit using because the interface was complicate or out of date? Think about it." she makes a gesture with her right index finger.

Now we can see some flashes in the almost dark auditorium.

"Our company is composed of these competent ladies here. Hailee, 'The Designer', is the responsible for this stunning app design. Lily is the 'Finance Girl'; she handles numbers and money, and she controls them. Emma is 'Ms. Marketing'; well, you all know what she does." she smiles. "Ellen is our 'Lady Code', she makes the magic under the buttons." Elle winks with a mouth snap. "And last but not least, this is Anna, 'The Manager'. She's the boss!" Elle whispers these last words and smiles. "Most of us are experienced professionals in the software industry and other fields."

Now we can see no one typing on cell phones. Some whispers, some flashes here and there, no side conversations. Then, Elle begins to speak again.

"Do you need to talk to doctors and they are not coming so fast? Do you need something else to notify to your patient's relatives? Do you need to improve this specific communication at your hospital? We certainly have a value proposition you should listen to. Moreover, new features are coming to upgrade our product. Just access our website, as you can see on the screen, and let us your e-mail for news and releases. Thank you very much for your attention and have a nice day!" she gives us her best smile.

Cheers. Many. Flashes too – a lot of them. Elle gives one step back and gets closer to the team.

"Wow! You were great, Elle!"

"You don't know through where I'm sweating right now, Lily!"

"Oh, my God!"

"I didn't know I had a nickname, Elle!"

"I've just created it, Ellen! Now you're Lady Code!"

The girls laugh discreetly – they are still on stage – and applaud the founder. Elle applauds too, because they all have made the perfect work.

Chapter Twelve – Version 12.1

Later, on the same day, Saturday, the girls are having a meeting (maybe a celebration). They are not qualifying to the next stage yet, but...

"Yeah, we did it! WE DID IT!" says Lily.

"Yippee! We're in the finals! I know we are! Tell me who are in the finals!" Hailee says.

"Wow! I don't believe that, ladies! We finally made it!" says Emma.

"Wee! Let's make a party!" Anna says.

"It's already a party!" says Elle.

"Yeah! Let's get lost, ladies!" Ellen says.

Suddenly comes some silence between the laughs and smiles (and shouts).

"Hey, I've just remembered something!"

"What is it, Ellen?"

"We have a party next week, Anna!"

"We are having a party now, Ellen!"

"No, it's serious, Hailee! We'll have a costume party. I was talking to Lily earlier. Right, Lily?"

"Yes, the costume party! We need to pick some princesses costumes!"

"What? We didn't choose yet, Lily!"

"We're almost done, Ellen! Princesses forever!"

"The contest sponsors call this... let me see... 'Networking at a Party.' It's on the website. 'Come as you are' is the slogan. Are they paying royalties to Nirvana? Jesus! This is gonna be weird!"

"This is gonna be cool, Emma!"

"Okay, so I was talking to Lily about that. It's a costume party, right? And our costumes will be?"

"Princesses, always. Always!"

"We've heard it already, Lily!"

"I'm just reminding you, Hailee!"

"Okay, so what do you want to do? Voting?" says Anna.

"Yeah, we'll vote. Any other options?" asks Emma.

"Fine, ladies! Take your cell phones and run some note or list app; anything you can write on it. We write and then we show the cell phones screens, okay?" Anna suggests.

"Fine, I'm writing 'princesses' already."

"Jesus! She's obsessed!" someone whispers.

"I've heard that, Elle!"

They keep silence for a while. Then, someone starts to laugh. They are in the living room, at headquarters or Anna and Lily's house, by the way. I forgot this detail.

"Done!"

"Me too!"

"Me too!"

"Ready to go!"

"One more second, please."

"Okay, ladies, show us those cute screens, please!" Anna asks.

"Princesses. In caps lock!"

"Badass girls." Hailee suggests.

"What?" asks Anna.

"Like Sigourney Weaver, in Aliens movies!"

"Oh, gosh! And who is the alien here?" Ellen asks.

"Huh... I choose marketing areas girls."

"God, Emma! And I thought 'badass girls' was a bad one..." Lily says.

"This is not bad, Lily! We can work in any area in marketing!"

"Dangerous professionals! Who's with me?"

"Huh... what exactly is this, Ellen?" Anna wants to know (me too).

"Well... firefighters, police officers, FBI, or maybe people who work with biohazard stuff. Elle?"

"Hmm... why not children?" she shows the screen.

"Excuse me?"

"Children! We'll dress as children, Ellen!"

"Do you mean old dresses, stupid hairstyle, and a lollipop?"

"No! I mean children! We can start with this lollipop you've just said!"

"Anna? Your vote?" calls Emma.

"Well, mine is simple, very simple: Lord of the Rings. I have a picture here. This is a 'Return of the King' picture. Everyone knows it! I'll be Frodo! Or Sam! I prefer Frodo!"

"Actually, Frodo is taller than you, Anna! Ha ha ha!"

"Ha ha ha!"

"Oh... grrr... I'll get you, Hailee! Just wait for it!"

"Ha ha ha!"

"Does anyone want to change the vote?" asks Elle.

Silence. For two seconds.

"Okay, let's try one more time. Write something, ladies, please." the manager says.

They spend some seconds and then someone starts to laugh again. Anna asks.

"Show it, please."

"Princesses."

"Jesus, Lily! You supposedly should change your vote!" laughs Ellen.

"Who said that? Anna said to write something; she didn't said to change. You're not paying attention!"

"Huh... 'Professional ladies' is my vote." says Emma.

"Professional what? You mean, prostitutes?"

"No, Hailee! I mean we can go dressed like doctors or lawyers! These kind of stuff!"

"Oh, my gosh! It's getting worse!" says Lily.

"Okay, I choose 'great movies'."

"Great movies? What is that, Hailee? That means 'Lord of the Rings' to me!" Anna asks.

"It means 'Gone with the Wind' or 'Citizen Kane' movies! I can be Scarlet O'Hara!" explains Hailee.

"Elle?" asks Emma.

166

"Huh… video games? I was pretty sure someone would pick video games! So we could finish this question!"

"Ellen?" asks Emma.

"Coders types."

"What? What is that?" asks Hailee.

"Well, there are many kinds of coders. You have the rookie, without beard; and you have seniors with a long hair and a thick beard."

"Huh… I'd like to remind you, Ellen… we have no beards… we're ladies, in case you don't know…"

"It's a costume party, Anna! And what is yours now?"

"Well, if you don't want 'Lord of the Rings', I suggest 'The Hobbit' movie! This picture is from 'An Unexpected Journey'! Did I win?"

"You supposedly should have changed your vote too, Anna!"

"This is different, Elle! There are thirteen dwarves in the movie! And Gandalf! And Gollum!"

"Oh, here we go again!" Emma says and lowers the head.

"This will not end, Anna!"

"It will, don't worry, Elle! Let's try harder, ladies! Write something, please!"

"Don't you write 'princesses', or Lily will win the poll."

"I'll change it, Hailee! Wait and see!"

A few seconds and they are ready to go again. This time, the manager Anna starts showing her cell phone.

"Tolkien's universe. Look at this! I've put an icon here!"

"Again? Oh, I can guess what Lily will say! You are really sisters! Nobody can deny that!"

"It's different, Hailee! There is an entire universe to tell! There are gods and deities!"

"I choose Disney princesses!"

"I told you! She didn't change! You both didn't change!"

"I've changed it, Hailee! Now it's a specific group of princesses! You can't dress like Princess Peach or Fiona!"

"Fiona is not a princess! She's an ogre, Lily!"

"She's a princess, Elle! She has a crown!"

"And now Emma is gonna pick something about jobs!"

"How do you know, Anna? I've chosen 'different women'!"

"Different women? What is that? Someone with three ears or four arms?"

"Of course not, Ellen! It's about jobs you don't see so many women working on! Like airplane pilot or carpenter!"

"My vote is for…"

"Some movie crap, I'm sure!"

"Jesus, Lily! Stop interrupting my vote! It's not about movies! I vote for cartoons!"

"Oh, very different, Hailee! Something you can watch on TV! Great!" says Anna.

"Huh… I choose Star Wars!"

"No way, Elle! There will be thousands of Star Wars fans there! I don't want to be mistaken with any guy!"

"There will be identical costumes, Ellen! How many people will go to this party? Five hundred? Maybe more!" says Elle. "So tell us your vote, please!"

"I choose great minds of history!"

"God! I'm afraid to ask you to explain that…" says Lily.

"What? Einstein? Socrates? Da Vinci? Hello?" Ellen makes a gesture.

"Oh, this is not working, ladies…" says Anna. "We can be here for hours!"

"And what do you suggest, Anna?"

"If everyone is the boss, automatically no one is the boss."

"What?"

"Excuse me?"

"Huh… English, please."

"Exactly what I've said, ladies. If everyone rules, no one rules. If everyone is in charge, no one is in charge. If all the people are commanding this, there is no command. People don't know where to go. You don't have two generals in the front; you don't have two CEOs at a company. Because you can have different commands; opposite ones, by the way. We all have a vote, right? And we want different things. Then, there is no solution."

"And?" says Emma.

"And we need one person to rule this all."

"Uh-huh… as 'one Ring to rule them all', right?" Ellen asks.

"Yes, right, Ellen."

"Okay, we'll vote." says Lily.

"Again? No way!" Hailee says.

"Yeah, voting is not working!" says Elle.

"We won't. We'll choose based on logic, attributes and meritocracy. I choose Elle, because she's the founder. She has started all this." says Anna.

"But she's not so experienced, Anna. No offenses, Elle!" says Ellen.

"Emma? What about you? You can handle marketing and presentations; you know how we must look to the people, to the marketplace and all stuff!"

"Huh... I don't know many things here, Hailee... coding, for example. I didn't know the entire process; Ellen taught me a few days ago. What about you, Lily?"

"Me? People will quit this company in less than a minute! Ellen?"

"Huh... I don't like to handle with people... I like to talk, sometimes I like to be with, but... managing is not my cup of tea. Sorry, ladies!"

"Well, don't look at me, because I didn't even finish the graduation, right? Just like Elle." says Hailee.

"Not finishing college is not an excuse, Hailee."

"But I still don't have so many professional experiences, Lily."

The girls turn to Anna.

"What?" the manager says.

"I think it's chosen, Anna." says Hailee.

"What? Why?"

"Because you are a senior professional; because you understand the whole thing here; because you can make a nice speech. And you're the manager already. It's done." Emma says.

"And we don't want to see you angry anymore." says Ellen. "Because you can become a big green creature, you know?"

"Ha ha ha!"

"Ha ha ha!"

"Oh, I was not expecting that..." regrets Anna.

"We're done here, Anna. Yeah..." says Ellen.

"Yes, it's a natural choice! Like, huh... I don't know! It's so obvious that I have no words!" confuses Elle.

"Don't worry, we'll help you, Anna! We're a team, right?" Hailee says. "Come on, give me five!"

"Okay, so what's your costume choice, Anna? Be reasonable, please! We have only this week to buy costumes!" asks Emma.

"Yes, pick something nice like... princesses!" says... oh, you know who said that!

The manager – and now the super boss – lowers her head. She smiles. Anna looks at the girls, and now she knows the responsibility. From now on, Anna Kelly needs to handle not only with her own will, but with all the team will. With great powers comes great...

"Fine, ladies! I'll think about it and I'll send you a message."

"When?"

"Tonight?"

"Later?"

"Tonight later?"

"Why not now?"

"It will be a surprise! Just be alert and don't wink!"

Chapter Twelve – Version 12.2

"Did you get the message?"

"What message?"

"From Anna."

"Did she choose the costumes already?"

"Yeah!"

"Let me see!"

"Not so good as I wanted, but it's fine to me, Hailee."

"Oh, I could have chosen that!"

"And it's not so hard to find these ones!"

"Yeah, we have no time to look for costumes around the city!"

"Yes, just imagine searching for an alien costume!"

"I was going as Ripley!"

At other house.

"Good morning, Dad!"

"Hey! Good morning, Ms. Blonde! Did you sleep well?"

"Yeah, very well, Dad!"

"You did a great job yesterday, Mary Elle!"

"Thanks, Dad! I think things are happening now!"

"Yes, you've just started, a few months ago. It doesn't look so long. And now you're with your friends, with this company... I'm proud of you!"

"Thanks, Dad! I could never make it without you! Thank you very much!"

"You're welcome, Ms. Blonde!"

"But, huh... we're not having so much profit yet, Dad..."

"Was this on the scheduling?"

"Huh... I don't think so..."

"It should be. But it doesn't matter, honey. You'll learn. You are learning, by the way, right?"

"Yes, Dad! I'm learning a lot of new things! Things I could never imagined!"

"That's how people grow up, Mary Elle. Sometimes it's hard, but it's great in the end. I mean, when you're passing through everything, it's hard. Maybe you see no options, no solutions. But after all this, you just laugh. And you realize you've just grown up. That's how life goes on."

"Thanks for teaching me so much, Dad! You're doing great without mom!"

"Well, I don't have this gorgeous blonde hair like you both have, but I'm trying hard here!"

Father and daughter laugh. Charlie "The Fox" Panning is trying to be a good father, every day. After losing his wife Deborah Annie, four years ago, he knew it would be hard to raise his daughter alone. When people get divorced, most of times the children still have visiting. Not in his case. It is harder to be single parent, especially because Deborah was a great mother and person.

Charlie looks his hands, he still can see some scars and callus from the time he used to play football. He was a great captain. Then came the injuries, the heart disease, the troubles, the life insurance, the team support – Mr. Jones included – the help from family and friends. Then came the life in a quiet neighborhood and the monotony. Charlie took a time to get used to. Maybe that could explain so many health abuses that took him to the hospital over and over. And the big father became just a father. Elle and Deborah, of course, did not care – they did not see like that. But it is hard to a man when he cannot do what he loves. Not everyone can truly understand this. It is not only the social pressure like "be the keeper, the guardian" or "a man must be strong, always." It is something inside men's mind. The feeling of impotence hurts more than any pressure from anything.

But he is still good. The large forehead, which means intelligence for some people, the thick beard – he does not like to shave every day – he still looks a good man for some women. Elle loves the sincere smile. Charlie looks really happy when he smiles – it is his trademark. A short dark brown hair in a modern style and light brown eyes certainly helped to get Jennifer's attention. Elle's father and Ellen's mother are dating for a short, but joyful period. And fortunately, neither the founder nor the coder is jealous of that relationship. The entrepreneurs are not kids anymore, they are growing up. Good for all.

"Well, I got to go, Dad!"

"Really?"

"Yeah, today is the day two in the competition. I'll meet the girls there. We'll watch the other teams' presentations."

"The rivals?"

"Hmm… a kind of that! And then we'll wait for the result. Are you coming?"

"Oh, I'm a little busy this morning, honey! But I'll be there later!"

"You and Mrs. Fage?" the blonde girl closes the mouth and gives a suggesting smile.

"Yes, Jennifer and I… We'll be there!" the father shows his sincere smile.

At Fage family's house.

"Hi, Mom! Good morning!"

"Hi, Ellen! How are you? Happy?"

"Well, despite the last night, when the girls definitely should have drunk something, I'm fine."

"And why didn't you drink?"

"Oh, not all the girls drink, I'm included. So we just talked a little, we just celebrated a little more, and we voted."

"Vote? What for?"

"We'll have a costume party, Mom. We have voted, but Anna will choose the costumes. I need to check messages, by the way."

"Oh, no cell phones at table, Ellen, please!"

"Just a second, Mom! I need to see only this! I promise!"

"Okay, but only because you have made a wonderful presentation yesterday! Congratulations to your team, Ellen! I'm very proud of you!"

"Thanks, Mom! We're having a great time there! The team is really working as a team!"

"I've heard you had some disagreements back there. Now you all are fine?"

"Who said that, Mom?"

"Huh… I just… I just heard it."

Ellen looks to Jennifer and keeps some silence. Mother and daughter smiles.

"Oh, I got that!"

"What?"

"Probably Elle told Mr. Panning about that. And, you know… you and Mr. Panning… okay, I got it, Mom!"

"No! Charlie just said a few words!"

"And you asked a little more, right? I know you, Mom!"

"Ellen! We need to know what our daughters are doing! We're still parents, did you know that?"

"Okay, okay! And Elle likes gossip…"

"It's not gossip, Ellen! Come on! We were just talking!"

"Okay, Mom. It's only Elle and Mr. Panning… I just reminded that right now."

"But they are happy, Ellen. As you and I."

"Yeah, Mom! Thanks for supporting me every day. I know sometimes I'm an idiot and I don't do housework. But thanks."

"I'm your mother, Ellen. That's what mothers do."

Jennifer knows that Ellen is a good girl. Maybe the coder does not go out so many times as Jennifer used to do at the same age, but the mother thinks that is how it is nowadays. Their ages are not so different, only sixteen years. Yes, Jennifer had kids when she was sixteen years old. It was a bad time to the conservative Jennifer's family. Her father did not live with that so easy. And the green eyes girl has cried for long periods when she was pregnant. But neither this had taken away the joy of being a mother. When Jennifer's husband has left her, all the hard times came back. She felt the loneliness and the helplessness again, as she did when her father did not support her.

But now it is different. She lives with her daughter Ellen, they are happy. Not all the families look like a margarine or cereal advertisement – they do not have to. The deep voice woman and the outspoken coder girl have a good living – thanks to straight talk every day and to the honesty between mother and daughter.

"I have to go earlier today, Mom."

"Okay, Ellen! The contest again?"

"Yeah! This is the day two!"

"With results, I guess!"

"Yes! We're so anxious, Mom!"

"I see an upside, Ellen! You know, you're different."

"Why?"

"You're saying 'we' more times than before…"

"Yeah… I think I'm growing up. I'm afraid I'm growing up…"

"It's not a big deal, Ellen! I grew up when I was sixteen."

Ellen lowers the head and agrees. She smiles.

"Yes, Mom… thanks for not giving up on me. I could be at an orphanage or something alike."

"No way, Ellen! I'll be always with you! You're still my baby, remember that!"

"Okay, Mom… I got to go now. I'll meet the girls at the contest. The results comes out today."

"Fine, I'll be there later, right?"

"Do you have some hot date, maybe?"

"Not a hot date, just a date!"

"At morning, Mom? Jesus, you're very busy!"

"Ellen!"

"Okay, okay, just enjoy it and make it safe, please!"

"Ellen! I supposedly should say that to you, and not the opposite!"

A cell phone rings.

"Oh, I got the message from Anna!"

"About the costume party?"

"Yes, she also sent me a picture of my costume. Check it out!"

"Wow! Are you ready for this?"

"I hope so. And I hope you help me with this, Mom."

"Always, Ellen! Always!"

Chapter Twelve – Version 12.3

"Hi! What's up?"

"Hi, Elle!"

"Where is everyone?"

"Hailee and Emma are on their way. Lily and Ellen are around here. So, tell me, are you eager like me?"

"Oh, my gosh, Anna! Do you think we did it?"

"Hmm… I don't know, Elle! I've never seen these judgments! They say 'a judging commission' will choose and this commission is formed by 'recognized professionals in the sector'. But they don't say what exactly will be judged. Most of times the organizers and sponsors say the result will be based on creativity, impact and other subjective values. We don't know what they will rate."

"I have a good feeling, Anna!" she smiles.

"Oh, that's good, Elle! Keep it!"

"Hey!"

"Hi, Lily! Hi, Ellen! What's up?"

"Did you sleep well, Ms. Nice Speech?"

"Oh… like a princess, Lily!"

"Well, tonight you'll sleep like a queen!"

"Oh, I hope you're right, Ellen!"

"Hey, I got a message from Emma! She and the little sister are at the entrance gate already."

Then, they watch some presentations. In the day two, there are many good teams to see. The girls get a little nervous. There are groups formed only by men (the most), mixed ones, of all ages. Maybe not all ages, but from very young people to seniors. The underage competitors must have a parental permission, and they are accompanied by someone of legal age in the same team.

"Hi, ladies!"

"Emma! Hailee! About time!"

"Oh, don't tell me! The traffic is so bad even on Sundays!"

"Well, let's wait!"

The last team finally finishes its presentation about an app for sustainable economy at schools. The host comes to stage and announces a sixty minutes break time.

"Oh, my God! Sixty minutes? I'm gonna die here!"

"Don't die, Hailee! We'll need you next week!"

"We'll need you too, Ellen!" Anna says.

"We'll need you all! Don't die, anyone!" says Lily.

"Hmm... there are interesting competitors around here..."

"What? This is not a club, Emma!"

"Emma's right! We need to make friends! Or something else... who knows?"

"Oh, Hailee... didn't you change your boyfriend this month? Or maybe this week?"

"I'm not even hanging out, Elle! Zero boys to me! I'm going through a withdrawal symptom here!"

"Withdrawal? God! It's serious!"

"Hello, ladies!"

"Hi!" they say.

"I've seen your presentation! I'm really impressed! Congratulations!"

It is a man, about thirty years old, good-looking and tall.

"Huh... I've tried to access your website, but I don't think it was online."

"Really? Let me see." Ellen takes the cell phone.

"When was that?"

"Yesterday, at night. Maybe the website was sleeping already!" he laughs.

The girls laugh too. The man is trying to be nice. He does not stop looking Emma.

"It's online, huh... what is your name, please?" asks Ellen.

"I'm Anthony. Glad to meet you, ladies!"

He is a very good-looking now I can see him better. And Emma looks interested – she is biting lips a little bit. Or maybe she is just eager – there are not so many men in this story.

"Oh, I'm giving you my business card. I don't even know if this is usual nowadays! Just in case. I've seen you are the marketing girl, just like me. I mean, I'm the marketing guy, I'm not a girl... You can call me to talk about marketing, Emma. If you want, of course!"

He gives the card to Emma and shows his best smile. Anthony says goodbye and leaves with a gentle nod and other smile.

"Wow! Well done, Emma! Well done!" Anna says.

"Oh, come on, ladies! He was talking to all of us!"

"Sure! Can you see his business card in my hand? In my empty hand?" says Elle.

"Nice work, sister! Maybe he has a little brother!" Hailee winks an eye.

"Go, Emma, go!" says Ellen.

"Can I see the card?"

"Sure, Lily!"

The finance girl tears the card.

"What? What is that?" asks Emma.

"Lily! What are you doing?" says Anna.

"Huh... what was that?" says Hailee.

"It's only us, ladies! No one else in this team!"

The girls are astonished and with no words (that is rare). Later, the finance girl can explain to Emma what that means. Maybe something on some Saturday night, after so much alcohol, in the chapter seven – who knows?

The lights go out and the host comes on stage again and interrupts the... "tearing action." The girls keep silence and wait for the announcement. A bald man in a showy black suit starts to say.

"Ladies and gentlemen, it's good to be back here! Thank you for waiting! We had great competitors this year! And we had a very hard work to select these finalists! But, as you know, only ten of you will go on here! And next week, only one team will go to the glory! I'd like to thank to all people involved in this contest: competitors, organizers, and sponsors. It's good to remind you that I will announce these ten names, but they are not in a particular order. That means there are no positions today, right? Now, without further delay, I'd like to announce... the finalists!"

"Almost sleeping here..." says Ellen.

"Almost peeing here!" says Hailee.

"Almost dying here!" says Elle.

"Blah, blah, blah…" says Lily.

"Ladies, whatever it happens, we are winners, okay?"

"We want more, Anna!" Emma says.

The host says five names. The Dad's Home Team is not in these first part of the announcement. The girls are very worried now, and I do not need to say they are impatient. They are holding hands and almost hugging themselves. The bald man speaks again with his deep voice.

"Well, ladies and gentlemen, as you all know, we had a very hard time! So many teams, so little time! All of you here are winners already!"

"Jesus! Someone can kill this guy?" says Ellen.

"Yeah! And take that paper in his hand, please!" says Lily.

"Easy, ladies! We're almost there!"

"Or not, Anna!" says Elle.

"Ladies and gentlemen, the sixth qualifying team is… Alfa Dogs!"

"What is this team? An app for pets?" says Lily.

"And here comes the seventh finalist!"

"I'm passing out here!"

"Ask Anthony to hold you, Emma!"

"I don't have his card anymore, Lily! And do you know why?"

"The Super Supers team is the seventh finalist!"

"Super Supers? What is that? Do they think they are superheroes?" Ellen says.

"WE are superheroes!"

"We will be, Emma! Next week!" Elle says.

"Yes, we will!" says Hailee.

"What? I lost that!" Lily says.

"Oh, I don't know what to say anymore…" says Anna.

"Why don't they show a spreadsheet on the screen?" Lily says. "I hate all this suspense!"

"Ladies and gentlemen, and the eighth finalist is…"

"Oh, God! My fingertips are sweating! Look!" says Elle.

"The Dad's Home Team!"

The girls are in a big hug, and they do not realize what they got in the first moment.

"What?"

"It's us!"

"Is it?"

"Yes, it is! He said our name!"

"Oh, my God!"

"We made it! We made it!"

"I told you! I told you, Anna!"

"I can't believe this!"

"It's true, Hailee! It's true!"

"We're in the finals! We're in the finals!"

The host still announces two more names and we can listen some celebration from the crowd. The bald man in a showy black suit thanks to everyone, shows some sponsors logos, and then he leaves the stage. Lights out and the second day in the entrepreneur competition is over.

The girls are still working on believing. Even when they leave the building, even when they get in the cars, even when they get to that large and famous bar to celebrate. They will not forget that fresh and fantastic night. However, at the moment, they want more.

"Ladies, I'd like to propose a toast!" Anna raise an arm.

"Yeah!" they say.

"To what?" asks Ellen.

"Oh, you tell me, ladies!"

"To friendship!" says Elle.

"To money and profit!"

"Okay, Lily! To marketing strategies!" says Emma.

"To a good design, then!" suggests Hailee.

"Jesus, stop thinking about work, ladies!" warns Ellen.

"Okay, seriously now! My arm is hurting already! Come on! Say something!" asks the manager.

"I was speaking seriously, Anna!" says Elle. "To friendship!"

"To us!" says Emma.

"To friends, united, forever!"

"Forever? Like a marriage, Lily?" Ellen asks.

"Oh, yeah, like that!"

"To family!"

"Seriously, Ellen?"

"Yeah, Hailee! Pretty seriously!"

"Okay, to a good life from now on and forever!" says Hailee.

"Wow! Someone here is dreaming high! Nice one, sister!" Emma says.

"To our new life!" says Elle.

"To our new life!" Anna strengthens and shakes her head positively.

They toast, they drink, they smile and laugh. The girls are having a good time (finally). Next week, the finals: thirty minutes to present again the project. In the next stage, however, it is not only a two minutes elevator pitch. They have to explain details about marketing strategy, finance, and even coding – if the judges ask it. The judgment will be based on – yes, they have explained – the overall performance. That means agility and speed when they are speaking and explaining their project. Technical knowledge will also count many points, of course. In addition, the jury will not be there for kidding. They are formed by a group of very rigorous investors, experienced entrepreneurs, and qualified business people. The audience, in fact, is not formed by students and some casual observers anymore. The people at the auditorium come from big companies. They are checking if a group can be part of their own business. And a contest like that is a chance to meet competent professionals and creative projects. Then, if the girls did not grow up until now, next week, they will.

At nine o'clock, Anna stands up and says.

"Okay, ladies, it's time! I've got to go!"

"Oh, come on, Anna!"

"No! No way, Anna!"

"You stay, Anna! Sit down and have another drink!"

"No, it's serious, ladies! My boyfriend is waiting for! It's almost two months we didn't date! I promised him!"

"Oh, no, Anna! Come on! A man can wait one more day!"

"We can celebrate next week, ladies! Same bat-time, same bat-channel, okay?"

"Okay, Anna…"

"Yeah, have a nice night with Jesse, sister!"

"Make good choices!"

"See ya soon!"

The left girls stop talking for a while (only a few seconds). They have drunk a lot already, but they are still good (I am not so sure about that, actually). Suddenly, someone takes a glass of wine and drinks.

"Elle! What are you doing?"

"It's a party, Emma!"

"Oh, my God! She's drinking! Someone call the police! Hey, underage drinking alcohol here!"

"I'm not underage, Lily! I'm twenty-two!"

"Okay, so let's do it!"

"Jesus Christ, Ellen! You too?"

"The founder says it's a party, Hailee! Then it is!"

"Oh, my gosh! Someone is gonna sleep on the sidewalk tonight!" says Emma.

The girls drink and drink more, for hours. Near to midnight, it is time to go. Some of them must wake up soon on next day. But they are not caring so much. As the founder said, it is a party. The ladies have the last drink for that special night and they leave the famous bar.

"Let's walk a while!"

"Walk? It's almost midnight, Elle!"

"She's drunk, Lily!" says Emma.

"Okay, let's walk!"

They find out another bar, some blocks away, with karaoke machines.

"Hey, let's get in there!"

"Karaoke? Are you sure, Lily?" asks Emma.

"It's late, ladies, let's go!"

"No, it's open until morning, Ellen!" says Elle. "I vote for getting in!"

"Yeah, let's go!" says Hailee. "We're wasting time out here!"

The girls get in the karaoke bar, they have a sit. A polite waiter comes to serve them, and they ask for more drinks – alcohol, I mean. Now they are having wine, vodka and tequilas – a not good mixture. Despite the fact of two of them – Ellen and Elle – do not drink, the other girls drink a lot – more than some men. Lily, Emma and Hailee are almost drunk. No, I am lying. They are drunk already, about twenty lines ago.

"Let's sing just one song, ladies! Who's with me?" stands up Elle.

"The founder says sing it! Let's sing it!" says Lily walking with some difficulty.

The song is "I will survive." They sing a little, some verses. The group almost cannot stand up, but they keep going. The bar is not so full of people. Some couples here and there, some group of boys and girls, young and older ones. They are on a small stage, some meters wide and higher.

"I neither know this song, Lily... it's too old..."

"Oh, just sing it, Hailee... nobody cares..."

Hailee goes to the karaoke machine and choose "It's my life."

"Oh, that's a very new song, Hailee! It's a new release!"

"I can't read the small letters, Ellen! My eyes are closing!"

Elle takes a bottle and drinks. With no cups, directly from the bottle.

"Jesus, Elle! Are you drunk?" says Emma.

"I don't know... who is Jesus?"

"Ha ha ha! She's drunk! SHE'S DRUNK!" laughs Ellen. But Lady Code falls on the ground.

"Ellen! Oh, my God! Are you okay? Are you hurt?"

The fallen girl raises the thumb and the others do not worry – how could they help, by the way? Lily changes the music. Now it is playing "Smells like teen spirit". And now they are going wild. I neither can correctly describe the scene! Ellen takes a bottle from a near table and drinks. Emma starts to take off clothes. Lily likes it, and she begins a sexy dance with the Ms. Marketing. Hailee takes a mug (full of beer) and throws to the audience. Some people stand up and start to leave the place. Elle is still singing and drinking directly from the bottle. The founder does not know what is inside, but she does not care. She is young, she is drinking and drunk, she is with her friends. And…

"We are in the finals, bitches!"

"Yeah, we are in the god damn finals!"

Someone recognizes the words and starts to film. Soon, there are more than ten persons shooting the drunk girls. However, those ladies do not care anymore. Lily takes the bottle from Elle's hands and throws on a camera.

"Shoot this, you jackass!"

We have a situation here. The customers are leaving the place. The owner of the establishment comes and asks them to leave the place or he will call the police. The girls stop singing because the waiter has turned off the sound system. Lights are turned on in the entire place. Someone is lying on the ground, I think it is Emma. Ms. Marketing is still dressed, at least. Hailee is seated on the ground next to her sister. However, the design girl does not know who is at her side. Ellen is fighting to the karaoke machine – Lady Code is kicking, punching, and asking why it is not working. The founder Elle is drinking another bottle of something – she does not know what it is, neither do I. And the finance girl… Oh, no! Where is Lily?

The night is almost over. They get a taxi and go home – do not ask me how five drunk ladies did that. But they do not go to their own houses: all of them go to Anna and Lily's place. Anna is not home yet and she is not watching all this… event. No, I am being nice. The manager is not witnessing this scandal, this moment of disgrace. The entrepreneurs sleep right there, in the living room, some of them on the ground, full dressed (I mean with shoes). Another one is sleeping on the sofa with two empty bottles. Someone is sleeping seated. The night is over, finally and fortunately. Phew! I need a drink… No! I need an aspirin!

CHAPTER THIRTEEN – VERSION 13.0 – WHAT A WONDERFUL WORLD...

Networking

Saturday night. The entrepreneurs have an appointment at the headquarters, or Anna and Lily's house (I know you know that already, but I am still writing, just in case). The big sister is in the living room; the little sister is not home.

"Where is Lily?"

"She's coming, Ellen! She's at Gal's home, our cousin."

"What cousin? Do I know her?"

"I don't think so. My cousin used to do some awesome cosplays. Lily probably is getting some stuff over there."

"That's nice! Did she get the message?"

"I think so."

"And where are the others, Anna?"

"Well, the superheroes are coming, Ellen!"

"Who are these superheroes? Tell me the other costumes, come on!"

"Wait and see, Ms. Green!"

Anna and Ellen talk a little more while they are waiting for the team. It is Saturday night, and the girls are exciting for the party. It is a great opportunity to make networking. Anna believes they can make more progress in their business if they have more professionals contacts. That is important to every company: the trade marketing, as Emma has told, is related to supply chain. It is the "upstairs": it is not about the consumer, it is about retailers, distributors, and wholesalers. Anna says that if they can talk to more professionals, someone can help them to reach more clients. Maybe a good contact can introduce the girls to a new potential consumer. That is the manager's first goal in the party, which is almost beginning.

"They are late!"

"Women always get late in parties, Ellen! Don't worry, they are coming!"

"I'm not late, Anna!"

"Huh… maybe you're not doing right, Ellen… you should go home and get late, just a little…"

In the meanwhile, at another house.

"Dad, where are you?"

"I'm in the kitchen, honey!"

"Close your eyes, please!"

"What? Why?"

"Just close!"

"Okay!"

"Are you looking?"

"No! I'm not!"

"Really?"

"Yes, I'm totally blind! Like Daredevil!"

"Daredevil can feel things, Dad! Don't look!"

"Okay, okay! I'll cover my eyes with my hands!"

Elle comes to the kitchen.

"Ta-da!"

"Wow! What is this?"

"It's my costume, Dad! There is a party tonight! Remember?"

"Sure! I have to take you to Anna's house, right?"

"Yes, we'll take a cab from there. Anna has no car anymore..."

"Yeah... Jennifer told me this story... so sad..."

"People are making sacrifices for this business, Dad."

"Yes, I can see it, honey. What about you? Are you making sacrifices?"

"I think so. Sacrifices of time, wishes, some shopping... I'm still studying correctly, by the way."

"Everything is gonna be fine, Ms. Blonde. Just give some time."

"Is this really necessary, Dad? All this hard work? Why can't things be easier?"

"Well, it depends on what is important to you."

"I didn't get that."

"People want the easier way. But when they have it, they don't give so much value. Some people want the hard way, so they value the goal and the path. They appreciate it."

"The path? Why not the goal? Is it wrong to think only about the goal?"

"Are you thinking only about your goal, Mary Elle? Your objective?"

"Yes, Dad. When I see all this work, these nights without sleeping so much, my friends making sacrifices like Anna did... I think about my objective. That's what makes me keep going."

"This is right, Ms. Blonde, but there is another way to see this. Your target is what make you keep going; it's what make you try over and over. But don't forget the path, the journey. This is important too."

"The journey?"

"Yes, the journey. Think about life, our lives. We all know how this is gonna end, right? We all know we'll be dead someday. This is the end, or you can see this way. Then, we need to enjoy the journey: the life. Even the bad things, because we learn with them. The bad things make us stronger, experienced and ready to face the next challenge. The journey, the life, is always great, anyway you see."

"Oh, I got it…"

"What have you learned in these few months, Mary Elle?"

"Oh, so much, Dad!" she sighs.

"Is it enough?"

"No! I want more!"

"You were talking about bad times. But look how much you have learned."

"Yeah, now I can see, Dad."

"So… don't worry about the end, because you already know what it is, right? Just enjoy the journey, Ms. Blonde! You still have your entire life!"

"Thanks, Dad!"

Elle has no words anymore. She hugs Charlie, the best father of this story, for a long time. Now she is ready to face the world.

"Well, I'll take you to Anna's house! I think you're late already, honey!" he checks the watch.

"Thanks, Dad! I'll get my purse; just a second, please!"

"Are you sure you don't want to go to Krypton?"

"Krypton is dead, Dad!"

"Oh, sure! It exploded! Maybe Metropolis?"

At Anna and Lily's house, someone knocks the front door.

"Hi!"

"Hi! Aquaman? You must be kidding? Why I'm not Aquaman? I want a trident too!"

"Because I'm the manager, Hailee! I'm a queen!"

"But we're not under the seas, Anna!"

"It doesn't matter, Emma! Come inside, come on!"

They go to the living room and meet Ellen.

"Green Lantern? Oh, my God! I want a ring with a green light!"

"Wow! You look great, Hailee! You too, Emma! Why did you take so long?"

"Oh, they don't sell this! They just have Batman and Superman costumes! I hate this exclusion!"

"Did your mom help?"

"No, just me and Emma! We made it! Look!"

"What is this, Hailee? Your ear?" asks Ellen.

"No, it's like an aerodynamic stuff! To run faster, you know?"

"I liked it! I like the red too! Wow, you're stunning, Hailee!"

"Thanks, Ellen! I like yours too! And green is your favorite color, right? Anna did a great choice!"

"What about you, Emma? You're quiet."

"She's in the dark, Ellen." says Anna.

"I'm in the dark now, Ellen. I'm evil!"

"Oh, come on! Show me your costume! Stand up!" asks Ellen.

"I can't! I'm in the dark, watching and taking care of my city."

"Jesus, she has embodied the character, Anna!"

Someone else is at the front door again. There is a bell, but people knock. Hailee goes to see who is there – she is the fastest girl in this story now.

"Hello! Superman? Oh, my God! I want to fly!" says Hailee.

"Hi, Hailee! The Flash? Oh, Jesus! You're so wonderful in red! Is everyone here already? Sorry, I'm late!"

"It's okay, Elle! We were almost sending you a message, but I think Metropolis is offline!" Anna says.

"Hey, Ellen! Oh, she's Green Lantern! I hope you make better than the movie!"

"Oh, come on! My mom has made this joke already! Please, forget that movie!" asks Ellen.

"And who is this? Is that you under this mask, Emma?"

"She's in the dark now, Elle! She's not even talking." advises Anna.

"And Anna has a trident! Why?" Elle asks.

"She said she's the queen. Anna is the queen manager now." says Hailee.

"Well, we're all here... oh, wait! Where is Lily?"

"She's coming! I'll send her another message. She's late." Anna says.

An almost imperceptible sound comes from the front door. Someone is unlocking and opening it. However, the girls are too noisy and they do not listen to it. Suddenly, something spherical crosses the air in the living room. A spherical, white, red and blue object, with a star in the center. It is not adamantium, but it sounds like metal.

"What was that?" says Anna.

"I don't know! But I've heard a sound!" says Hailee. She is seated on the sofa with her back turned to where the sound has come.

"I don't think it is what I'm thinking it is." says Elle.

"What did you see? I didn't see anything." says Ellen on the sofa, beside Hailee.

"Was that… a shield?" says Emma.

Hailee stands up and goes to the other side of the living room, behind the sofa. She takes the object and brings to the girls.

"Ta-da!"

Lily comes to the living room and shows her costume. A white, red and blue costume, as her shield. There is a mask too, with an "A" on the forehead. Red gloves and boots and a white star in the chest complement Lily's costume. The finance girl looks at the team; she stops smiling.

"I think something is not fitting here, ladies…"

"Lily, what are you doing?" asks Ellen.

"I… huh… have a shield… where's my shield?"

Hailee gives the spherical object back to Lily.

"Lily, didn't you get the message?"

"I did, Anna! Wait!"

She takes the cell phone and runs the message app.

"It's here! Look! I'll read for you. 'Come as a superhero!' "

"Huh… there is a scroll button here, Lily…" Hailee shows her on the screen.

"Come as a superhero. A DC Comics superhero. That's what I've said, Lily!"

"Huh… there is an attachment here, Lily… this icon means that…" Hailee shows again.

"Oh… I can't believe this! This anxiety is gonna kill me someday…"

"Well, we can't go to the party like this!" says Ellen.

"No way! We are Justice League or Avengers. We can't be both!" Hailee says.

"Why not? It's a crossover! They make crossovers events in comics!" says Lily.

"But they don't make crossovers in the movies, Lily!" Emma says.

"Why not?" Ellen asks.

"Because they are fighting for rights and copyrights! And because they can't see the great chance to make an unforgettable movie!"

"How do you know that?" Ellen asks again.

"I'm Batman!" says Emma.

"Okay, so what now? I think we should go, anyway." says Elle.

"Why didn't you choose something easier, Anna, like Harry Potter?" says Lily.

"No, not Harry Potter!" says Emma.

"Why not, Emma?" Hailee asks.

"I don't like it!"

"Why?" Hailee insists.

"Because the girl looks smarter than me!"

"Okay, ladies… I'll fix this!"

"How, Lily? It's late!"

"I'll go back to Gal's house, Anna! Our cousin must have something to help me. Well, to help us!"

"We're late, Lily! The party has begun already!" says Elle.

"You can go; I'm after you! Don't worry, I'll be there! It was my fault, and I won't let you down, ladies! This is still a team!"

Chapter Thirteen – Version 13.1

The building is full illuminated. Some red and blue lights adorn the entrance gate, as the front door. It is a party night! Teams from all over the country have come to the contest, and now they can have a nice time to network with each other. We have the finalists, we have the other groups there. If you are not a finalist, at least you can enjoy a costume party and make some contacts. The organizers believe the objective is not only a trophy or glory, but a sustained growth of this industry. Tonight , they are all winners.

"Wow! Look this! It's so crowded!"

"Yeah, all the city is here, Elle!" says Anna.

"I hope you meet Anthony, Emma!"

"Really? I think I don't care anymore, Ellen! Whatever…"

"Hey, girls, did you see the Chewie over there?" shows Hailee.

They get inside the main hall. It is a large place, with red and blue balloons hanging from the ceiling. The walls are blue too. The floor is white and bright, but the lights are off. There are some small red and blue lights on the sides. The place is almost in a dim light, but you can see people. It is costume party, and you go to see and being seen. There is a stage at the end of the hall, where a band is playing a happy song, "Jack Tequila".

"Look who's there, Emma!" says Anna.

"Oh… it's Anthony! Oh, my God! What should I do?"

"Go there, Emma! Come on! And bring some hot guys with you!" asks Hailee.

Ms. Marketing walks nicely through the hall. She comes close

Anthony, but he does not note her. Emma gets closer and pushes him with her hip – a very small push, almost an unintentional touch, because, as we know, she is a lady.

"Hey! Emma! Nice to see you again!"

"Hi, Anthony! How are you doing?"

"I'm fine, thanks! You?"

"I'm fine too, Anthony, thanks!"

"Hey, guys, this is Emma! The marketing girl from… huh… I'm sorry, what is the name of your team?"

"Dad's Home! Hi, guys, nice to meet you!"

"Well, you have a drink already, I can't offer you! Wow, you look great, Emma! You can arrest me, by the way, Batman! I'm a criminal!"

"Okay, Anthony, I'll do that!"

They talk for a while. Emma calls the other girls to join the group. Soon, they are having… huh… networking. I do not think I like this (but maybe I am jealous). Anthony has a nice talk, he really can entertain a group – or the marketing girl. At least, someone in this story can get married – but we still do not know that.

Approximately one hour later, someone comes to the place. The band is having a break time, and the DJ is playing some hip hop music. Then, the DJ sees someone at the hall entrance and asks for lights. Now we can see who is there. Half the people in the place stop talking and look at the entrance. It is a blue, red and golden costume. Not so shinning as seen in comics, just a little darker – or updated. There are small stars and an eagle, a big one, in the chest. And we can see a navy blue topcoat with golden details on the edges. The costume is not low-cut. However, there is a cut in each side of it. This cut starts on the thigh and ends near to the chest – bust, by the way. Because we are talking about a woman, a wonderful one.

"I don't believe it! She made it!" Elle opens a wide smile.

"About time!" Emma says.

"Wow! Look at her!" says Ellen. "She can turn me!"

"Do you know her?" a new friend asks.

"Justice League is complete now!" says Anna.

"I want a topcoat!" Hailee says.

Some men are speechless. And they do not stop looking at her. Lily uncover the head and she is wearing a golden crown too – she did not forget anything. Lights on her, the DJ announces.

"Ladies and gentlemen, Wonder Woman in the house!"

188

Suddenly, a man comes to Lily and kneel. He is wearing a golden and red costume, it looks an iron armor.

"I'm the CEO of my company, lady! Marry me, please!"

Lily sees the Iron Man kneeling at her front and say nothing. At the same time, another man comes to her side.

"I don't think she likes iron, buddy! Are you a CEO? I'm a god!" he shows the hammer, the red cape, and the blond long hair.

Lily sees the other man at her side. How can she say "no" to Thor? Or even to Iron Man?

"Huh… I don't think we belong to the same universe in comics, guys! Could you excuse me, please?"

She leaves the men and goes to meet the girls.

"Lily, you're great! No, you're wonderful!" says Emma.

"Oh, my God! I don't believe it's you!" Elle says.

"Look this costume, ladies! This is professional!" says Hailee.

"Nice work, Lily! Where did you get that? Warner Bros. Studios?" Ellen asks.

"How did you get that so fast, Lily?"

"Oh, it's a long story, Anna… Our cousin is gonna be mad!"

"Why? Did you steal that?"

"Huh… more or less… a kind of…" Lily shows a forced smile.

"What?"

"She had visits, Anna! And I… huh… I said I needed a belt… then I borrowed this for a while…"

"Lily! Gal is gonna kill you!"

"She would never borrow this one, Anna! This is almost a professional clothing to her!"

"Oh, God, Lily! You should have asked her anyway!"

"I hope she doesn't notice something is missing in her closet!"

The sound gets loud and the girls start dancing. Now they look normal: they are talking to boys, they are having fun in a party, they are drinking moderately – or safely. Next day, on Sunday afternoon, they will face the competitors, the final, their fate (but not with so much drama). However, tonight, they are growing up in a different way. Tonight, they are just girls.

CHAPTER FOURTEEN – VERSION 14.0 – THE ULTIMATE CHALLENGE.

Show time

"Lily? Wake up!"

"What? Let me sleep…"

"Lily, wake up and check your messages!"

"What messages, Anna? What time is it?"

"It's almost nine o'clock! Come on, lazy, wake up and see your messages right now!"

"What happened, Anna? Jesus…"

"There is a video in all my messages apps, and I'm not counting e-mail and social network!"

"What video?"

"You tell me, Lily!"

Anna sits at the edge of the Lily's bed – she was standing up at its side – and shows the cell phone screen. It is a video, a well-known video, recorded at some night, when Anna was not with the girls. When the manager had to leave around nine o'clock to meet her boyfriend Jesse. When some girls like Elle and Ellen have drunk – and got drunk – for the first time.

"Shoot this, jackass!" the girl in the video says.

Anna pushes the stop button. She is not believing. The manager leaves the girls for a couple of hours and… what do they think they are doing? They are entrepreneurs – and ladies. What were they doing? That was only a celebration, but it became a one million views video on internet.

"Just check it out, Lily! Over than one million on YouTube! Do you know what that means?"

"Huh… someone is making money?"

"Close. Someone is making money with our shame!"

"God, Anna! Did you call the girls?"

"Not yet. I was expecting you explain me this first."

"Oh, Anna… we just had a lot of tequilas… and wine… maybe some vodka, beers or unknown drinks too…"

"Just tell me one thing: why Elle and Ellen are on this video? Look this!"

The manager shows a scene where Elle is drinking directly from an unidentified bottle. In other scene of that creepy show, we can see Ellen falling on the ground with a glass.

"They don't drink alcohol, Lily! What are they doing in there?"

"Oh, Anna, it's a long story... someone has started to drink... I think it was Elle... so, Ellen started to drink too... and things went out of control..."

"I can see that, Lily! Look this: one million and ten thousand views. Ten thousand people have seen the video only in these few minutes we are talking!"

"I don't know what to say, Anna... it happens... it's done... let me sleep for five minutes, okay? Just more five minutes..."

"I'll call the girls!"

Chapter Fourteen – Version 14.1

Later. Everyone is awake.

"Someone can explain me this?"

Silence. For a long time.

"Anyone? No one?"

Still silence.

"What about this? Oh, this is a new one! This is like a... 'best moments' edition!"

Silence and silence.

"Does anyone in this group know that you cannot drink so much alcohol? I mean, in your entire lives!"

Nothing can be heard.

"Does anyone know you cannot drink so much alcohol when you start to drink alcohol?"

If a strand of hair falls right now, we can hear it.

"And did you know that drinking alcohol is not the best habit to start?"

Nothing, still nothing.

"And don't tell me about what socially acceptable is! That definitely isn't! Look at those people at the bar! They are running away! From you! Can you see that?"

Neither a breath sound.

"Emma? You're the marketing here! You supposedly should take care of our images!"

"Huh... I think I was too drunk to remind that, Anna..."

Someone says.

"I'm sorry, Anna. It was my fault. I've started that."

"You, Elle? Why?"

"We were happy, Anna… that's all…"

"That's what you do when you are happy, Elle? You destroy a karaoke bar?"

The silence comes back. The manager starts to calm down.

"I'm sorry, Anna… we just started… and we didn't know how to stop…"

"I can see that, Ellen…" Anna takes a deep breath.

"We were so happy, Anna… yes, we have gone that far… but… I, huh…"

"Okay, Hailee…"

"I'm so sorry, sister! I know this is one more big headache to you…"

"Fine, Lily…"

"Well, sorry for not doing my job, Anna…"

"It's alright, Emma…"

"It was my fault, Anna, I'm so sorry."

"Don't worry, Elle. We'll be fine…"

Silence, lowered heads, some sadness and blame.

"Oh, God! I'm looking like a mother here! Don't look at me this way!"

"You're the manager and the boss, Anna. You're like a mother!" Hailee smiles.

"I'm not! When is your birthday, Ellen?"

"February."

"I was born on August! See? Ellen is older than me! I'm not the mom here!" says Anna.

"But I was born one year earlier. Because this year, I'm twenty-six, and you'll be twenty-seven years old. Right?" Ellen points Anna.

"Oh… crap…"

"Congrats, Anna! You're a mom of five drunk ladies!" smiles Lily.

"Oh…"

The other girls start to smile too. Soon, they are all laughing.

"Well, I hope no one in the contest sees this. I mean, no one in the jury." reminds Anna.

"Can they disqualify us?" Elle asks.

"I don't know! There is nothing in the rules about that!" informs the code girl.

"We didn't show any logo there! Nothing from the contest, I mean. We'll be fine." Emma says.

"Well, we made a mistake, we'll wait for the punishment." says Lily.

"If it comes! And I don't think it's coming. Anyway, we still have a presentation. Nothing happened that night!" Hailee says.

Chapter Fourteen – Version 14.2

One more time, they are at that building. This time, it can be the last or the best. Because if they get a first prize, it will be the glory. If not, I do not know what they are going to do or where they are going to.

However, it is not so dramatic, in fact. It is just a contest, a national one. It is just a competition where they can meet business people from all over the country – and some from all over the world too, because the companies are transnational nowadays. You can see it just like a simple contest, but it is not. Let's make this clear: this event is really important to those girls. Because, for the first time in this story, they have a chance. The team have a good product with a true story, they have already a client, they have skills to rule the company. The girls are ready.

In the living room, at headquarters.

"Anna? Is Ellen there already?"

"Yep! She's taking care of tech stuff. Elle and Hailee are on their way."

"Does she have the files?"

"I don't know, Lily! Call her!"

"Okay."

Lily calls Ellen.

"Hello? Ellen? It's Lily. Do you have all the files?"

"Oh, thank God, you called me, Lily! I have only the powerpoint! I need some development process files, but I don't have them here. They're at my home. Can you go there?"

"Yes, sure! But why don't you get there?"

"Because these stupid newbies can't even connect a laptop to a projector! They are here for hours! And I need to watch this because they need a team member here and blah blah blah!"

"Why don't you connect by yourself?"

"Because another stupid manager here said 'for staff only', and I can't even touch the hardware! God! This is taking too long!"

"Don't you have these files in the cloud, Ellen?"

"No, I don't trust in cloud for these important files, Lily! Okay, call me old-fashioned, if you want!"

"I'll go there, don't worry, Ellen! Emma and I are coming!"

"Thanks, Lily! I'll tell my mom you're going there!"

Lily hangs up and calls Emma.

"Emma, we have a mission!"

"What is it?"

"We need to go to Ellen's house to get some stuff!"

"Okay, let's go!"

"Anna, we're leaving! We'll meet you there, right?"

"Sure, I'm almost done with my hairstyle."

Ms. Marketing and the finance girl go to Lady Code's house.

"Good afternoon, Mrs. Fage!"

"Hi, Lily! Hi, Emma! Call me Jennifer, please! Ellen told me you were coming! Please, come in!"

"Sorry for this inconvenient, Mrs. huh… Jennifer!"

"It's okay, Emma! You're in a rush today, right?"

"Yes, totally, Jennifer! We need to get some files. Where is Ellen's bedroom?"

"Oh, I'll show you!"

They go to the bedroom. The house is large, despite the fact it is only for two women. Actually, a man used to live there, but he is gone – much better to the mother and the daughter, because he was not a so good man. Some flowers pots here and there, and a beautiful picture on the wall shows Jennifer and Ellen. It is a cozy place – why can women build so cozy places? Men's houses used to be functional: you can have all stuff in the right locations. But women adorn houses to make homes – it is different!

"Well, here it is! Be my guests, ladies!"

"Thanks, Jennifer! We'll be brief here!"

Lily calls Ellen.

"Hello? Ellen? It's Lily. We're here already. Where is your laptop?"

"The desk, Lily. Go to the desk."

"I'm going. I'll put you in the speakerphone."

Lily and Emma goes deeper in the bedroom. It does not look like a girl bedroom. We cannot see posters on the walls, or anything pink. There are many green things, because that is Ellen's favorite color. We can see a Green Lantern lampshade, a Bulbasaur garnish (a Pokemon), and a Hulk action figure (it is not a toy). There are no Barbie dolls. We can see some computer components empty boxes too: motherboards, video cards and power supplies boxes. There is a workbench with some tools like a soldering iron – this is heavy for ladies, but the code girl can handle it.

"I can see it, Ellen. But there is no laptop here."

"It's not a laptop, Lily. It's a desktop computer."

"I still can't see it, Ellen. There is nothing on the desk. Just a keyboard and some papers."

"Can you see the desk?"

"Yep!"

"The desk is the computer, Lily!"

"What?"

Emma is listening and she starts to look for a power button. She crouches under the desk and touches the back, but there are no buttons there.

"Can you see anything, Emma?"

"Nope! Still looking for!"

"Oh, wait, Lily! You need to turn on the UPS first!"

"Okay, where is it?"

"It's out there. I mean, out of the bedroom. There is a white wall out there."

"Okay, guide me. Why is this so complicated, Ellen? I feel like a 'Mission: Impossible' guy here!"

"Oh, I need to fix that, Lily! The desktop pulls too much power! It's temporary!"

"Okay, I'm out of the bedroom."

"Oh, wait! Do not turn on the desktop before turning on the UPS!"

"What?"

"Just don't! It's too much power!"

Lily runs to the bedroom and shout.

"EMMA!"

The marketing girl smashes her head harder – she is under the desk.

"OUCH!"

"Oh… you… are you okay?"

"I hope this is important, Lily…"

"Oh… I need to turn on the UPS first!"

"Tell that to my head, Lily… and my hairstyle… ouch!"

"What are you doing there, you both?" Ellen asks. "Are you destroying the bedroom?"

They finally turn on the computer. The upper side of the desk opens and a display comes up. A green light turns on from the middle of the desk and shows the hardware: we can see all the components there, through an acrylic cover.

"Wow!"

"Wow! Is this gonna fly or something?"

Then, Lily seats and starts to type while Emma is standing and checking the lights inside the desk – it is cool! Ellen directs them through files and windows, until they find what the code girl needs. That girl is really a hardware enthusiast!

"Okay, Ellen, we got it!"

"So come over here! Elle and Hailee are close!"

"We are coming!"

"And don't forget to turn off the UPS, please!"

The code girl hangs up the phone and sees the technicians, supposedly the IT guys. They are still trying to connect things over there. Ellen starts to type on the cell phone, on some social network. Suddenly, she realizes that she cannot say anything bad about the organizers – the group can be disqualified. And, by the way, it is not the best practice for professionals.

Before running out of patience, Ellen goes to the restroom. She opens the toilet door and gets in. The girl seats. After few seconds, after doing what she had to do (you know what it is, I do not know why I am describing it), Ellen stands up.

A plastic object falls down inside the jar, but Ellen does not see. She pushes the button, and then she realizes something – a very important thing – is there, inside the jar, going away – I mean, it is lost.

"Oh, my God! Oh, no, no, no!"

In the movement, she drops the cell phone too.

"Oh, no!"

The code girl almost puts her hand inside there, but there is no time for that. She puts the hand on the forehead, opens her mouth, in vain. Ellen still can save her cell phone – it is too big to go down the drain. However, Lily's flash drive is gone, with the presentation slides. The finance girl is going to go mad twice.

Chapter Fourteen – Version 14.3

Later, on backstage.

"Is Anna here already?"

"No, she's coming!"

"Oh, my God! She's late!"

"Where's the file, Lily?"

"Oh, it's here, Ellen! Take it! Where is my flash drive?"

"I don't have it! It's gone! I lost it in the drain!"

"What?"

"I lost it, Lily! I went to toilet and... I lost it!"

"And the powerpoint was inside of it?"

"Yes, it was!"

"And why did you take the flash drive to toilet, Ellen?"

"And what should I do? Leave it here, where someone can take it?"

"I don't see any difference, Ellen! It's gone!"

"Don't you have a back-up, Lily?"

"Nope. Wait! I have it in the cloud!"

"Huh... but we don't have any internet connection available for the next two hours, maybe more. The IT guy said."

"Oh, God! This only happens in the movies!"

"Well, this is not a movie, but it's happening, Lily!"

"Where are Elle and Hailee?"

"They are talking to the organizers, Emma. I think we'll be the first group to present. Elle and Hailee are trying to delay it."

"Oh, I hope they can do that!" says Emma.

"Emma, can you call Anna, please? My cell phone is gone too."

"In the drain? Oh, my God!" surprises Lily.

"It's just soaked, Lily! I think I can save it, but not for now."

"Jesus! Is everything going down?"

"Don't worry, Emma! Everything is gonna be fine!" says Ellen. Elle and Hailee comes.

"So what?"

"Huh... we didn't get it, Emma... we'll be the first group..."

"Oh, God! Now tell me the bad news, please!" asks Ellen.

"Huh... we don't have internet connection yet. Anna is late. We don't have the powerpoint. And I've seen the other competitors, they are very calm..."

"They are faking, Elle! Don't worry about that! Everyone is nervous!" says Lily.

"Yeah, just think about our job, Elle!" says Emma.

"Who is in charge there, Elle? Who is managing the presentations?" Ellen asks.

"It's a man called Bryan. He is in a dark grey suit. But Hailee and I just have tried. He denied any change."

"I'll talk to him. Lily, Emma. On me." Ellen makes a military gesture.

"Yes, sir!" they say.

The three girls ask for the man, and they go to an office in the back, after a row. Before knocking the door, Lady Code says.

"Just make lovely faces. Got it?"

The finance girl and Ms. Marketing do not understand, but they agree.

"Hello! Excuse me! Are you Mr. Bryan? I'm looking for the manager!"

"It's me. Can I help you?"

"Oh, I have a situation here, Mr. Bryan! I think only you can you help me!"

"What is it?"

"My name is Ellen, these are my friends, Lily and Emma. We'll be presenting our company soon!"

Lily turns to Emma and both of them do not believe Ellen could make that pretty, sweet and calm voice. The code girl looks like a teenager speaking – her 1.55 meters tall certainly helps on that.

"Oh, Mr. Bryan, my grandmother is coming to watch this presentation! I know she is late, but she really needs to see me at this so great event!"

"Well, what can I do for you, Ellen?"

"Oh, Mr. Bryan, unfortunately, my team is the first to go to the stage! That is so terrible! My grandmother is coming from the other side of the country! She is travelling for more than ten hours! She is on her way now, but the traffic is so horrible! Oh, I don't know what to say, Mr. Bryan! My grandmother said her last dream was watching me at a business contest! And she is eighty-nine years old! Could you help me, please, Mr. Bryan?"

"Well, in this case, I think I can, Ellen… I need to talk to the other groups first. But I'll change the programming, don't worry. Huh… 'Dad's Home Team'? I got that. And, please, tell your grandmother to take it easy; she doesn't have to rush. I'll put your group in the end, right?"

"Oh, Mr. Bryan, I'm so grateful! Thank you so much! My grandmother will be so happy! Thank you very much! Thank you!"

"You're welcome, ladies! We are here to help you! And good luck!"

They thank the manager and leave the man's office.

"Ellen Fage, you're full of surprises!" says Lily.

"I have no words, Ellen!" says Emma.

"I can play the cute girl when I need, ladies." says Ellen while straightens the dark green dress.

They go back to the backstage, Anna has come.

"Oh, about time, Anna!" Lily says.

"Did you get something there?" Elle asks.

"Yes, we'll present in the end of the day!" Ellen says.

"What? How?" asks Hailee.

"Oh, don't ask me, Hailee!" Ellen says.

"Don't ask me too!" says Emma.

"Me neither! The job's done! That's what matters!" Lily says.

"Okay, ladies, what we got here?" asks Anna.

"Huh... we don't have the powerpoint slides; Ellen lost her cell phone. If we had internet connection, we could make another powerpoint or access the files. Or even show our website. But we have nothing to show on the screen. And we have no brochures or T-shirts too." informs Emma.

"Oh, my gosh... Any bad news?"

Chapter Fourteen – Version 14.4

Lights off and drums. The host comes to the stage and starts to call the groups. A spotlight follows him. The first group is a team called "Higher." They present a solution to schools, particularly colleges. It is a system to help students to find cool places to have fun. The second team also has a solution for colleges: the group shows a system like Ebay, but only for registered students. The third team is called "The Super Supers" (yes, they have come). The Super Supers group brings an app to find lost pets. It is like a virtual wall to put your warning.

"I'm going to the restroom!"

"Take care of cell phones, Lily!" advises Anna.

"I'm going too." says Ellen.

They soon are in the large and white restroom doing what they need – I mean makeup. Lily checks the light blue blouse, with three-quarter sleeves, everything is clean. The dark blue skirt is not so short (Anna's advice) but it is a little shiny – Lily's choice, as the pearl necklace. Suddenly, someone starts to speak about a video. If you consider the voice, it is a young woman. The toilet's door is closed, then Lily and Ellen cannot see who is talking on the cell phone (you also consider no one could talk on a public telephone inside a toilet). The girls are in front of the mirrors and they can listen to that weird conversation.

"Did you get that? The video? Yeah, the drunk girls on the video! Just search for 'drunk girls contest' on YouTube! Yeah, more than one million, and counting! I'm making money with this! I've sent you the link, John! It's funny! They are totally out of control! No, I don't know! But I think they are here, those idiots! No, they don't have any chance! A group of little girls playing business? No way, John!"

You cannot imagine what faces Lily is doing right now! She is almost possessed! Also Ellen, of course. The girl inside the toilet definitely messed up with the wrong... huh... ladies.

Lily sees a locker and walks to it. She opens the door and, look this, there is a bucket there! Wow! This is going to be funny or tragic – it depends on which side of the toilet door you are! Ellen makes a gesture; the code girl shows some cleaning products. Oh, this is going to be evil – but I do not care!

Lily fills up the bucket with water and the cleaning products. She even shakes well the containers – it is written on the packages and the finance girl likes to follow instructions – she is a right girl.

Ellen goes to the restroom door and beware if someone is coming. The young woman inside the toilet is still talking and laughing. That makes the girls more insane, poor young woman! Or maybe she deserves what is coming.

Lady Code turns the head to Lily and makes a gesture, like cutting the neck with some fingers. The finance girl throws the bucket over the door. Someone starts shouting inside there. The girls leave the restroom very quickly. Nothing unusual is happening in a beautiful day at the entrepreneurship contest.

On stage, the host calls a new competitor. Then comes the fourth group. This team is formed by three men and two women. They present a solution to companies: an app for business training, and they have already four clients – and some profit.

The Alpha Dogs, the fifth team to come up, shows an app to read books and magazines anywhere. Like a "Steam of books and magazines," as they say. Their competitive advantage? Partnership with major publishers.

The sixth group, three women and three men in business clothing, comes with a solution for hospitals, and the girls pay attention. This is Anthony's team, and the handsome man presents a new way to make schedules for physicians on duty.

In this meanwhile, Hailee and Emma are walking on the aisles. They stop in front of a large mirror, before a bend. The older sister checks her white blazer and skirt with a wine shirt. Hailee sees herself inside that dark blue and shiny white dress. She wanted a black one, sleeveless and turtleneck, but Elle took it first – the blonde founder even shouted firstly for that clothing! The sisters are trying to spend time – they are stressed and anxious too. Suddenly, the girls start to listen some people talking. Hailee can recognize the voice.

"Hey, did you see that group? That 'dad something' group?"

"Yeah, what is it?"

"That girl, Hailee, she's gorgeous!

"Really?"

"Yeah, she's hot!"

The brunette girl, with smokey and dense eyes, smiles.

"It's him, Emma!" she whispers. "I told you about him already!"

The little sister smiles. That man was in another contest. The younger sister has a crush on him.

"Oh, but I've heard about her…"

"What?"

"Oh, you don't want to know, James…"

"Just say it, Nicholas!"

"I've heard she has a lot of guys, like a… you know! She likes to change boyfriends, I think!"

"Oh, that's bad, Nicholas! I'm looking for a stable relationship. You know: wife, kids, family and all stuff… cute but naughty? Too bad…"

"Yeah… girls have changed, James! Now they are hunting men!"

Hailee does not know what the worst thing is: the frustration or the prejudice. Why cannot a girl have some boyfriends? How many boys can she have? Is there any number, anywhere? Based on what? Show me statistical numbers, please. Neither all people change their minds at the same speed.

The tall brunette lowers the head and almost starts to cry. Emma comforts her. They are not there to cry, neither to listen to stupid comments. Some men are still living in the Neolithic, they guess. Hailee thinks and makes a promise to herself, in her own silence: she will not cry anymore, for any men. Most of men do not cry (or they hide), why should she? The clock is ticking, and things seem to be worse and worse. But they do not bother. The entrepreneurs are involved with their business, and those small matters must come later.

In the front, we can listen the host announces the next group. The seventh team have an idea for cars: you run the app to find the closest place to buy parts, gasoline, or even mechanical services. Anna likes it and the manager smiles. Ellen liked the eighth presentation. It shows where to find places to buy computer components, with scores, prices and an overview of every shop. The app has also product reviews from customers and discount coupons if you are a heavy user and buyer.

On backstage, a cell phone calls.

"Hello?"

"Hello? Anna? It's Jennifer!"

"Jennifer? Hey!"

"I can't talk to Ellen! No one answers! Is she there?"

"Yes, she's here! Oh, she had a problem with her cell phone! Do you want to talk to her?"

"Actually I need to talk to Elle! Can I?"

Elle feels some sweating on her fingertips. Anna gives the phone to her.

"Hi, Jennifer! This is Elle! What? When? Oh, my God!"

The girls stop talking.

"It can't be true! Where is he? Is he okay?"

The girls keep silence.

"Where are you, Jennifer? Oh, my God! This is not happening! I'm coming, Jennifer! I… huh… I have a presentation in few minutes, but… Oh, no, no, no! This is not happening! No, no!"

The girls are concerned now. What is going on, Mary Elle?

"I'm coming, Jennifer! Oh, no, wait! I can't leave here! Oh, no! Wait!"

She puts the phone on hold, she turns to the team.

"What happened, Elle?" Anna asks desperately.

"Don't make this face, Elle! Talk!" Lily yells.

"Oh, my God! She's gonna cry!" says Ellen.

"My father! He was not feeling well! He's at the hospital! Jennifer is with him! But…"

"Wait! Don't cry, Elle! Do anything you want, but do not cry! You don't have time to make up again!" advises Anna.

"Oh, God, what should I do?"

"We need you, Elle! You must present this!" says Lily.

"I think it's better you go to the hospital, Elle! It's your father!" advises Emma.

"Oh, Jesus! Is this presentation so important, ladies?" says Hailee.

"Sorry for saying this, but I think it is, Hailee!" Ellen… says.

"Oh, my God! I don't know what to do!"

"Just don't cry, Elle!" says Anna.

The founder takes a deep breath. Then, she listen to the girls. What has happened? Few days ago, everything was going so well: they did a good presentation, they got to the finals, they were happy.

There was a drunk situation in between these happy moments and someone has made a video, but it does not matter at the moment. The contest is happening right now, and it cannot wait for fathers, diseases or people holding back tears.

Elle must choose between friends and business, or family. What would you do? You certainly would choose family, as I would, but I am not so sure about you – I do not know you. However, what about that loyal team? What about all the sacrifice they did? All the nights without sleeping? Sold cars? Frank conversations about life, feelings and wishes? What about friends forever stuff? And all that work, gone? Wasted time?

Elle takes the phone again.

"Jennifer, I need you to speak to me very straightly! Is my father okay? Is he talking?"

"He's unconscious, Elle. He's under sedations. I'm so sorry."

Elle feels a tingling on her fingers. The tingling becomes a sweating. She raises the head and sees the girls – her team. She talks to Jennifer a few words and soon she hangs up.

"Okay, Jennifer, thank you! I'll call you later!"

In the meanwhile, on the stage, people are watching the ninth group. It has boys and girls, which present a new dating app, but only for gamers. You must input your achievements from every game you have. These achievements will increase your level. That means you will be in the "trend topics" in the app. The audience asks some questions and the ninth team is almost finishing its presentation.

On backstage.

"Fine, ladies, let's go!"

"Elle, are you sure?" asks the manager.

"We still don't have internet!" says Ellen.

"And we don't have the damn powerpoint!" says Lily.

"We're against all odds here!" says Emma.

"It's our turn now! The host is calling us!" warns Hailee.

"Okay, ladies! It's only us and them! Let's do this!"

"Elle, please! We can drop out now! It's not a shame! Just think!" says Anna.

"We are doing this, Anna!"

"She's right! I'm tired of crying and trying hard for nothing! No matter what happens, ladies, Elle is saying we are not leaving! We are doing this!" says Hailee.

"I have not come this far to give up, ladies! Few months ago, I was just a kid trying to understand my father! Then came the idea, the app, then you came in my life! I'm not giving up! Not to all this! It doesn't matter how good we are doing over there, we'll try! We don't have slides or internet! But we have each other, and we'll help each other! We'll do our best! Whatever happens from now on, we do not give up! I'm not quitting on you!"

On stage.

"Oh, maybe they are not listening to us, ladies and gentlemen! Let's call them again! I'd like to introduce you the Dad's Home Team!" says the host.

Here comes a new challenger: the tenth group, the Dad's Home Team, my girls. Push start button… Oh, so many clichés…

"Good evening, everyone!" she waits for an answer to try out the audience.

People answer.

"My name is Mary Elle Panning, I'm the founder of this company. It's a pleasure to meet you all. These ladies here are my team, my partners, and my friends." she smiles.

Some people smile too.

"This is our product." She takes the tablet with the app, but she cannot count on the screen – there are no slides. "I know you can't see it on this small screen, but I'm not here to show a screen; I'm here to show my company and to talk about details. You can access our website later." she spells the website address.

Some persons get their cell phones.

"I'd like to tell you a story first. Don't worry, it's a short story! Please, don't sleep!" she smiles.

People smile and laugh discreetly.

"This app is about incompetence. People have appointments, meetings and so many tasks nowadays that the day should have more than twenty-four hours. We are not able to manage so many jobs. And then what do we do? Do we ask for more hours in a day?"

She walks nicely on the stage, people follow her with their eyes.

"In the other hand, what do we do when we have a little time? Do we spend our time with our families? Or we waste time on internet? Who goes to internet? Please, raise your hand!" she teases again.

Many people, more than half, raise hands.

"As I said, this app is about incompetence. We have no competence to manage so many tasks in only twenty-four hours. And when we have some spare time, we don't make it useful. Now, what happens when you have someone at a hospital? You don't have enough time for your everyday tasks; and you didn't take advantage of your time when you could, right? So, what can we do now? We need some help, and our app is here for this: saving time."

Some people start to think.

"My company would like to make you an offer. We help you with your little time, and you take care of your relatives at a hospital. Everyone wins. This app allows you to communicate to the doctors directly. These doctors will send you a report of your relatives at the hospital. You don't waste your time with phone calls, you don't wait for doctor's hard scheduling, you don't go to a hospital and wait in line to listen about remedies. Everything is in here, in this app."

The audience starts to whisper.

"Or maybe you want to visit your relatives! Oh, that's really important, I give you that. Patients need to see people! I mean, every day! This app is not cancelling visits, it's just saving time and patience for more and better visits. Because now you can go to a hospital without the concern about schedule. You can go with pleasure, and not thinking 'Oh, how long I'll wait to talk to that late doctor?' " Elle makes a fun gesture.

People laugh and smile (I think they are liking).

"So, this is the deal: we can help your hospital in communication. And you can help your clients and their relatives. You are not helping only people; you are helping families. Any questions until now?"

No one answers, the blonde girl keeps speaking.

"Our team is formed by these experienced women"–she uses the word for the first time–"This is Emma Charlotte; we call her 'Ms. Marketing'. Please, don't call her by this title. This is an inside joke!" she smiles.

The audience smiles a little, and we can listen a few laughs in the back.

"This is Ellen, the 'Lady Code'. You can call her this way too, but ask her first, please." Elle smiles.

As well as the audience.

"This is Lily Jane, the 'Finance Girl'. Lily has the best part of the business: she takes care of money. Don't send her an e-mail, send a spreadsheet, please. This tall girl here is Hailee, 'The Designer'; she is the responsible for the gorgeous things you can see on our website. Have you accessed it already? It's friendly for mobile devices, by the way. You can access it right now!" she repeats the website address.

Some people take their cell phones.

"Now I'd like to introduce 'The Manager'. Anna Kelly is not like a mother as you can think. She's our big boss! Well, some of us have a large experience in this software industry; some of us have a large experience in contests. And, I can tell you that, this is not for rookies." she winks with a mouth snap.

The audience smiles.

"Now, if you wish, we can answer some questions from the audience. For now, thank you very much."

We can see more than five hundred people in the auditorium. They are not all seated. There are tables and chairs on the sides, but most of people are standing up in the middle of the place. That is strategic: business men and women can loosely walk and meet the others. The day three of the competition is a free presentation, like a showcase. The major part is for questions and answers, like a business serious game.

The first man asks about the age of every girl. Elle answers nicely. She does not understand why someone is saying that, and she prefers not to think about it. All the team prefers that way. The second question comes from a woman.

"What is your profit forecast?"

Elle looks at Lily, and the finance girl comes to the front.

"Well, firstly, in our company, we don't sell profit; we sell benefit. However, we know you all want to see numbers, because there are investors here. I love numbers too! We still don't have accurate values, lady, and I can explain that. This is a new business, and we don't have so many consumers yet. We have a preliminary estimate, but it would be a lottery if we would reveal – I could say any magic number here. The most important thing right now is: we have a business model. We're not here trying to catch audience, or page views. We don't need to sell advertisements in our app. We sell our service, we get profit. We're not here for playing, waiting for the general public find out our app. We don't expect Google or Apple buy our company. Because we have a sustainable business model already. This is the major feature in our business, and it's not a button with malfunction."

The woman thanks and starts to typing on her cell phone, like taking note. Not long after that, a man raises his hand. He is about fifty years old, bald, in an expensive grey suit with a red and white tie. He looks a rich man (maybe because he is bald). The man asks.

"Why did you choose this type of software? I mean, accessed via web-browser?"

Ellen comes to answer.

"We believe this is how the apps should work, mister. In a near future, we will not have so many native apps, I mean, for local installation, in your own desktop computer, laptop or cell phone. The most part will work based on internet. In our case, that is the most advantageous and convenient."

"How long is this what you call 'near future', lady?" the bald man continues.

"Less than ten years."

"Oh! Do you have a crystal ball or a magic mirror?" he laughs, as well as the audience.

"No, we don't. I actually think it's stupid to fill my local hard drive when I can access and use some apps in the cloud. And, in my opinion, I think it's stupid to go against the tide. Parts of the marketplace are already working like that, and we are not blind."

"I agree with you, lady. A local installation is unusual for some software." the man says.

"No, I didn't say local installation is unusual, I said it's stupid in some cases."

Anna covers half the face with a hand, turns to Ellen, and discreetly says "Calm down!" to the code girl. They do not want to make them angry, but that man deserved that – he was just teasing the girls!

Someone raises the hand. She looks like a serious woman in her thirties, in a serious navy dress, in a serious hairstyle.

"I didn't like the design. It's an orange and blue logo, but it's for hospitals. Why didn't you choose white and red? It's just an opinion, but I really don't like these colors."

Hailee rises and starts to answer with a little laugh.

"Thank you for asking and commenting! That's a funny question, lady! Last month, I was talking to my mother about that. She said to me 'Why don't you try out pink?' and I told her 'Because Barbie is not gonna buy this app, Mom!' This is what happens when you make things the way you like: you don't satisfy the client, only yourself. Everything you make in design must be explained. You can't insert a square because you like squares, or because it's cute. Squares are not cute, by the way, they are just sexy. So, you don't create a green icon because your boyfriend has green eyes. Design is not what you like, or even what your mother does; design is for your customer. And this customer must love it, not only like it. Because it's your client who is going to buy it and pay the bills." she smiles.

The auditorium smiles too. The designer goes on.

"But, I didn't explain what you've asked, right? You've asked about the logo. Please, everyone, visit our website to check it." she says the address. "You'll see there is a secret message inside our logo. Don't tell anyone, please! In the back, you can see shapes, blue shapes. Those images represent the world, the 'men world'. That's why these shapes are blue, because it's the color commonly connected to men. We also have this blue in some variations that means emotions, honesty and integrity – we still believe in these values nowadays. As you can see, these shapes are patchy, they are not perfect. Because the world we live is not; it has flaws. We can say this world is not perfect, but there are still good principles here. In the middle, you can see the 'Dad's Home' title in orange. This is us, our team, in this blue world. Orange means energy, vitality and optimism. That's what we need to face this world, I mean, every day. Orange also is the color of adventure, and we see our business like that: a fantastic journey with action and challenges – our greatest adventure."

The woman smiles and thanks with her head and the audience whispers a little. It is still too early for cheers, because the investors and business people did not finish yet. Suddenly, the bald man in an expensive grey suit with a red and white tie raises his hand again.

"How can you be so sure this product will be a success? A best-seller in the market? Because you look very excited about your product. I can see your smiles, that's very good. But how can you know?"

Ms. Marketing time. Emma comes and smiles to the audience.

"Good question, sir, very good! Before replying this, I'd like to ask you some questions. Can you predict a hit? A best-seller? Anyone here? Can you?" she says and starts to walk. "How can you know a product will be a successful sale? Apple, Microsoft, Google, Amazon, they all do market researches. They also have all kind of specialists working at their headquarters. We could show you some charts and spreadsheets, with beautiful colors and effects, with nice and lovely cells and fonts. We could quote or highlight specialists opinions about our product. We could even say we have a hunch, a good feeling. Or our female intuition is telling us something. But all this would not be true in the marketplace, ladies and gentlemen. You asked how we can know this product will be a hit. Well… we can't. Because you can say a product – any product in any marketplace – is a success only when you launch it. This is the single method to know. Maybe this is not the answer you want to listen. We could lie to you all here, but this is not what we do. We just listen to what the marketplace tells us. Then, we use this to help and improve our company."

The man thanks and asks again.

"I don't see your manager speaking! Is she up there?"

Anna comes smiling and making a gesture with both arms.

"Hello, there! Well, I think that's because I'm not so tall, mister! Thank you for asking!" she laughs.

The audience smiles, some people laugh. Anna keeps going, captivating smile included.

"Well, my job here is about giving resources to my team, these ladies. I don't hold or oppress them, this is not my job, neither me. I just listen to them, and I see what they need to make things done easily and quickly. I also verify who they want to be in this company, and where they want to go in few years. Then, I provide what these girls need. Besides, look this: I do not ask for their jobs – we all know the deadlines! I inform the dates to them; they tell me how much time they need; we negotiate. There are no children in this group, we all know how to handle with deadlines. In addition, I try to get the best from them. How can I do that? Oh, I have a straight talk to each one of these ladies. We're not only co-workers, we're friends. There is respect between us. You've said I'm not here, mister! Well, my job is not being here, it's getting things well-done, and on schedule! But if you still want to see me, I'll try high heel shoes next time, okay?" Anna smiles.

The man in the grey expensive suit thanks. The audience talks louder now. Another man raises a hand.

"I see your app is very beautiful!"

Hailee thanks discreetly with her head, as well as the team. The man proceeds.

"But I see many pretty apps that do not work properly. How do you see this, huh… trap?"

"Well, sir, if your product is not good, put it into a pretty package. That's what some people do, unfortunately. Our app is not only beautiful, it's working properly. And it's not a trap, by the way." Hailee smiles.

"What if my product is good?" someone yells in the back.

"If your product is good, ask more for that, mister!" Lily states.

The entrepreneurs start to answer quickly and the audience asks the same way. Soon, the presentation turns into a questions and answers business serious game I said before.

"Do you really think a good design can sell a product?"

"Yes, sure! Ask iPhone's maker about that!" says Hailee.

"What about marketing? Do you believe marketing is the solution for everyone?"

"The best product in the world, if you don't sell it properly, is just the best product in the world. It's not a hit; you don't make money with it. So, yes, we do believe marketing is very relevant in every company." says Emma.

"I see your app sends messages. It's a very simple app."

"Sorry, I didn't hear the question, sir." says Ellen.

"I mean, anyone can make it!" he smiles.

"Well, Google is just a searcher, and Facebook is just a social network. Our app? In a short version, yes, it's a messenger; an e-mail client for doctors and families. But, has anyone made it before?" the coder asks.

"It's all about market niches, mister. You don't need to be good, you need to have a market niche. We can see many corporations in specific niches that other ones don't operate. Sometimes it's not profitable, sometimes other companies just don't want to act there. Then, a company works alone in a market niche, even if its product is not so good. Our app is simple, but we have no competition from other companies yet." Emma explains.

"Nothing is so good that it is unanimous. We know our product is not perfect, that's why we are always researching to improve it. In the other hand, nothing is so bad that cannot be sold. So, we still can sell our app, even if it's not perfect." Anna says.

"And who would be your competitors?" a woman in a light color blazer says.

"They are not enterprises, lady. Doctors' resistance to the adoption of our product is one of our competitors; families' resistance to install and learn a new app is another one. And, of course, hospitals can simply refuse this new way to communicate." Emma says.

"Everything looks beautiful when we are here, well-dressed, talking to you on this large stage. We know where we are going into, I mean, the dark side of the Force. The real deal is when you meet a potential client and show numbers." advises Lily.

"What if someone copies your app?" a man in a brown suit asks.

"This happens, mister! I can see a man with the same nice suit you are wearing!" Hailee says and laughs.

The audience laughs loudly. The designer keeps going to tell the joke, I mean, to reply.

"There is competition everywhere, and there is no escape from that. What should we do? Improve our service, of course. Maybe prices, maybe design, but certainly new features in our app." says Hailee.

"You know many things about marketing for a designer, lady!"

"Oh, I have a good teacher! Ms. Marketing here is my sister!" Hailee winks with a mouth snap.

"And what if those improvements are not enough?" an older man with beard asks.

"We'll try harder, mister. We are able to improve our app, because we have a consumer inside our team, actually. I mean, we do use our own service. This is the best way to understand what the client needs." Anna says. "Dropbox, by the way, has a lot of huge competitors with the same product, but the company has not been sold yet." she completes.

"Why don't you have a powerpoint back there?" a man points the large screen.

"Oh, did you note that? We didn't! Really!" Anna makes a gesture as well as the girls; they smile.

"Have you thought that the marketplace cannot accept your product?" says another man with a green shirt and a tie with small drawings.

"The marketplace will not change; you will. This statement I've just said is intentionally ambiguous, mister. If no one buys our product, we'll change it, we'll adjust our app. In the other hand, and we can understand this in the same sentence I've said, if the marketplace doesn't accept our product, we'll change the marketplace." Emma teaches.

"How can you do that?" the man asks again.

"Oh, that's another question, right? That's classified, mister…" Emma winks with a mouth snap.

"What about coding? Did you have too much work?"

"It's hard to explain coding, sir. Coding is like speaking; and only a few people can make an unforgettable speech. Well, I think we had our moments making good speeches here – no pun intended."

"Why does Ellen use these odd comparisons when she talks about coding, Anna?" Elle whispers to the manager.

"Because people are too stupid to understand what she really does, Elle." Anna answers in low voice.

"You have experienced competitors here. What do you expect for this contest?" someone asks.

"There is no second place: we're here to be the first. We believe in good experiences, but we're not coming to play business." says Anna.

"I've seen your first presentation last weekend. Did you change anything to improve security in the app? Like a password or something?"

"Yes, sir, we did. But forget long passwords and virtual keyboards. You'll swipe a finger, as you unlock the touch screen of your cell phone." Ellen informs.

"I can see some of you are still very young. What about everyday business? It can be stressful. Are you ready for this?" a man in a white shirt asks.

"Yes, we are, sir! Completely! People used to listen to seniors, because they are experienced. This is right, we can't discuss. But as older as you get, you start to put barriers in your life. Someone calls you to make something, and you have many excuses – you don't even try. Young people don't. You call them, they are ready. They have the impetus, the rush. Young people make the noise sometimes we need. Why shouldn't we believe them?" teaches Anna.

The same bald man in an expensive grey suit with a red and white tie raises a hand to speak again.

"I have some stupid questions, and please, tell me if I'm being impolite, ladies. Do you really think a group of young girls can understand what a company does, its significance? Or the marketplace you are getting into? Any company, I mean. The point is your core business. At least, do you understand the core business of your company? Because, huh… you're pretty, lovely, you're well-dressed… but I still can't see you as a company. Sorry for this comment, but it's true. That's what I'm feeling right now. And maybe other people here can feel the same."

Elle turns to the girls and looks at Anna. The manager is a few meters far from the founder, as well as some of the other girls. Anna's royal blue dress is showy; it is a deep and vivid color and she is gorgeous. Then, Anna Kelly looks quickly to the team. The other girls do not look apprehensive, not anymore. There is no strain of ideas, design, code, management, marketing, and finance. They got as far as they could – the girls feel free. There is no powerpoint, no internet for them; there is just a father at a hospital. Those ladies are presenting their business on a blank huge screen, only using their intelligence.

The manager looks at Elle and moves her head down and up once, discreetly. The founder knows all about that movement: "Finish him," Anna would say. Elle turns to the audience.

"Well, thank you for asking, sir! First, there are no stupid questions, just stupid people asking. But, that's a good question, and I think I have a good answer." she says and smiles. "We see the problems in the marketplace, we create products, and we sell them. We help people; we work to them. We solve problems in the marketplace and we solve people's problems. That's what we do: helping people. WE do that. You asked us if we understand the core business of our company, sir. We don't. We ARE the core business of our company."

The audience keeps a long silence (five seconds or more) to analyze – and assimilate, and believe, and swallow – what the blonde young girl has just said, until someone in the back starts to applaud. In few seconds, everyone is doing the same. The bald man in an expensive suit looks embarrassed and he does not talk anymore; he just shows a forced laugh to people around him.

The girls made it, and they feel good. All that last days stress has ended. The Dad's Home Team just has to wait for the final result. However, Anna, Elle, Ellen, Emma, Hailee and Lily are not concerned about positions anymore – are you? Under all those circumstances, they did a great job, as good as they could, and that was what mattered. It was a great night.

CHAPTER FIFTEEN – VERSION 15.0 – LEFT BEHIND, ROUND TWO.

In God we trust

She desperately goes to the hospital while the girls take the stuff after the presentation. Hailee comes together.

"Hi, Jennifer! Where is he?"

"Oh, thank God you came, Elle! He's fine! The doctor said he's gonna be okay!"

"Who's the doctor?"

"It's a woman, Doctor Alice!"

"Oh, I know her! Is she here?"

"Yes, I think… She's around here!"

"Hmm… we should create a feature to locate doctors inside the hospital, Hailee!" Elle smiles.

"Hey, you're talking like a business woman now!" Jennifer notes.

Doctor Alice comes.

"Hey, I know you, young ladies!"

"Hi, Doctor Alice!"

"How are you doing, Elle? Hailee?" she winks with a mouth snap.

"I'm fine, thanks, Doctor Alice! Huh… is my father okay?"

"Yes, it was just a little scare, Elle! But, luckily, he came here fast! Thanks to Jennifer!"

"Well, and what is the bad news?" Elle asks.

"He has made a health check, and he's fine. I think he can be discharged tonight. I have no bad news to you, Elle!"

"Oh, that's so good, Doctor Alice! Thank you very much!"

"Huh… sorry for asking this… Were you in a party?" Alice sees the dresses.

"Oh, no! We were at a contest! We are coming from there! The other girls are still there, by the way!"

"Okay, and how was that? Did you get it?"

"Huh… we don't know yet… but I think we did fine, right, Hailee?"

"Yeah, we crushed it over there!"

"That's nice! Congratulations, ladies! Oh, I also have some news to you! Your app is being used by, let me see… where did I leave the number? Oh, that's it! Seventeen patients are using your app, ladies! Great work!"

"Seventeen? Oh, my God! The girls will go crazy!" Hailee says.

"Wow, I don't even know what to say, Doctor Alice! We are having a great night!"

"Well, congratulations again, ladies! And... I need to tell you something. I have a cousin, Rodrigo. Paulo Rodrigo Santos, actually. He's an investor and he has seen you at the contests. Huh... I'm not sure if he was watching you tonight... but he certainly knows your company. Here."–she takes a card–"This is his business card. Talk to him someday, right? I'll tell him you'll call."

"Oh, my God! An angel investor?" celebrates Hailee.

"What?" asks Jennifer.

"It's a kind of investor, Jennifer! He invests money in companies that can be profitable. It's a... it's almost a bet! People give a company's stake, the investor gives money. It's an angel, really!" Hailee teaches.

"Wow! You're entirely inside this start-up business, Hailee!" Jennifer surprises.

"Oh, I can't make you promises, ladies; it's better you talk to my cousin! And... I think you can see your father now! I have some urgent tasks, okay? You know my job here..." Alice smiles.

"Okay, thank you, Doctor Alice! Thank you very much! I'll share this contact with Anna and the girls!" says Elle.

The three women go to the room to see Charlie.

"Hi, Dad!"

"Hey, Ms. Blonde! Hi, Jennifer! And this gorgeous girl inside this dress must be Hailee!"

"Hi, Mr. Panning!"

"Hi, again, Charlie! I've heard the girls have made a great job back there!"

"Really? What was that?"

"Oh, Dad... I think we really did it! Right, Hailee?" Elle shows a stunning smile.

"Totally right, Elle! We made it, Mr. Panning! Tonight we really made it!"

"The first prize? Really?"

"Huh... we don't know yet... the girls are there, waiting for the final result!" the daughter informs.

"Well, anyway, I think it's a party night!" Charlie says.

"We are just waiting for you to be discharged, Dad! The night will be complete!"

"That will be soon, Charlie! We've talked to Doctor Alice." smiles Jennifer.

"Well... thanks to you all, girls!"

Chapter Fifteen – Version 15.1

Later.

"Thanks for everything, Jennifer!"

"You're welcome, Charlie! You're my boyfriend, in case you don't know!" she smiles.

"Okay, I'll remember that!" he smiles back.

Jennifer leaves the house; she gives a ride to Hailee.

"See you tomorrow, right, Hailee?"

"Yeah, I'll come here before we go to college!"

Then, it is just father and daughter. Elle helps Charlie, and soon he is on the bed. The blonde girl thinks it is a great night – everything is fine for the first time in this story. Her father is home, and he is healthy, recovering. The company has a client, and now the client is paying enough money. The team is working fine, united, not like a company, like friends. The blonde girl is happy – how couldn't she?

She says "good night" to Charlie and leaves his bedroom. Elle has some things to do before sleeping. Checking the cell phone, for example, to know if the Dad's Home Team really did it at the competition.

Do you want to know something?

It does not matter anymore.

She lets the cell phone on the bed and goes to take a bath. Elle turns on the shower, some warm water flows. Now the long blonde hair is wet. Soon, the skinny body is the same way. She wets the face, all the stress is not there anymore. There is only happiness in the shower room – and at that home. The shampoo starts to make a white and consistent foam. She closes her eyes, and feels the warm water again. To Mary Elle, bath time is one of the best moments in the day – she loves it. The blonde girl feels free, with no clothing, no strings, just her and the warm water. Soon, the foam is gone, as well as the tiredness. She lather the body, long legs include, the clear skin looks almost pale. Elle washes her face properly – there are at least five products to do this – and now she is ready to face everything. Even the contest results.

However, that is not important, not anymore. She dries herself with a pink towel. The girl takes care of her face with some products (nine of them), and then she leaves the shower room. Elle checks Charlie's bedroom, the father is fine, already sleeping – she can listen his breathing. The blonde girl smiles nicely.

The founder finally goes to her bedroom. She looks to the cell phone, there are messages from Hailee and Anna. Mary Elle turns off the device and goes to sleep.

Chapter Fifteen – Version 15.2

The day starts with a weaker sun. The autumn is almost ending, as well as the year, and the blonde girl is waiting for more good news. The weekend was great, she can remember. Elle wakes up, Charlie is already waken.

"Dad, are you in the kitchen?"

"Yes, I am."

"Can I cook today?"

"Are you sure? Any special reason?"

"No, I just want it!"

She goes to the kitchen and starts to cook. It is not anything special, she just want to say thank you to everything in her life – that includes her father first. She is not an expert at kitchen, and Charlie keeps watching the new blonde adventure.

"That button, honey, you can turn off heat. I think something is burning. Please, don't incinerate the kitchen, okay? We're using it at dinner!"

"Don't laugh, Dad! Help me!"

She finishes cooking – they do – and now they can have a lunch. Father and daughter talk about everything: work, family, and Deborah, beloved wife and mother. Elle tells about college, friends, and even about business – now she is experienced. Charlie teaches football, leadership and life to his daughter. He also speaks about perseverance, patience and resiliency. Elle asks about true friends.

"You'll know when you'll meet them, Ms. Blonde."

Then, the founder says she has true friends already.

"That's nice! I mean, meeting them so young! I took some years to meet my true friends."

Elle smiles. She knows she is a luck girl. A great father, a great mother, true friends. Maybe her mother could be there to watch her, that victory. However, the girl is not sad. Elle understands her life. It is not perfect as a romantic comedy, but she does not bother.

"That happens only on movies, Mary Elle!"

Or a book.

"So this is life, Dad? You finish college, you start to work… what now? Marriage, kids and it's over?"

"Hey, this looks boring to you!"

"I'm just asking, Dad!"

"Life is complicated, Ms. Blonde… I think you know that already."

"Yeah, until now… it was a little complicated…" she smiles.

"But now it's working, right?"

"Yes, now it's working, Dad! I have a job, friends, I'm finishing college this year."

"So you should start to plan from now on. What do you think?"

"I think I'm gonna miss these days, Dad… all this rush time! As I missed the time mom was here with us…"

"So, don't miss!"

"Is that possible, Dad?"

"Impossible is nothing, Ms. Blonde! Look at you! Twenty-two years old, almost graduated, a success entrepreneur!"

"Well, the real life is not so beautiful like that, Dad! We're not profiting so much as the big companies…"

"But people don't know! They only see your title, 'entrepreneur'."

"I think I'll miss this… this innocence too, Dad."

"Don't miss it. Do you know what I do?"

"Is it a secret?"

"Yes, it's my most precious secret."

"Like a Gollum thing?"

"Yeah, it's my precious." he makes a funny gesture.

She smiles.

"I don't miss anything in my life anymore, honey."

"What? How?"

"I just don't miss."

"Even mom?"

"Even your mom."

"How? This is impossible, Dad!"

"No, it's not! Everyone here has a moment. I mean, on Earth. I'm having mine, you too. Deborah? Yes, she also had her own moment. But all the time she was here, with us, I've enjoyed a lot. I've made everything I could to see her happy, to make us happy, as a family. Of course I had my faults, I'm not perfect! But we've lived together all these years, Deborah, you and I. And we were a happy family; we still are! So, when Deborah's time has come, I just took it, I didn't cry. It's not my choice or hers. When she died, I accepted. Because I knew her time has come, and all those years together were worthwhile."

"So this is it? Enjoy it? No regrets?"

"Yes, enjoy the journey! Because when all this is over, you can say to yourself: 'I have enjoyed my moment.' And you don't regret, and you don't miss it. Because you lived."

All that was complicated to accept in the first time. Elle did not know that Charlie's "way of life." She thought her father was very sorry for Deborah's death, maybe some blame too. In the first view, all those words look like so cold to her. However, when the blonde girl started to reason, she could see Charlie was right. Her mother died four years ago, it was time to move on. Elle still had something to make for her mother – a very important mission – but she did not tell me.

The blonde girl keeps talking to her father while both are finishing the lunch. Soon, Hailee will come again. The founder and the designer must go to college. They need to go back to real life: studying, exams, classes, teachers, and so on. They have to leave the entrepreneur life for a while.

"Sooner or later, you'll leave the college, Ms. Blonde. The business will call you." Charlie advises.

She listens to those words and expects for the best. Then she starts to think how entrepreneur life is.

"It's a life, honey. Salaries, taxes and bills. In the other hand, you'll have profit, promotion, even prizes." Charlie says.

She cannot wait for it.

"Hey, be a good girl, okay?"

The good girl smiles and keeps that in mind. However, at the moment, she needs to finish the lunch and goes to college. The class is a little later that day, and the girl can wash the dishes. Just a fair favor to her father Charlie. After washing, Elle goes to her bedroom, and Charlie goes to take a nap. It is around midday and the father is still recovering from the last night.

Elle sits down in front of the computer. She turns on the device, there is some time to update. The blonde girl does not know what is going on in the world. Sports, politics, wars, entertainment, she did not read anything about that last days. What are the new releases on movies?

Some minutes later, she goes to the kitchen to have some water. Elle passes in front of Charlie's bedroom. The girl sees her father, he is still sleeping. She smiles and go to have some water in the kitchen.

Then, she comes back to the bedroom, to the computer. Elle wants to search some new companies, start-ups, and what they are doing. Now the blonde girl has a new interest: business. She is growing up.

About four hours later, she gets a little tired. It is a pleasant afternoon, and Elle could even get some rest – her bed is so near… right there… She looks the blankets on the bed, blinks a little, rubs her eyes. However, the girl goes to the kitchen again. It is time to have something to eat. She opens the fridge, there is an orange juice there. Elle also finds a cake in the food cupboard. Now the girl and her father can have an afternoon snack. In some minutes, she must go to college.

The young entrepreneur goes to Charlie's bedroom. She opens the door widely, and calls him.

"Dad? Can we have a snack? I found some cake!"

He is not lying in his usual position. Charlie lays on his side, crossing the bed, in a weird way to sleep.

"Dad? Hey! We have a cake!"

The twenty-two years old girl touches that body once, twice. Charlie does not answer. Maybe he is in a deep sleep.

"Dad!"

The almost graduated girl swings the father's body.

"Dad! Hey!"

The founder of Dad's Home company touches her father again, in vain. He cannot answer.

"DAD! DAD!"

His eyes are open, but still. The body is not rigid, and it is still warm.

"DAD! Dad…"

Charlie cannot answer to his daughter anymore. He cannot tell her how to face life. Charlie "The Fox" Panning cannot show how everything can be good, even when bad things happen. Because, as he said, you can learn with your bad moments. You get stronger, experienced and ready to face the next challenge.

The loving father will not tell his young daughter how to enjoy the journey, that great journey called life. How can she grow up from now on?

"DAD!"

Elle wakes up and her body is all sweating; she throws away the blankets. Quickly, the founder goes to the father's bedroom – she is desperate and breathless. The girl opens the door, there is no light.

She turns on the light, the switch is on the well-known place. Elle goes to the bed, no one is there – but the blanket is a little messy. Where is Charlie?

"Dad?"

The young girl comes closer to the bed. Elle is afraid of what she can find in the other side of the bed, but she goes on, not so fast. The founder comes and sees nobody. Where is Charlie?

"Dad?"

No one is in the bedroom, only the young lady. She turns back, and goes out of the place. The bedroom is a little dark or maybe the girl is not reasoning so fast as she can. Elle goes to the door and knocks into...

"Dad!"

"Hey! What happened? Are you okay? You're trembling!"

"I thought you were dead, Dad!"

"Hey, I'm alive! I'm here!"

"I had a bad dream, Dad! I thought you were dead! It was so real, Dad!"

"Hey, hey! I'm here, I'm alive, I'm not leaving you, okay? Did you sleep in front of your computer?"

"No, I was on the bed... Oh, I don't remember going to bed..."

"Hey, look at me! I'm here, Mary Elle! And I'm fine!"

Charlie hugs his kid; Elle is afraid – with all the reasons. Now it is only father and daughter; they must be together for the rest of this story. That is why it is named "S.H.E. Edition" – it is Sweet Happy Ending Edition. Oh, I have just told you everything – or not! Do not worry, we will have much more than this "father and daughter happy stuff."

"Hey, don't you have to go to college? You can stay home, if you want. Are you okay?"

Her body is still shaking.

"You're sweating too, honey."

And still breathless.

"Oh, bad dreams... I remember when your mom was here. You used to have bad dreams sometimes. I remember Deborah took you into her arms when that happened. And you calmed down in few seconds..."

The young girl closes her eyes and the breathing is almost normal.

"Don't worry, Ms. Blonde. I'm here for you. I'm your father."

"Thanks, Dad."

CHAPTER SIXTEEN – VERSION 16.0 – STARTING... OR NOT!

The real life

Few days later, a phone call (it is unusual to them).

"Hey! What's up?"

"Hi, Hailee! Long time no see! Huh… ten hours, maybe?"

"Yeah… we need to talk!"

"What is it?"

"What are you doing right now?"

"Huh… I'm having a lunch. Well, it's not a real lunch, it's a sandwich."

"Hey, are you eating unhealthy food?"

"No, it's just a sandwich…"

"Stop eating fast food, Elle!"

"Okay, Mommy Hailee! I got that!"

Hailee invites the friend to come to her house. The brunette girl with smokey eyes and Emma are going to Lily and Anna's house, and there is always something good to make at Davelman sisters' house. Like business and fun.

"Right now?"

"Yes, you can eat your sandwich on the way! Come on!"

Chapter Sixteen – Version 16.1

At Davelman sisters' house.

"Hi, ladies!"

"Hey, Elle! How are you?"

"I'm fine! Thanks, Lily! You?"

"I'm fine too, thanks!"

"Where is Anna?"

"Oh, she is talking to Rodrigo, Doctor Alice's cousin! You gave his business card to Anna, remember?"

"Yes, I did that last week. So what?"

"Anna is arranging a meeting with him. I think we'll have excellent news soon, Elle!"

"Wow! That's great! Hey, where is Ellen?" Elle asks.

"She's coming." Emma answers.

"Is Jennifer fine?" Elle wants to know.

"Yes, I think… Isn't she with your father?"

"I don't know, Emma; I didn't talk to him. Hey, I was wondering…
I'm going to be Ellen's step-sister! Can you imagine that?" smiles Elle.

"Yeah! I didn't realize that!" says Lily.

"Watch out, Elle! Lily is gonna fight to your step-sister!"

"Who said that, Hailee? We don't fight in this company anymore!"
says Lily.

"Ha ha ha!"

"So, what's the good news?" Elle says.

"Emma and I… you know… we, huh… how can I tell them,
Emma?" starts Lily.

"You what?" says Elle.

"Just say it, Lily!" asks Emma.

"Wait! Is this something I don't know?" Hailee asks.

"Huh… I don't know how to tell you that…" says Lily.

"Just tell them, Lily! Be a man!"

"How am I supposed to be a man, Emma?"

"Just be it! Stop being fussy and say it, Lily!"

"Okay! Well, it's not a big deal. Emma and I are delivering
lectures at a college. It's a nice place, and we can present new things
to students. And we have already a special group of young girls.
They are very committed, they always want to know more and more,
and they don't stop asking… I have a good feeling about them! I'm
speaking about finances, of course; Emma is teaching marketing.
That's the big secret…"

"Phew! I thought you would say you and Emma were dating!"

"No! Where did you get that, Elle?" Lily laughs.

"I don't know! I'm just saying! I thought you and Emma were kissing
each other or something! My fingertips are sweating! I don't know why!"

"Elle! We don't kiss each other! I'm not gay!" Lily says.

"Of course not, Elle! Not when we're sober!" Emma says.

"What? Oh, my God! Ha ha ha!" Elle laughs.

"Jesus, Mary and Joseph! Ha ha ha! Nice work, sister! You got Ms.
Eyebrows!" Hailee laughs.

"Emma! Stop saying this crap! Ha ha ha!" Lily asks.

"Ha ha ha!"

"Hello, ladies! What is so funny?"

"Ellen? Where did you come from?" Lily says.

"Huh… front door, it's not locked, and not even closed… you
know, when you have some space, you can pass through it…"

"Ha ha ha! Ellen being Ellen!" laughs Hailee.

"Ha ha ha! Welcome, Ellen! How you doing?" Emma laughs.

"I'm fine, thanks! You? Well, I think you're fine, because you're laughing, right?"

"Yeah, we're fine! Lily and Emma are telling jokes!"

"Really? That's something I've never seen before!"

"Ellen, is Jennifer okay?"

"Yes, she's with your father, I think. You?"

"I'm fine; I'm even laughing here with these funny ladies. Gay ladies, by the way…"

"I'm not gay! Oh, come on!" says Lily.

"Hey! What is this gay talk here?"

"Hi, Anna!"

"Hi, ladies! Okay, nobody move here!"

"What happened, Anna?" Hailee asks.

"Nobody breathe too! I've lost my AK ring!"

"Your what?" Emma says.

"My AK ring! It's like the One Ring, from 'Lord of the Rings' movies! With all inscribed words! But inside, there is my name, 'AK Davelman'! That's my Anna Kelly Davelman ring!"

"Is it a gift from Jesse?" Lily asks.

"Your boyfriend Jesse?" Hailee asks.

"Yes, it's a gift from him! Oh, my God! He's not gonna marry me anymore!" she is worried.

"What? Only because of it?" says Emma.

"It is a special gift, Emma! That means a lot to me and Jesse, because he is a huge fan too! He has the same ring with his name! And he gave me when we were watching the movies for the fiftieth time!"

"Did you watch 'Lord of the Rings' fifty times?" Elle surprises.

"We make movie marathons! Extended versions only! You all are invited to the next session already!"

"You lost that day we went shopping, Anna! Inside your car! No?" reminds Lily.

"And your car is… Ouch…" says Ellen.

"Oh, no…" says Elle. "This is not happening…"

"Okay… Let's think it's still inside the house! I'll look for it again!"

"Sorry for that, Anna…" says Emma.

"But we still have good news today, ladies!" Anna says.

"So, tell us, Anna! Come on!" asks Hailee.

"We have an appointment with a big investor here in the city. He saw us at the last competition, he likes us. And…"

"And…"

"And… what?"

"Spit it out, Anna! I hate this suspense! Oh, God!" Lily complains.

"He will probably invest on our company! But he wants to talk first, of course!"

"Really? Oh, my God!"

"So, it's up to us!"

"Huh… do we need a powerpoint, Anna? Oh, my God! It was traumatic back there!" Hailee is concerned.

"When is this, Anna?"

"Next week, Emma! We have time. And we don't need any slides, Hailee, don't worry! He saw us at the contest, he knows what we can do with a blank huge screen!" Anna winks with a mouth snap.

"So… let's get ready!" says Hailee.

"What do we need for now?" Lily says.

"We need to talk, ladies."

"About what, Anna?"

"About our company, Emma."

"And what is this? Why so much mystery?" Lily hates suspense.

"We need a serious conversation, ladies."

"What conversation, Anna? We'll have this meeting, and we're fine, I think."

"We must decide if we want to sell company's stake, Ellen. Investors mean that someone from out of the company can say what we can do; these people can even impose conditions to us. And maybe this investor will have someone working with us, as an advisor. We get money and valuable networking, we lose autonomy and agility in decisions. But, it's not completely bad. All investors have a profile. Some of them want to rule the entire business. In the other hand, there are the 'partner type' investors: we can trust them, because they want to improve the business in a different way. They want to help, not giving orders. We need to find out Rodrigo's profile. It's our next quest."

Chapter Sixteen – Version 16.2

Few days later, they are going to the meeting. It is a big place, with a beautiful garden in the front. This garden is almost a forest, because there are even tall trees. But the girls entrepreneurs cannot recognize any types – they are not botanists or gardeners. In the middle of the large garden, we can also see a fountain, which uses recycled water –

someone from staff will tell that to the girls some lines below. After the garden, there is a free area, with places to seat, like a park. A gardener is working there, and the girls are amazed.

We can see three buildings. The highest is round, with twenty floors, at least – the girls did not count it. The others are like squares: they are exactly two cubes near the highest structure, positioned in a ninety degrees angle. Like one cube on north side and the other on the west side of the main building. These smaller constructions are not so high as the main, but they have ten floors and heliports – we can see a helicopter landing.

When Anna, Elle, Ellen, Emma, Hailee and Lily get in the entrance hall, everything changes. The green from the garden is replaced by a blue ambience, full of glasses. The girls can see a very high ceiling, and a large glazed area. Through the glasses, they can see the rest of the garden, this time with many colorful flowers.

In the entrance hall, they identify themselves. A lovely receptionist treats them with respect and a smile. She informs the floor and says.

"Be welcome, ladies! Mr. Santos is waiting for you!"

Security guards on each ten meters greet and watch them while they go to the elevator.

"Wow! What is this place? Google headquarters?"

"I've heard Apple is beautiful too, Lily!" says Ellen.

"I don't know about you, but I'm very impressed here!" says Hailee.

"Yeah, this is the most beautiful building I've ever seen!" Ms. Marketing says.

"Don't get so impressed, ladies! This is a strategy to buy our company!" Anna smiles.

"Oh, God! They do that, Anna?" Elle wants to know.

At twenty-sixth floor, the girls pass through five doors until they meet Mr. Santos, Doctor Alice's cousin.

"Good afternoon, ladies! Please, come in, have a sit, be my guests!"

The ladies sit down at the meeting table with places for twenty people or more. Mr. Santos is seated at the edge of the table. In his left, we can see Hailee, Anna and Elle, in this order. In the other side, Lily, Emma and Ellen are seated.

The forty years old man is tall, 1.9 meters at least, and he has a big forehead – he looks intelligent. The skin is tanned, like a surfer skin. He does not look his actual age. His dark brown eyes are not so big, and he looks a honest person. The thick beard attracted Anna's attention, but the manager has a boyfriend already. All the girls are attracted, by the way. Mr. Santos has dark brown hair in a modern style. The man seated at the edge of the table looks young, but he must be very powerful to command that building. Size matters here.

He starts to present his company. It's a technology transnational enterprise. He supports many small companies and invest on them. Then, when these small and promising business can stand on their own feet, the investor sells his stakes. One thing is very important: he does not abandon the companies, he keeps supporting them. However, he does that in a different way: providing a co-working space. In this place, inside the cube buildings you have read before, the entrepreneurs can do what they need to grow up their companies. They have a different office environment, where they can talk and network with people from all over the world. It is a favorable ambience to have ideas and solve problems of all kinds and complexities – that is the reason Mr. Santos has built it. The investor has thirty-five companies working inside his company – it is a lot of people.

The girls start to explain their business too. Elle tells the story, the beginning. Then comes Hailee with design, and how she called his sister Emma.

"Are you sisters?" Mr. Santos asks.

Then, Emma tells about marketing strategies and the moment she called Lily.

"Best friends? Nice!"

Lily talks about spreadsheets, numbers, presentations and, of course, the sister Anna.

"Sisters too? Wow! Everything in family here!"

Anna tells all the complexity in managing that business, and even the fights.

"Really? You look so adorable, and I'm not calling you little girls, okay? I mean, I can't imagine you fighting, ladies!"

Finally, Ellen explains the development, the obstacles, and the coding.

"Yes, you can use those technical terms, I can perfectly understand you, Ms. Fage. This is an IT company." he smiles nicely.

The girls are very impressed and surprised. An investor, a big one, believes in their company. They are proud and happy. All that "playing business" talk looks so far away at that moment. It is like a dream.

"Huh… Mr. Santos…" says Anna.

"Call me 'Paulo', please."

"Okay, sorry! It's because you are calling us 'Ms.'!" she smiles.

"Oh, I like that! I feel like I am in 1950s or before! But I'll call you by your names from now on, okay?"

"Okay! Huh... as I was saying, your surname, 'Santos'. It's not American, right?"

"No, no, it's not! The origin is in Italy and France. But my father gave me this surname in Brazil."

"Oh, are you Brazilian?" asks Hailee.

"Yes! Do you know Brazil?"

"Huh... not so much... soccer, Carnival..." suggests Hailee.

"Amazon! Huh... not the e-commerce, the forest." says Ellen.

"Anything else, ladies?" he asks.

"Rio? San Paulo?" Emma says with accent.

"Huh... touching Olympic Games? I mean, the opening ceremony." says Lily.

"Yes, all that! Soccer, Carnival, Amazon and creative people!"

"Creative people? Sorry, I've never heard that before!" says Anna.

"Well, sometimes we need to work under hard circumstances, especially in politics and economy. And even like that we make a profit in our companies. We need to be creative. We need to make more with the same investment."

"Wow! How interesting! One more thing to learn!" says Emma.

"Because you, here, you have a stable economy and good conditions to grow up your business. I'm not saying it's easier, not at all. I'm saying it's... huh... less hard. Well, that's why my headquarters is here, not in Brazil. But I also have a small place there."

"Oh, we can't imagine what you call a 'small' place, Mr. Paulo! Because this building is wonderful!" says Anna.

"Thank you, Anna! And... I can recommend you some books about Brazilian entrepreneurs. If you want, of course."

"Yes, please!" asks Anna.

"Well, ladies, I'd like to ask you something. I've seen your presentation. You've made a great work over there. Congrats! But something has attracted my attention. I could see you had no powerpoint, nothing. I didn't believe you were doing all that with a blank screen. Only you and the audience. That was very challenging."

"Huh... we had some unforeseen events, Mr. Santos... I mean, Paulo." Elle says.

"We lost our file, the powerpoint file..." Lily says.

"And there was no internet connection to get a new one." Ellen smiles.

"And no time to make new slides." Anna says.

"Ellen lost her cell phone too, but this is not so relevant." Hailee says.

"And Elle's father was hospitalized. We had many troubles, Paulo." Emma says.

"At a hospital? Even under those circumstances, you continued. This is good. Persistence, resilience."

"We couldn't give up, sir." Elle says.

"Who's in charge here?"

"I'm the manager, but Elle is the founder, Paulo. She's the leader." Anna says.

"And did you continue, Elle? Even with your father at the hospital?"

"Yes, sir."

"Why? Why didn't you give up? Is your business more important than your family? I don't believe you can tell me that. You were against all odds."

Elle lowers her head and takes a breath. She looks the girls around the long table, and the business man in the edge. Then, she remembers Charlie's words.

"I'm the founder of this company, sir; I'm the captain. I do lead people here. To me, there is no such 'impossible' word, I can't work with that. WE can't."

The forty years old man looks impressed. He smiles.

"This is the kind of speech I like to hear, ladies. Congrats."

The girls smile. The man keeps talking.

"Well, one more reason to have you working here. So, this is my proposal: I want to invest on your company, you can sell me a stake. I'm thinking in five percent. You can use the co-working space here, and you'll have five million dollars to start. Or how much you need to improve and develop your app. I have many contacts here. So, you can sell your app to the entire world."

"And what about our autonomy, Paulo?"

"Oh, this is very important, Lily! You still decide everything in your company, of course! If you don't know what to do, or where to go, you can come to me, or some advisor. We have many experienced directors and specialists. We can talk anytime about decisions. But the final word is always yours, because it's your enterprise, not mine. Everything that happens to your company is your merit and your fault. Don't forget that."

"Well, Mr. Paulo… oh, sorry! Paulo! The proposal is very good, but we'd like to have some time to think. Can we?"

"Sure, Anna! I'll give you… ten seconds. Wait. Okay, counting here." he looks his watch.

The girls do not know what to say. They look each other, but with no answers.

"I'm kidding, ladies! Sorry for that!" he smiles.

"Oh, my God! You scared us, Paulo!" says Lily.

"I've heard about quick business decisions, but I wasn't expecting that!" says Anna.

"Yes, you said that so seriously! I'm stressed already!" Hailee says.

"I'm not waiting for a quick reply, ladies. This takes time, and you'll have it to decide. Please, don't be rushed. Maybe one week or two? I'll wait for your contact. Just call me or send me a message, okay?"

"Sure, Paulo! Thank you very much!"

Mr. Paulo thanks the girls and reminds them about the answer. But he does not rush them – he is not this kind of investor. The Dad's Home Team leaves the stunning building with good impressions.

In the garden, they see the fountain again.

"Look that! It's so beautiful!"

"Yes, but it looks like waste of water, Hailee…"

The gardener is near, and he can hear them. He is a man in his forties, black hair, blue eyes.

"Excuse me, ladies! I presume you are talking about the fountain, right?" the man starts talking.

"Yes, we are!"

"Well, let me tell you, if you do not mind. The water is recycled. The fountain is totally sustainable. These buildings are almost there." he points the towers with his hand.

"The buildings?"

"Yes. On the top of each structure, we have solar cells. The upper windows have cells too. The use of energy is minimum here; these buildings are almost sustainable. Can you see that covered parking over there? It's a rainwater collection system." the gardener teaches.

The girls thank the gardener for the lesson and they leave.

"I want to work here!" Hailee whispers.

"Me too!" Lily says.

"Well, if the gardener knows all that, just imagine what a director can know!" says Anna.

"Yeah! They look so proud to be there!" Emma says.

"I don't know about you, ladies, but now I'm totally impressed!" says Ellen.

"We all are, Ellen!" Elle says.

Chapter Sixteen – Version 16.3

Later, at headquarters (it is still Davelman sisters' house, but this can change soon).

"Well, ladies?"

"Well, ladies? I'm still very impressed, really!" says Ellen.

"What about you, Anna? You're the most distrustful here!"

"I'm not the most distrustful here, Lily!"

"Okay, you're the most experienced... is it better?"

"Fine, Lily, thanks! Well, it's a beautiful place, we'll have all support and networking. But forget the beautiful place to decide, okay? Let's think rationally."

"Can we? After seeing those buildings?" Hailee says.

"Yes, we can, Hailee. We need! So, forget the wonderful garden with those gorgeous flowers, please!" says Anna.

"And the sustainable fountain!" reminds Emma.

"I'd like to say something, ladies." asks Elle.

"Yes? What is it, Elle?" Lily says.

"Huh... I was wondering... We've made so fine till now. I don't know if I want an investor in our company... and we are starting to make some money. Well, it's not five million dollars, of course. But I think we should try, I mean, by ourselves."

"But what if we don't make it, Elle? What if we lose everything? It's business, it can happen." advises Lily.

"Well, we still can try again. And we can work as employees, of course! I'm finishing college this year."

"This can be hard, Elle. You know? From entrepreneur to employee, trainee... starting down there... this can be hard."

"But this is life, Emma. We win, we lose, it happens. Now I see what my father was trying to tell me. Maybe we should try out, I mean, take a risk. It's business, right?"

"I agree with you about business, Elle. But we need to think about our condition too. Is this risk worthwhile?" Lily asks.

"It's a calculated risk, Lily. We still can get a job. We are not gonna lose everything. And we can work as employees, what is wrong with that?" Elle says.

"I have to agree with her, Lily." says Anna.

"Me too. I think she is being reasonable." Emma says.

"She is not being emotional. She knows the risks, she wants to invest. It's enough to me." says Ellen.

"And the most important: I believe in this business, I believe in you, I believe in me. That's why I want to invest. It's about friendship, but it's still business. We have made so fine till now. I mean, by ourselves! We had many people helping us, of course. Mr. Johnson, my father, Jennifer, Doctor Alice... but at the critical times, we were alone! We did that presentation without any stupid slide! I think we should try, but this is my opinion. I'll agree with you, if you decide something different." the founder says.

"You're so different, Elle... You're growing up." Hailee smiles.

"Oh, you'll never know, Hailee..." she sighs.

Chapter Sixteen – Version 16.4

In the same week.

"Be welcome, ladies! Mr. Santos is waiting for you!"

The lovely receptionist treats them with respect and a smile, and the girls are in the wonderful building again. They go to the same elevator, the same security guards are there. Soon, they are at Mr. Santos, oops, Paulo's office.

"Really?"

"Yes, Mr. Santos! I mean, Paulo! We talked and we decided that." says Anna.

"Are you sure?"

"Huh... yes, we are!" continues Anna.

"Don't be angry with us!"

"No, no, Hailee! I'm not! Zero angry here! It's not that! I mean, most of the groups accept to work here. Not all of them, of course. Do you have any particular reason? Anything you didn't like here? I'm asking because if people complain about something, I want to improve it. It's a kind of a market research."

"Well, we just want to try, Paulo." says Elle.

"Try? Be more specific, Elle, please."

"We're making a good work, Paulo. Not perfect, but a good work. We're having troubles and fights, of course, but we think these things are part of the business, right?"

"Completely right, Elle! And I still can't imagine you fighting, ladies! Just saying!"

"So, we want to try, we want to learn. We know this is the harder way... but we'll grow up."

"You have to be conscious that the market doesn't wait for you, right? I mean, the market doesn't wait that you learn, it moves on. And it changes fast. I'm not pushing you, just warning, okay? So, the advice is: get ready to learn fast, change faster and move even faster. Don't be still. Never."

"Okay, thank you, Paulo!" says Elle. "We really appreciated that!"

"Hey, you all are so quiet now! This is not a goodbye, right? I'll keep watching your work, for sure."

"Oh, I think we're feeling a little bad for that, Paulo..."

"Why? This is just business, Anna! Please, don't worry about that! It's not personal! I get many denials, I'm not perfect! This company isn't too! That's why I need to work hard every day! When you look all those buildings, you think everything is fine. But we need to work hard to keep this!"

"Oh, I can't imagine, Paulo..." says Lily.

"Okay, I've predicted this situation. I mean, you could deny my proposal, of course. Then, I still have something up my sleeve, ladies."

"What is that, Paulo? Some poker game?" smiles Hailee.

"Yes, a kind of that, Hailee! As I said before, there is a co-working space here, at the cube buildings. I'm opening this space to you. You can work here for free, you can networking. We even have a nice and healthy lunch every day. I take care of this personally, because I like to be healthy. This is very important in this company."

"And what is the deal? What is the payback?" Ellen wants to know.

"Networking, Ellen."

"Only this? We work here, even if we don't make any business with you?"

"Yes, if you see like that, Ellen. There is another point of view I'd like you to see. Networking is an essential element nowadays. How many jobs have you got because of your friends? Think about it, Ellen. Anyway, this co-working space is open to you, ladies. You can come here and work, you're welcome."

"Really?"

"Yes, really, Emma! I'm talking seriously here!" he smiles.

"But what do you get? I still don't understand, Paulo. We don't make business with you, but we come here? Where is your profit?" asks Emma.

"It's a business ambience, Emma. I truly believe this place can build better companies if we work together. Because one idea can inspire another, and so on. You can get a solution in a casual talk at an afternoon snack. Because you all are working in the same place. Sometimes, good ideas come from unusual and even weird places, conditions and situations. This communal space can inspire and create that."

"Hmm… synergy?" Emma tries.

"Bingo!" he winks with a mouth snap.

"Well, I think we can't deny this new proposal!" says Lily.

"Yes, and we don't need time to think about it!" Hailee says.

"Okay, we're in, Paulo!" agrees Anna. "Everyone?"

"Yes, we're in!" Ellen says.

"Sure we are!" Emma smiles.

"Yes, sure! I think we can learn faster here!" points Elle.

"Well, thank you, ladies! We finally made some business here! Would you like to visit the space? What do you think?"

"Do you mean, now?"

"Yes, now, if you have time for that! I still have some minutes before a new meeting. Shall we?"

The girls agree and they all go to the cube buildings. They take almost ten minutes to get there.

"Huh…. One more question, Paulo. Why did you choose us? I mean, there were many talented groups in that contest…"

"This is a good question, Ellen. I have a funny reply to that." Paulo smiles one more time.

"Funny?" says Hailee.

"Yes, funny. I have three kids, three girls. And, with my wife, they are four. I'm the minority in my own home! So, I've learned to respect and admire women. And your team was the single group formed only by women, right? This is one reason. The other one, I've said before: you've made a great work. Without any slide, I mean. And today, I found a new reason: you denied to be here. That means you're very confident with your business. I'm impressed!"

The girls agree. They remind the competition and the stress. Everything is being worthwhile now. All that happened for a reason, and the girls can see that. It is making sense.

They walk through the aisles. There are large glazed areas everywhere – this saves electric power. The girls stop at a place to look up to the garden. Ellen and Paulo stop a few meters from the girls. Suddenly, Ellen sees a known man in the other side of the aisles.

The man cannot see the girls, because he is busy with a child. The bald man, who Ellen and the girls have seen in an expensive grey suit with a red and white tie, is playing with a little girl.

"Huh… that man… Does he work here?"

"Who?"

"That man over there, playing with that girl." Ellen points with her hand.

"Oh, you mean, Harry. He has pushed you hard, right?"

"Does he work to you?"

"I don't have employees here, Ellen; I have partners. But, yes, he works here."

"Why? I mean, what is his job?"

"He is a hunter, Ellen. He goes to the competitions to look for good teams."

"Oh, I didn't know this job could exist!"

"And when he finds a potential group, he pushes it hard. Just like he did to you."

"Yes, he has pushed us really hard, Paulo!"

"But you survived, Ellen!"

Ellen agrees. Now she sees people can be good or bad. It depends on what side you are seeing; and most of times, we do not consider the entire situation. Ellen looks at the bald man with that little girl. He does not look evil now. He looks just… human.

"So, was it a test?"

"Everything in your life is a test, Ellen! In our lives, by the way."

"Sometimes you look like a father, you know?"

"I am a father, Ellen! I have three kids at home!" Paulo smiles.

They finally get to the co-working space. It is a large place, with colorful walls. Every wall has its color. You can seat near your favorite color. We also see many desks. Some desks are communal, for six or more people. There are, of course, many windows to save electric power. Through the glasses, we can see some gardens with red, yellow and white flowers. In the back, there is another fountain which uses recycled water. Some doors are closed. It indicates that people are having a meeting inside the rooms. The girls and Paulo stop at the entrance. Then, Emma sees a known man.

"Anthony?"

"Emma? What are you doing here? I mean, wow! Are you coming here?"

"Yes, I'm just visiting for now! But, I'll come here!"

"Well… I think we'll be colleagues!"

"Yeah… that's nice, Anthony!"

"Huh… I have to work now! Good to see you again!"

"Yes, me too, Anthony! See you!"

They walk through the place for a while. Paulo shows every detail. He has personally planned that space. It means too much to the investor – it is the place where ideas and solutions come true.

"Well, I think we finished our tour, ladies! What do you think?"

"I have no words, Paulo!" says Anna.

"Me neither!" says Lily.

"When can we start here, Paulo?" asks Emma.

"Hmm… someone is eager to meet someone…"

"Oh, come on, Ellen!" smiles Emma.

"You can start whenever you want. Just send me a message. There is an informal introduction when new people start here. We're open at six o'clock."

"So soon?" asks Hailee.

"Yes, business doesn't wait, Hailee!"

"And what time do you close? If you close, of course!"

"Yes, we do, Elle! The space closes at ten o'clock at night. People have time for happy hour. It could be open for a longer time, even for twenty-four hours, but it's not good when you work for so long. We need some rest too."

"It seems people like to be here, Paulo." says Anna.

"Yes, they do. As I said before, it's a communal space. People help each other here. I don't call rivals to work, that could be unproductive."

"And you have very experienced people working here."

"Have you talked to someone, Hailee?"

"Your gardener knows a lot about the facilities." Elle says.

"The gardener?"

"Yes, a man we met last week."

"Can you describe him, Elle?"

"Huh… about forty years old, black hair, blue eyes."

"Oh, Jonathan is not the gardener, he's a director; the Human Resources Director."

"Excuse me?" Lily says.

"Every month, we change jobs for one day; we draw lots for that. It's funny, I can tell. People can see how their colleagues work. So we can work better, because we can see exactly what our co-workers do in their jobs."

"Wow, that's very interesting! I can't imagine how this works in real life, but it's cool!" says Anna.

"Of course we don't do that in specific times, like pay day, for example. There is time to try out, and time to play seriously."

"You're really a different CEO, Paulo."

"Well, I don't want to change things, Ellen. I just want to make things the way I believe they work. You can try out that too."

"Is this really necessary, Paulo? Because we're not so many persons in our company. And I think this can become a mess if we try! That's what I'm afraid!"

"Huh... I don't like to say 'you should' or 'you must', Anna. I think these words can limit people. I prefer to say 'you can do' or 'you can try'. It's up to you deciding what is the best to your company."

They walk again through the aisles. Soon they are at a large hall, and they can see the sun through the windows. After they have a seat, Paulo asks.

"Anna, I've just remembered something. Your surname is Davelman, right?"

"Yes, why?"

"And your full name is?"

"Anna Kelly Davelman. Why?"

"I think I have something yours."

The investor puts a hand in the suit pocket, he takes an envelope."

"I think this is yours, right? It's your name inside of it."

Anna takes the envelope and opens it while Paulo stands up and walks to the window. There is a round object inside. She sees some words in Elvish language. Inside of the object, the manager can read a name, "AK Davelman." She does not believe.

"Where did you get this?"

"I'm looking at it right now." he says in front of the window.

The girls run to the window. There is a parking few floors down there. In this place, the girls can see a small and very powerful thing. It is not a pink or purple thing, it is black with silver five rims wheels with car wrapping – that is a little out of date, but Anna Kelly likes it (and it protects the paintwork). The girls can see the ghost or something from the shadows – according to Anna's thinking. It is something very special – the manager girl has worked for almost one year to buy it.

"Last month, a partner came driving that car. He didn't like it. He said the car looks... soft. He thinks the previous owner was a woman." says Paulo.

"I don't believe that!"

"Well, my partner didn't like the car, so I bought it from him. But I'm not driving every day, because I'm using bicycle now. You know? Ecology, health, saving time…"

"Huh… can you sell that car? I mean, do you want to sell that car?" Anna desperately says.

"Well, I'm not driving it so much. Yes, we can talk about that."

"It's her very first car, Paulo! I mean, in her life!" Lily informs.

"Really? Wow, so we definitely must talk about this!"

"Oh, my God! I don't believe that! Can I see it? I mean, can I get into it? Just for a while, please!"

"You can even drive it, Anna! Here are the keys. I can take a bicycle today."

"Oh, my God! Thank you! I don't know what to say!"

"Saying 'thank you' is enough to me, Anna!"

They leave the magical place, and soon they are at the exit – the cube building is not so high as the main one.

"Well, I'll wait for you, ladies! Thank you for now, thank you for the pleasant afternoon! I really enjoyed it!"

The ladies thank the investor and leave the building. They go to Anna's car – she is amazed. She almost cried, but do not tell that to anyone. Everyone is happy.

That place must be really magical. So many good people there, so many nice things inside, so many surprises in every suit pocket. The girls leave the place and go home. Do not ask me how six girls got into only one car.

Chapter Sixteen – Version 16.5

Some days later.

"Hey, where are you going?"

"First day, Mom!"

"Really? Congratulations, Ellen! Don't let the kids annoy you, okay?" advises the mother.

"Okay, Mom! I'll remind that. It's just some high school kids."

"Yes, but you remember what you did at high school…"

"Yeah, Mom… I do… I was a stupid kid…"

"But, well, congratulations for becoming a teacher, Ellen! You're making the next developers over there! It's a great responsibility!"

"Thanks, Mom! I'll do my best!"

In some other house.

"Lily, wake up!"

"What now? Let me sleep…"

"Check this out, Lily!"

"Oh, come on, Anna! Just five minutes…"

"Okay, you'll not be invited to the wedding party!"

"Wedding?" she throws away the blankets.

The big sister shows pictures of the last night. Jesse, Anna, engagement rings, a happy couple.

"Oh, my God, Anna! I'm so happy for you!"

"I don't believe that, Lily! It was so wonderful! He kneeled!"

"Did he? Jesse? Wow! Where are the pictures of this epic moment?"

Anna slides the cell phone screen and shows the rest of the special moment.

"Wow, congratulations on your engagement, Anna! Have you decided upon big day?"

Anna says a date, she is not sure yet. They are not sure, by the way. Now it is her and her fiancé.

In some place near from there.

"Hi."

"Hi, Emma. Hmm… someone is not so happy today…"

"I'm happy, Hailee."

"I don't think so, sister… I know you…"

"Huh… it's me and Anthony… We're not so well…"

"That's very complicated, Emma. But I think that's how things work between men and women. You know? We don't talk the same language."

"Oh, so I think I prefer women and women, Hailee…"

"Don't bother, sister! Everything is gonna be fine! As always!"

"Thank you for supporting me, little sister! What about you? I don't see you with so many boys anymore…"

"Huh… that's a new me! Fully updated Hailee!"

"Why?"

"I'm just choosing wisely people I date, Emma."

"About time, Hailee!"

"Yeah… about time… I've enjoyed all that, but… I want more than enjoying boys, Emma. Now I want to enjoy me and my life. I'm loving myself!"

"Good for you, Hailee! Welcome to your new world!"

At Elle's house.

"Now, I need to focus on this. Oh, that's so hard! Why should I use this? Do people use this nowadays? Okay, it's not comfortable, but it's necessary. I have to call Hailee too. Is she home now? I'll send her a message. Did Doctor Alice call me already? I need to talk to her too. We're making some great business! Yes, she is a great partner! She looks my mom too, but I can't tell her that! She can feel offended, because she is not old. Yeah, now I need to take care of everything I say, especially on social network. That counts when you're an entrepreneur. Well, that counts on everything, but people don't care, I think. Yes, people definitely don't care about what they are saying on internet. But I don't care about what people say on there too. Why should I worry about that? Okay, fine. My hair is beautiful. It's done! And now all the grades are here, all the grades are good! I got it! Now I need to call Hailee. She is not gonna like I got a higher grade in Art History. But we made it, anyway! We are graduated from college! Mom would be proud, wherever she would be... I know she is proud..."

She stops and calls.

"Dad! Where are you?"

"Living room, honey!"

"I'm graduated!"

"What?"

"I'm seeing my grades now! I'm graduated, Dad!"

"Wow, congratulations, Ms. Blonde! Let's have a party!"

Charlie comes to the bedroom to hug his daughter.

"Congratulations, Mary Elle! You really deserved that!"

"Thanks, Dad! I never would have made it without your help! This achievement is for you, Dad, and Mom!"

"She would be proud, Elle!"

"Yes, she would, Dad... All these nice things I'm living... it's because of you both, Dad. Thank you!"

"That's your hard work, Ms. Blonde; I'm just giving you a little help. You're my daughter, don't forget that."

"I won't." she smiles with the red lips.

"But, hey, have you told this to your partners already?"

"I'll meet them today, Dad!"

Father and daughter hug each other. And that was the very important mission Mary Elle had: being grateful to her mother. Deborah is looking all that from some place out there.

Chapter Sixteen – Version 16.6

Some days later, they are all at headquarters.

"So?"

"So, we're engaged, Elle!"

"Really? Congratulations, Anna! Jesse is a nice man! I'm sure you'll be happy!"

"What about you, Elle?"

"Well, there will be a graduation ceremony in few months! You're all invited, ladies!"

"Wow, congrats, Elle! You too, Hailee! You're graphic designers!"

"And entrepreneurs, Lily!" Hailee says.

"And... I was wondering... I'll leave this house when I'll get married, right? Lily is gonna be alone here. I'm thinking... you all could move here! What do you think?"

"It's not a bad idea, Anna. What do you think, Lily?" says Elle.

"Oh, sure I don't want you here, Elle! We have fought already, remember?" Lily jokes and smiles.

"Ha ha ha! Fights at home now!" Hailee laughs.

"I think it's a good idea. Well, firstly, we need to talk, because there are rules here, lady." says Lily.

"Uh-oh! Rules are coming, Elle... in spreadsheets! Watch out!"

"Oh, come on, Hailee! It's not a spreadsheet!" Lily says.

"She's lying, Hailee! She has all the rules, times and dates in a spreadsheet!" reveals the big sister.

"Come on, Anna! It's only one single spreadsheet!" says Lily.

"Sure, with ten tabs!"

"Ha ha ha!"

"Ten tabs, Lily? Really?" asks Emma.

"Eight."

"Ha ha ha!"

Someone knocks on the door.

"Ellen? Wow, now the team is complete!" Emma says. "Hey, look this teacher clothing!"

"You look an adult woman, Ellen! This is dangerous; you should take care! How is teacher life?" Lily wants to know.

"Yeah, Ellen, tell us! Did anyone ask whether you work or you just teach people?" Elle asks.

"Ha ha ha!"

"An exam? Today? Why, Ms. Fage? We didn't do anything wrong!" says Anna with funny gestures.

"Ha ha ha!"

"Why do you come every day to the school, Ms. Fage? You never miss!" Hailee says with a child voice.

"Ha ha ha!"

"I was absent yesterday, Ms. Fage. Did I miss something?" Emma imitates a student.

"Ha ha ha!"

"Okay, ladies, that's very funny! I'm laughing loudly here, really!" Ellen sits down on the sofa, she leaves the purse.

"Well, it's not that bad… good students, bad students… just like life. What about you, ladies? Anna has a new ring, I've heard that!" the new teacher smiles.

"Graduation ceremony in few months, Ellen! Hailee and I are inviting you!"

"Congratulations, you both! Now you can even work! I've heard about a new company, Dad's Home. They are doing a great job! Send a resume to them!" Ellen says ironically.

"Ha ha ha!"

"What about the company, Ellen?" Anna asks.

"I'm working as a teacher only two days every week, Anna. I'm fine. But it's just an experience, I think. But I like it. It can be a plan B. You should have one too."

"Yeah, we all should have one of that, Ellen." Lily says.

"What about you, Emma? You're quiet."

"Oh, she is not good with that guy, Anthony…" Hailee informs.

"Really? He looks a nice guy, Emma!"

"You only get know people when you get closer, Ellen. I can tell you that." Emma says.

"Well, I hope this doesn't interfere in your jobs there."

"I can handle that, Ellen. Thanks for worrying." Emma answers.

"So, what's next, ladies?" Anna wants to know.

The girls look each other, they smile. They are working at Paulo's company, they have four clients now. The Brazilian investor has introduced the girls to a great friend in other country. This new friend will present the app to the European Union – the Dad's Home Team will be there.

Ellen is teaching coding at a high school. Not every day, as you have read, but she likes it (you have read that too). Jennifer is fine, and Ellen's mother agrees on that new teacher life. At least, the daughter does not stay for many days inside the bedroom.

Lily and Emma are lecturing about finance and marketing to students – they want to spread their knowledge, especially to girls. Emma is still looking for a great love, but she does not care whether it will be a man or a woman. Lily Jane? The finance girl does not have time for that. It is written on her spreadsheet – she showed me.

Elle and Hailee have finished the college grade – you are invited to the graduation ceremony in few months. Now they are graphic designers, and they already have a large experience at a start-up company to put on their resumes. The girls did not decide whether someone is coming to Anna and Lily's house – anyone probably will move, but in the next book, maybe – who knows?

Anna is engaged. Jesse, her boyfriend, did not give up on her. He would propose to her anyway, with or without the "AK ring". Anna is also taking care of her new old very first car. She is very happy.

Hailee is choosing wisely her boyfriends. It is like a hiring process now, not that... huh... I do not know how to call that! She is enjoying her new life, as well as the entire team.

Are they done? You tell me.

At the moment, Anna, Elle, Ellen, Emma, Hailee and Lily are understanding their lives. Just like you and me. The girls have lived a big adventure, but only a small part of this great journey called life. They do not think about changing the world anymore, because they are already evolving it.

From now on, the entrepreneurs will try to understand themselves, with tolerance, patience and goodness – because they are true friends now. The girls will also try to know who they are and where they are going to.

Do you want to know who they really are?

They are my girls.

And they have just grown up.

THE END.

INTENTIONALLY BLANK

CHAPTER SEVENTEEN – VERSION 17.0 – EPILOGUE.

Who am I?

She goes to the last page and then she finishes reading in few words. The new girl in town has read her entire writing to that new class, in a new college, somewhere in a new state.

"Well, this is the story of my last holidays. As you all know, I'm new here, I've just moved. But I'm not here to ask for your acceptance. I'm not begging for you friendship. Because I have already true friends, those girls in the story I've told you. This is the most beautiful friendship story I've ever heard. And I'm telling you this because I believe we can live better if we do things together, as friends. You never know where you will meet a new one. Maybe this is not important to you, but I really want to share this, because we're going to study together here; and because it's important to me. Thank you for listening." she says.

The teacher asks for some applause, some people do what the senior man asks for. The new girl goes back to her desk, someone smiles to her. She is not home yet – she does not feel at it –, but she will be.

INTENTIONALLY BLANK

CHAPTER EIGHTEEN – VERSION 18.0 – POST-CREDITS SCENE.

What?

The girls are playing a zombie cooperative game.

"Hmm… I was wondering…" Elle says.

"Uh-oh! Trouble's coming, ladies…" Hailee warns.

"No, it's serious, Hailee!" Elle says again.

"What?" Lily says.

"Wait! I'm trying to have an idea here!" Elle says and smiles.

"Oh, my God! Somebody call 911!" Lily advises.

"Someone call the Army!" Emma says.

"Just pray, people! We're cursed!" Ellen says.

"She is thinking, ladies! It's hard to her!" Hailee laughs.

"What is this about, Elle? Are your fingertips sweating again? Jesus! This is bad… this is bad!" Anna says.

"Just say it, Elle! I hate this suspense! I hate when you do that, you know?" Lily tells.

"Maybe a new idea for a company! Wow! How about that, ladies?" Emma says.

"I don't think I'm ready for another company! Really! But I'll help you, you can count on me." Ellen says.

"Okay, we're ready to go, Elle! We're alive and breathing! Whatever you say, we're here!" Anna says.

"Ellen?" Elle calls.

"Yes?"

"Have you ever coded a videogame?"

"Huh… more or less… but…"

"But…" all the girls say but Lily.

"Just say it, Ellen! I hate this suspense!"

"But I know a girl. She has moved from here. I can call her."

INTENTIONALLY BLANK

CHAPTERS – OVERVIEW

DISCLAIMER
It looks funny, but it is serious.

ABOUT THIS EDITION
What is so different?

PREFACE
This book is about business. Business girls.

INTRODUCTION
Who is the protagonist?

PROLOGUE
I would like to introduce myself.

Chapter One – Version 1.0 – Who I am and how I got that. Meeting Elle and Hailee

This chapter introduces Elle's story: who is she? Where does she live? What does she do? What is her trouble? It also introduces Hailee, Elle's best friend.

Chapter Two – Version 2.0 – What do I need? Hailee, we have a problem – having an idea

Elle has a problem: her father has heart complications and he cannot do much physical effort. Then, she creates an app for cell phones called "Dad's Home." Off course, Elle calls her best friend Hailee. The friend is almost a talented graphic designer (and she is almost finishing the graduation as Elle). They present the app to a professor but it is still too poor. They have just a sketch, but the idea is good.

Chapter Three – Version 3.0 – Who are my friends? Where are they? Emma and Lily

The best friends start to look for people to help. The first option is Hailee's older sister. Emma has a graduation in Marketing and she knows how to sell and present the app. They start to talk about business and why not a start-up company? Emma calls her best friend (all the girls in this story have a best friend): Lily got her graduation in Management, especially Finance. Now we have four girls, and counting.

Chapter Four – Version 4.0 – How can we organize this mess?
The Manager

They present the app in a contest at Elle and Hailee's college – but they still have only sketches. The judging commission likes the idea, but they need to improve the app – or starting coding. They got an eleventh position in the contest. Elle thinks the presentation was a mess. Lily calls her sister Anna – The Manager!

Chapter Five – Version 5.0 – Lady Code.
Introducing Ellen

Now we meet Ellen, the coder. Hailee is a coder too, but not so experienced as Ellen. We also know who Anna Kelly Davelman is.

Chapter Six – Version 6.0 – The dinner.
About marketing, leadership, design, team work, friendship, ice cream and pizza

Now we know Anna loves cars. They are having a dinner, with pizza and ice cream and they start to talk about the business. Anna and Elle talk about how the blonde founder can lead the company and how to make a presentation. Anna teaches Elle how to be a good leader. Emma explains about what she does at the company, marketing – Ellen has asked about to her. They talk frankly about feelings and they became friends.

Chapter Seven – Version 7.0 – One chance.
Climbing

The girls talk and adjust all the arrangements. Then they go shopping. Because the team have worked hard. Everyone talks about dreams and feelings. When they come back from shopping, they celebrate and drink (and got drunk too). Emma and Lily kiss each other.

Chapter Eight – Version 8.0 – Consequences.
Why didn't you tell me?

This chapter starts with the girls talking about the fourteenth position they got in the state contest. They present the app to a larger audience. There is some discrimination and prejudice, Emma and Hailee talk about that. About the fourteenth position, firstly, they think it is a step back because in the other contest they got an eleventh place. However, this time they are in a bigger one. In addition, they do not have any client yet – that matters. Anna and Lily talk about improving the business, that means getting clients. Gossip not so gossip: Jennifer, Ellen's mother, is dating Charlie, Elle's father.

Chapter 9.0 – Version 9.0 – The Finance Girl.
Girls triumphant

The girls invest money and start the company for real, as a partnership. Then they look for clients and the first option is – yes – the hospital where Elle was always going to take care of her father. They meet Alice, a director of the hospital. Alice Bragan likes the app and she wants to test it. The girls get their first win! They have a consumer to give a proper – and real – feedback about the app.

Chapter 10.0 – Version 10.0 – Where is the money?
Bills and yells

They start to work in design because they believe a good design sells better. They have "sold" the app to hospital, but where is the money? The hospital is testing the app, but not paying so much for that.

Elle, Hailee and Ellen borrow the company's money to Ellen's friend. The guy does not return the money, and the girls do not have money to pay all the bills. Then, Anna sells her first car.

Chapter Eleven – Version 11.0 – Another competition.
Hiring

Hailee is pregnant, or she thinks she is, and the brunette girl is at a hospital. The girls hire a boy to make a design freelance job. Hailee says this boy is not a good professional, but no one listens to her. With Hailee at the hospital, they can test the app. The girls can finally try out the app. The entrepreneurs are getting ready for the contest, but the freelancer boy does not deliver the job. Hailee comes back from hospital.

Chapter Twelve – Version 12.0 – Hope and glory.
Fail

The girls go to a huge competition – and this time it is a national one. Investors, entrepreneurs and business people from all over the country will be there, and it is a chance to introduce the Dad's Home company. The contest has two stages, in two weekends.

There will be a party and they vote to choose the costumes. And the girls are in the finals! They go to a bar to celebrate; they get drunk and make a fuss at the bar. Someone record a movie and put on internet.

Chapter Thirteen – Version 13.0 – What a wonderful world...
Networking

The Dad's Home Team goes to the costume party. Next Sunday, they go to the finals.

Chapter Fourteen – Version 14.0 – The Ultimate Challenge.
Show time

On Sunday morning, Anna gets a message with the drunk girls video. It is a hit on internet, with thousands of views. They regret and wait that this scandal will not have influence on the final result.

The girls go to the contest and they have their greatest, their biggest challenge. Now they have to justify their choices to a group of very rigorous investors, experienced entrepreneurs, and qualified audience.

Chapter Fifteen – Version 15.0 – Left behind, round two.
In God we trust

Charlie is fine.

Chapter Sixteen – Version 16.0 – Starting... or not!
The real life

The Dad's Home Team gets a proposal from Paulo Rodrigo, Alice's cousin. The girls deny and decide to invest in the company by themselves.

Elle and Hailee have finished the college grade; Lily and Emma start to lecture about finance and marketing to students, especially girls; Anna is engaged; Ellen is teaching coding at high school. They are happy, they are fine, they are my girls.

Chapter Seventeen – Version 17.0 – Epilogue.
Who am I?

Who is really telling this story?

Chapter Eighteen – Version 18.0 – Post-credits scene.
What?

Sometimes, a great movie has a post-credits scene.

Chapters – Overview

You are here.

P. S.

In the last competition (Chapter Fourteen), the girls got a fourth position.
But, seriously?
They do not care.

INTENTIONALLY BLANK

www.ingramcontent.com/pod-product-compliance
Lightning Source LLC
Chambersburg PA
CBHW060314260626
47160CB00007B/2601